reprise

The Spiral Series
Book Two

lisa silverthorne

REPRISE

Book 2: The Spiral Series

Heather thought she had escaped the Between with Ross but soon learns that he's trapped and enslaved by demons that have taken over the shadowy realm. The world is crumbling, overrun by soulstalkers, deadly poppy fields, and demons harvesting trapped souls.

Giving up her new life, Heather returns to save the man she loves. As she builds and leads an army of surviving pale angels and souls, Heather finds an unexpected ally in new arrival, Knox, a fierce former soldier. Sparks fly when she's drawn to his fiery spirit and commanding presence. As they embark on the dangerous rescue mission, Heather struggles with her conflicted feelings for Ross and Knox.

Can she save Ross and stabilize the Between before darkness and demons consume everything?

Reprise is the second book in a tense, action-packed urban fantasy series, *The Spiral* that will leave you on the edge of your seat.

SUICIDE IS PERMANENT

Trigger Warning: **This work of fiction is about suicide and its aftermath. Suicide isn't a solution. It won't fix anything.**

Suicide is ***permanent***. It isn't romantic. It can't be undone. It doesn't resolve your pain. Every person that jumped off the Golden Gate Bridge and lived said that they regretted their decision the moment they stepped off the bridge. But it was too late.

- **TEXT or CALL 988** for help
- **TELL** someone
- **ASK** for help
- **REACH OUT** no matter how much it hurts

There are ways to fix what seems unfixable. ***You are worth fighting for*** no matter how much it hurts or how much you think you don't matter. **You *DO* matter**. Your light is unique. Without it, the world's entire spectrum darkens.

If you feel suicidal: Text or Call 988
Because YOU MATTER

Novels by Lisa Silverthorne

Standalones:

ISABEL'S TEARS

LANDFALL

PACIFIC BLUE TATTOO

BEAUTY: CAPTURED AND FRAMED

A Game of Lost Souls series:

THE CINDERELLA HOUR

THE PRINCE CHARMING HOUR

THE EVER AFTER HOUR

THE FALLEN HEARTS SEASON

THE RISING SPIRITS SEASON

THE ETERNAL SOULS SEASON

THE ROYAL WEDDING HOUR

THE HEAVENLY HONEYMOON HOUR

THE DIVINE NEWLYWEDS SHOW

THE CELESTIAL COUPLES SHOW

The Spiral series:

BETWEEN

REPRISE

SHORT STORY COLLECTIONS

THE SOUND OF ANGELS

THE MAGIC OF ORDINARY THINGS

COMING SOON!

A Game of Lost Souls series:

*The Enochian Apocalypse Show, Book Eleven (**9/3/23**)*

The Angelic Anniversary Hour, Book Twelve

The Perdition Picture Show, Book Thirteen

The Spiral series:

Avenge, Book 3 (Coming Soon!)

Ruin, Book 4

Descent, Book 5

The Resurrectionist Papers:

A ROMANTIC FANTASY MYSTERY SERIES

Grave Reckoning, Book 1

Corpses Delicti, Book 2

Stiffed Again, Book 3

SHORT STORY COLLECTIONS

Timeless: 8 Time Travel Romances (Dec 2023)

SCIENCE FICTION WRITING AS L.S. SILVERTHORNE

Experiencing True Purple series:

*Splice, Book 3 (**8/13/23**)*

Cipher, Book 4

Renascence, Book 5

one

BEING HIT by a bus wasn't high on Heather Billot's list of ways to die. But she'd go through with it if it brought her back to Ross.

Heather's body stiffened and she tried to fold up inside herself, bracing for the oncoming pain. The air smelled like hot asphalt and burning rubber as the massive bus' brakes squealed like a cat with its tail caught in a door as it skidded across the street, trying to swerve and miss her.

She stood stone-still in the middle of the street, her brain screaming *get out of the road!*

Shouts rang out from the sidewalks.

"Look out!" someone screamed!"

Heather smashed her eyes closed, bracing for the impact. She felt Zakhart and Razasha beside her, squeezing her hands.

"I'm so sorry, Heather," Zakhart said, tears cracking his voice.

Razasha laid a hand against Heather's heart. Cringing as the bus slammed into Heather.

Agony was white hot, burning through muscles and strafing bones as the bus hit her broadside, unable to stop. It tossed her like a rag doll through the air until she slammed against the pavement.

Faces swam above her. Lungs burned, filling with water. Her heart fluttered and shook with uneven bursts as fire spread through limbs and organs.

She couldn't move. Couldn't breathe. Every bone and joint felt crushed, shattered, and broken.

Like her heart.

Razasha sat beside her, Zakhart cradling her head in his lap as a crowd gathered in the street around Heather. Both pale angels cried as they held her. The bus driver paced around her, a stout fifty-something balding man who wrung his hands, raving, looking despondent as he called 9-1-1.

A shadow fell across Heather. The mother of that little girl, Michelle. The one she'd given Charles the bear. With a pinched expression, the woman bent over Heather, tilting her head back.

"I'm a nurse," said the woman in a calming tone and laid Charles the bear against Heather's cheek. "I'll stay with you until paramedics get here, okay?"

Heather gurgled out an okay as the woman tried to stop the bleeding, pressing hard against Heather's upper thigh. The nurse smoothed a bloody, tangled lock of coppery brown hair out of Heather's face.

"Michelle said I should let Charles help you," said the nurse, tears in her eyes.

Heather gripped the nurse's arm with a bloody hand and nuzzled her little white bear. Charles sparkled against her face.

"Thank you," she whispered and gazed at Charles.

Maybe we'll meet again, little guy?

Pain ripped through every organ, the world turning hazy.

"Stay with me, now," the woman said, both hands bloody as she tried to halt the blood pouring out of the artery in her left leg.

But Heather was bleeding out. She was leaving now. This new life was over now, too.

Heather shook her head. "Don't...think I can," she whispered, her voice raspy and weak.

"No!" the nurse shouted. "Hold on, please! You're just a kid. Hold on!"

"This will help the pain," Zakhart whispered in Heather's ear.

A wave of crisp white light washed over her body and she relaxed into it. It absorbed the crushing feeling in her lungs and the overwhelming pain throbbing through broken bones.

"Was it an accident?" the nurse asked.

Heather felt the light settle into the pit of her stomach, the world beginning to rise, life siphoning away.

"No," Heather whispered. "But it was...necessary."

Looking horrified, the nurse glanced over at her daughter, Michelle, as her eyes filled with pain and tears.

Zakhart picked up Heather from the pavement, Razasha beside him as he lifted her essence away from the broken body lying on the road. That went still with all of Seattle flowing with life around her.

With every step, the sounds of living softened. Her skin cooled, the vibrant blue sky fading as a fog rolled in, immersing her in smoky images and growing quiet. Her eyelids were so heavy, the urge to close them too difficult to fight.

"It's time to go, Heather," said Zakhart, cradling her essence in his arms.

With a last, deep breath, Heather let go, the frantic beat of her heart slowing like a child's toy winding down. Beats. Growing softer. Slower. Blood halting. The world disappearing.

With. A last. Beat. Her heart. Stopped.

One more. Breath. And Heather. Died.

Again.

two

· · ·

TWIGS SNAPPED. Grasses swished in the cool, dirty breeze that scraped across silvery grasslands, dusk gathering.

Heather froze, tucking herself deep into the tall sea of silvery green whip-like grass as something screeched overhead.

She held her breath, hands trembling as a shadow beat the darkening sky with ragged black wings, combing through the reedy grasses. Searching. Its pointed face and needle-sharp features made its pallid eyes look wild and hungry. Spiky teeth in its leering mouth looked so sharp. It beat its fists against its bare, muscled chest and shrieked out a call as it flew in tight circles above the field.

She gritted her teeth, anger rising as she balled her hands into fists. A soulstalker!

To her, they were flying cockroaches. But this time, she wouldn't hesitate to fight them with everything she had.

The suddenly empty cavity of her chest unnerved her almost as much as the shrinking grasslands that had once filled the Between's horizon. Much of the sea of grasses had been overtaken by dusty fields of grey poppies that towered over the landscape like ashen skyscrapers.

Grey dust choked the air, the sky darker than she remembered, the forests shrouded and thinning. She looked for the twinkle of amber lights in the grasses or a distant glimmer of warm light from the woods. But the horizon was dark, not a glimmer of light anywhere.

The Between had grown much worse than she'd expected. And it was pitch black in places.

Her stomach sank, dread heavy against her hollow chest, the soothing beat of a heart absent again.

What had happened to Ross?

She felt sick and it made her hurt all over at the thought of what he must have suffered here after she escaped.

Alone. Broken. Still grieving the loss of Jessie.

Heather feared what had happened to the great tree. It had been the only refuge against soulstalkers—and the demons! Besides the Red City.

She winced. All those confused, lost souls. People that had just needed a little more time...a little more help.

Zakhart had warned her that the places she remembered were gone now. But she hadn't expected the souls to be gone, too.

She felt horribly alone.

Tall grasses rustled nearby.

Heather jerked her head toward the sound.

Nothing in the twilight as it began to darken. A burnt smell hung on the wind, the air dry and dusty.

Another swish of movement.

She turned, scanning for creatures.

Ross was out here somewhere. She had to find him! Figure out what happened here, where all the souls she remembered had ended up. Where the smoke people had hidden themselves.

Where had they taken Ross?

If she knew Avana, that woman had found a grand place to hide. Avana was resourceful if nothing else. She would have grudgingly taken the others with her—if she could.

But Ross never got that chance. Her chest ached. He was out there somewhere as the Between crumbled around them.

And what about Death?

Would she sense Heather's return and come after her with a vengeance? The one that got away? Had she already carried Ross away, giving Heather no chance to save him?

No! Zakhart would have known that! He wouldn't have brought her back here if Ross' spirit was gone. There had to be some small chance or he wouldn't have come for her.

And if there was any chance—any chance at all—she'd take it. For Ross.

A shrill voice pierced the silence. Brush rustled. Somewhere behind her.

Heather turned, crawling on hands and knees through the undulating grass, working her way toward the sound. Avoiding the beat of nearby wings. She kept her head down, getting as close to the forest as she could. She'd get as close to those trees as she could before running out of the tall grasses. Making a run for the dark woods. It was her best chance.

Again, a voice cried out. Desperate. Piercing.

Heather froze.

Wings fluttered past, surging toward the sound like wolves toward an injured animal.

Heather moved closer, keeping herself camouflaged in the tall grass.

Soulstalkers screeched, shadows rushing across the grasses.

She counted at least four of them. A hunting pack.

Several packs darted across the grasslands, way more than she remembered from her first time in the Between.

Zakhart was right. It looked so different now.

The grasslands and the soulstalkers were familiar, but she barely recognized the rest of the landscape. So much had changed.

For the worse.

"Let go! Let go!" a terrified female shrieked.

A scuffle broke out in the willowy grasses ahead, two soulstalkers diving toward it. Dark feathers and silvery grass flew up, scattering on the wind.

Another human shriek.

"No! Let her go!" a deeper male voice.

Two lost souls!

Heather crept closer, seeing the shadows scuffling among the broken stalks of grass. She shuddered, counting five soulstalkers.

They were outnumbered.

Heather gritted her teeth, scrambling to her feet as the rage washed over her.

Not for long.

Two soulstalkers screeched, trying to lift a man out of the grass. Heather leaped onto one of the soulstalkers' backs, ripping feathers out of its wings, and slamming her fist into its face until it let him go.

It turned on her, wings outstretched, teeth bared. Claws extended.

Heather set herself, arms raised as the soulstalker flew at her. When it was in range, she slammed the heel of her hand upward against its nose.

The soulstalker crumpled.

She kicked it in the face until it dropped unconscious into the grass.

Thanks to Hannah's mom for the ballet lessons.

Turning, Heather lunged at two more soulstalkers trying to carry the young woman off.

The four of them tangled into a ball of fog and feathers and careened into the sea of grass. Until something broadsided her, smashing her into the ground.

Everything went dark, black wings entangling around her. Heather grabbed fistfuls of feathers, tearing them out hard and fast.

The soulstalker screamed and kicked at her legs, trying to knock her over. She grabbed hold of its leg and smashed her foot into its knee and then its shin.

A shrill cry of pain echoed as she ripped out more feathers until the thing retreated.

Three left.

The young man was beside the woman now, backing away from the three remaining soulstalkers that advanced on them. He crouched beside Heather, shielding the young woman as the soulstalkers began tag-teaming them, trying to separate them.

When the young woman bolted, one soulstalker sprang at her.

Heather rolled underneath a soulstalker and ran after the young woman.

The soul stalker had cornered the young woman, its wings spread wide. Swooping.

Heather lunged at it, tearing free a fistful of feathers.

It landed beside her and she went for its face, gouging its dark eyes, and bending one of its wings backward.

A feathered arm wrapped around her throat, squeezing.

Another one grabbed her around her waist, pulling her off the other soulstalker. Carrying her into the air.

For once, she was glad that breathing was a remnant of physical life. He couldn't choke her out at least.

She slammed her foot into its body and grabbed hold of its coarse black hair with both hands. She jerked forward as hard as she could, ripping out handfuls of the thick hair as she squirmed against its hold.

Heather and the soulstalker plunged toward the grass. She hit the ground hard, shimmied out of its grasp, and crawled through the grass away from it.

Two soulstalkers rushed at her.

She ducked, rolling out of their way.

Turning, she grabbed hold of a wing, tearing out feathers, and bending the wing backward until the soulstalker screeched in pain. She didn't let up her assault until the thing skittered backward and launched itself into the darkening sky, away from her.

With two stubborn soulstalkers left, she moved slower this time, but she went after the nearest one, wrapping her arm around its throat. Squeezing.

This time, the two lost souls helped. The young woman tore out feathers while the man pounded on the remaining soulstalker. Didn't take much more battering to get it to flee into the thickening grey dusk.

After all, the soulstalkers were outnumbered now.

Chest heaving, Heather dropped down in the grass, the other two strangers collapsing beside her.

"Who the hell are you?" the man asked with a charming smile.

He was tall and handsome, muscular beneath silky grey robes, curly dark brown hair framing his chiseled face, perfect nose, full lips, and light blue eyes. For a moment, he took her breath away.

"Heather," she said in a thin voice. "Who are you?"

"I'm Knox." He motioned to the slight young woman beside him. "This is Zoe."

Zoe was all of ninety-nine pounds, silky grey robes hanging on her. She had thick, black hair and warm hazel eyes. Her skin was winter-pale, perfect, round lips soft pink beneath a small, upturned nose. But not a young woman at all. She was a teenager, looking about seventeen. Maybe she was older than she looked. This teenager looked traumatized. Knox was in better shape. He looked at least twenty-three, maybe older.

"What happened? Did you both just wake up here?" Heather asked.

Knox sighed, nodding, hands on his hips. He ran his fingers through his curly hair. "I uh...um—died, I guess. Thought I was hallucinating and that it'd all go away when I closed my eyes again. But it didn't." He motioned at the sea of grasses surrounding them. "I sure as hell didn't expect...this."

The girl named Zoe folded her arms against her chest, a faraway look in her eyes.

"Do you know her?" Heather asked, motioning at the slight teen.

He shook his head. "Found her in the grass when I—woke up here. She hasn't said much beyond her name."

Heather moved toward the slight teen and dropped down on her haunches. Smiling, she brushed the hair out of the teen's desperate hazel eyes.

"Zoe, for the moment, we're safe. But we need to get out of these grasses. This is where the soulstalkers hunt. Do you understand?"

Zoe stared at her, past her, and then back at Knox, her hands trembling. Tears reddened her eyes. She bit her lip, her eyes scrunching into an anguished look of despair.

"Help me," she whispered. "I don't like this place."

Heather took hold of the teen's hand, pulling her to her feet. The teenager gripped Heather's arm with both hands, cowering beside her. This girl wouldn't last long here if Heather couldn't find a safe place for her.

"Where are we going?" Knox asked, moving closer. "It's all just grass and darkness."

"Toward the trees," said Heather. "We'll be safer there."

"Why should I trust you?" Knox asked, frowning. "You could change into one of those—those things at any moment."

"And so could you," Heather snapped. "I'm taking Zoe into the forest. You can either trust me or take your chances out here. Your choice. But I'm leaving with Zoe. Now."

"All right!" he said with a growl. "Let's go."

Heather turned toward the sprawling forest with Zoe in tow and Knox rushed around to her left side, taking hold of Heather's hand. The warmth of his touch sizzled through her fingers and she gasped.

She tried to ignore the pulsing heat as she led them out of the grasslands. She had no blood flowing in her veins anymore and neither did Knox and Zoe. How was she feeling heat from his hand?

"Zakhart? Razasha!" she called, the perpetual dusk heavy against the almost skeletal trees.

"Ssssh!" Knox hissed, thrusting his hand toward her mouth.

Heather ducked under his reach. "Are you crazy? You'll bring a whole herd of those things down on us!"

"Relax," Heather said. "I'm calling for help."

Knox frowned, his chiseled face scrunching into a confused stare. "Help? How do you know so much about this place? You just got here like us. I saw you appear in the grass."

She sighed. "It's a long story. I'll tell you anything you want to know as soon as we find a safe place."

"Looking forward to it," he said, his pale blue eyes wild.

The flutter of wings whispered around them.

Zoe shrieked and threw her arms over her head, cowering on the ground against Heather. Knox set himself, face a mask of concentration, fists raised.

At the wink of pumpkin-orange eyes, Heather relaxed. Zakhart!

The pale angel landed beside her, flaxen-haired Razasha a moment later.

"Soulstalkers!" Knox shouted, swinging a fist.

He tried to lunge at Zakhart, but Heather held him back.

"No, they're friends! See the pale wings? Warm-colored eyes? That means they're creatures of the light, not shadows."

"What light?" Knox asked, dropping his fists against his sides. "There's no light here."

Heather nodded. "There is. Pale angels. But they're hiding because they're outnumbered at the moment. They're trying to help us."

Knox glared at the angels, his arms crossed. "What if it's a trick?"

"What if it's not?" Heather shot back at him. "Gonna have to learn to trust someone here, Knox. It's a dangerous place to walk alone with a chip on your shoulder the size of Texas."

Zakhart unfurled his wings and stretched his arms toward the sky, closing his eyes. Rays of light pierced the Between's dark and gloom, engulfing Zakhart and Razasha in the purest, whitest light that Heather had ever seen. A sense of peace and calm emanated from the light.

Zoe whimpered, shielding her face.

Knox gaped at her as he reached toward the tangle of light spilling onto the pale angels. It trickled onto his wrist and covered his hands as it rolled across his entire body.

"It's incredible," he said, smiling. "I feel...joy. Calm." He took Zoe's hand in his and held it out to the vibrant, white light. "Look, kid," he said. "there's still some hope left."

Zoe pulled away. "It's a trick!"

It took a moment or two before Zoe's face brightened with a smile.

"No, it's real...see!"

Knox held out his hands, letting the liquid light drip from his fingers into his other hand.

Letting go of Heather, Zoe stood up and walked past Knox, toward Zakhart. She stared at him a moment then lifted her hand toward the light, the soft glow washing over her face. Zoe stared into Zakhart's eyes, her face contorting in despair and fear. The pale angel reached for her, his sparrow-grey wings bending toward her, but she stepped back from him.

"I'm scared," said Zoe, tears on her cheeks. She hid her eyes.

"I know," Zakhart whispered. "But you mustn't give up."

"I'll try," she said with a moan.

"Promise me you won't give up."

Zoe wiped her eyes with the back of her hand and finally nodded at him, stepping back toward Heather.

"Zakhart, I need to get these people out of the grasslands," Heather said, hands on her hips, gaze scanning the horizon. "But there are soulstalkers and poppy fields everywhere! The poppies are growing like weeds now, choking off hiding places and spreading darkness. I don't remember the sky ever being this dark. Can we still get to the great tree?"

He shook his head. "The great tree is gone, Heather. Destroyed by demons."

"Destroyed?"

Shock washed over her and it took a moment or two to process that statement. She bowed her head, remembering how safe she'd felt that first night among the smoke people. And the thin wash of comfort from that small nook she'd carved out for herself in the great tree's upper branches. The three of them wouldn't last long out here, at the soulstalkers' mercy.

What happened after she and Ross got Thraecius and Shuying out of the Demon Veils? After they'd set out for the Spire?

A chill danced down her spine, remembering that journey into the Demon Veils. The demons seemed so...uninterested in what happened beyond their cave. She winced at the memory of those clammy, leathery-skinned demons. And Mulciber...with his mental attacks and the sticky gold cords trapping her in the Veils. Like a spider's web. Mulciber had seemed almost harmless until he'd brutalized Ross.

Was Mulciber behind this shift in the landscape? Or Death?

"What happened to all the lost souls here?" she asked. "The ones who didn't make it to the Spiral?"

Zakhart shook his head. "I don't know. Razasha, Halea, and I had to retreat when the tree fell. Everything was in chaos. Everyone from the tree scattered into the forest. That's all I know. Razasha, what can you add?"

Razasha laid her hand on Heather's shoulder and turned her to face the sparse line of trees in the distance.

"Do you see that line of trees?" she asked, pointing.

Heather nodded.

"That's where the great tree used to be."

"What happened to it?" Heather asked.

The pale angel's face contorted, shadows marring her perfect, oval face.

"The forest exploded with demons and soulstalkers. They came up out of the ground without warning, capturing souls. People scattered and ran from the tree, others hunkered into their little nooks. I grabbed as many people as I could carry and took to the air. When I looked back, the tree just...sank into the earth and disappeared. Halea was inside. I waited forever until she finally emerged with some of the lost souls."

Heather smashed her hand against her mouth, muffling her gasp. "All those people. Barb. Lamarr. Javier...Ross. No!"

"We saved as many as we could, Heather," said Zakhart. "We set them down in a ring of trees near the clearing and led the demons away from them. It was all we could do. I don't know where they all ended up. That's when I left to...find you."

Razasha opened her palm and flung a golden cord into the air. It slithered through the dark sky toward the trees.

"I'll search for them, Heather. My light can sense any creatures near it," Razasha explained. "Avana kept close to the trees, so that's where she probably hid. The other souls were all scattered."

"So, our first task is to find a safe place?" Heather asked. "And then find the scattered souls?"

"Yes," Razasha said, smiling. "Let my energy work on locating the others while we find a safe place among those trees. When we have a safe place, we'll lead the others there."

"And fortify it with light," Zakhart added. "I need to find Halea and call in as many pale angels as I can. This will take all three of us to summon them."

Heather's eyes widened. "How many pale angels can you summon?"

Zakhart's gaze turned toward the ground and he muttered to himself, counting on his fingers.

"Around thirty, I'd guess."

"What?" Heather cried. "Aren't there thousands of angels?"

"Yes, of course," Zakhart replied as he paced, tucking his arms behind his back. "But we can only summon certain angels for certain tasks. It's a complex, tiered system, Heather. Outside your physical world, the realms are phased, requiring specific skills and abilities. Angels assigned to each realm have to learn and train to serve there. The Between is...well, a lost—that is—transitional realm."

Heather folded her arms against her chest. "You mean, forgotten, don't you?"

"Misunderstood," Razasha offered. "Most angels accept that humans choose to go there. Choose to not find their way back. Zakhart defied the hierarchy to even come here."

Heather glanced at Zakhart.

"Razasha, hush—"

"What do you mean defied?" Heather asked Zakhart, stepping toward him.

He shook his head, warm pumpkin-orange gaze slipping away from her face. "I defied my hierarchy because I was curious."

"About what?" Heather asked, reaching out to his shoulder.

Zakhart flinched away from her hand.

"Curious to learn why creatures that have been favored above all others choose to extinguish the amazing gift they've been given." His voice trembled with anger, a shadow brushing across his face. "To give up hope. To throw away that gift so easily. And to expect emptiness on the other side—nothingness—is to receive it. A realm created and nourished by your own despair."

Created by despair? Had her suicide helped keep this place in existence? But how could she have known what was beyond her own physical world? Her own mind?

His features hardened, lips pressed into an angry line. His eyes darkened with anger, hands clasped into fists.

"To settle for the dusk and never imagine beyond it, to never see the wonders of the wellspring from which their lives emerged." He glanced at Heather. "Think of what you've already seen, Heather. Now, imagine what the dawn can bring."

"Back then, I couldn't see past the pain, Zakhart. The loss. None of us can. That's why we're here. I fought my own demons in this place. And when I saw hope, I recognized it, something I could never do in my physical life." She nudged his sparrow-grey wing. "Not without some help. From you."

"Zakhart was punished for defying the hierarchy, Heather," said Razasha. She pointed to his wings. "Turned grey by his—"

"Misguided arrogance, was the official term," said Zakhart, his wings drooping against his shoulders.

"Zakhart, I'm sorry," said Heather, her voice quiet now.

"I've been sent here indefinitely," he said with a sigh. "To finish my task of rescuing these forgotten souls." His face brightened. "You were my first success. Despite what's transpired here with the demons."

Heather nodded, remembering the moment that she, Ross, and the others entered the Spiral, drawing Death away. She winced. That tiny success had probably rallied the demons to attack the great tree.

"Because of my limited success, they've allowed me to seek more angels from the upper realms, but that will take time," said Zakhart, pacing now. "Time we don't have. I don't even know if they will get here in time."

"So, we'll have to make do with what we have," Heather replied.

"All of this is just more crazy talk!" Knox shouted, face red, eyes wild as he grabbed hold of Zakhart's robes and spun him around, baring his teeth. "Who are you, people? One minute I'm jumping off a bridge and the next, I'm running around this freak show movie set, running from flying assholes and talking about raising an army! I don't know who's on what side! Or why I'm fighting anyone! What the fuck's happening?"

Zoe sank to the ground and pulled her knees up to her chest, rocking, hands over her ears.

Knox whirled around, pointing a finger at Heather. "And you! You show up after me and start ninja-punching and yanking these flying bastards out of the sky until they turn tail and run. Who are you?" His face scrunched up and he gripped his hair as he sank to his knees. "I just want out of here, okay? Out of here! I shouldn't be seeing any of this! I died! Everything was supposed to just shut the hell up!"

Heather knelt beside him and slid her arm around his shaking shoulders. He didn't try to push her away.

"It's all too much, I get it. I felt just like you do when I woke up here. One minute, I stepped in front of a bus in Seattle and the next moment, I was here. Just like you, okay?"

His Adam's apple rose and fell as he sucked in a breath. He took her by the shoulders, his eyes intense. She felt the heat roll over her again.

"You killed yourself, too?" he asked, eyes wide.

Heather nodded, motioning toward Zoe who rocked and mumbled to herself. "So did Zoe. That's why we're here. In the Between. That's what this place is, Knox. It's where people end up when they kill themselves."

He winced. "Is this...hell?"

"No, it just feels like it," said Heather, offering him an encouraging smile.

She took hold of Knox's hand and squeezed, feeling sparks churn through her belly. He was so beautiful. She concentrated on her hands.

"This place is your last chance. To figure out why you gave up and to learn how to...to go on again."

"How do you know that?" he asked, shaking his head.

Heather sighed. "Because I was here before."

"You got out of here and then killed yourself again?" Knox replied and barked out a belly laugh. "Damn, you must be completely messed up!"

"Failed comedian in your former life," Heather shot back at him, eyes narrowing. "With jokes like that, no wonder you jumped off that bridge."

Zakhart muffled his laughter, turning away as Knox fell quiet.

"I came back here to help someone else get out, okay, smart guy. Believe me, the last thing I wanted to do was return here. Good thing I did, otherwise you'd already be in the endless sleep among the poppy fields."

"Okay, you're right," Knox replied with a sigh. "I owe you for saving me just now."

"You're welcome," she said and crossed her arms.

"Truce?" he asked, holding out his hand to her.

She stared at his thick, squared hand for a moment. Finally, she nodded and shook it, those sparks electrifying her skin for a moment as she looked into his light blue eyes. Like pools of warm Caribbean seawater.

"Truce. Okay, so we find a safe place and gather the lost souls there," she said, glancing at Zakhart. "Now, what happened to Ross?" She bit her lip, the empty space in her chest aching now. "I can't do this without Ross. Where do I start searching for him?"

"Heather, we'll talk about Ross as soon as we get these two to safety," Zakhart replied, looking troubled. "All right?"

He wasn't telling her everything. Had something terrible happened to Ross?

Had Death already killed him with her scythe and Zakhart just couldn't bring himself to tell her?

She was worried sick, imagining hundreds of horrible things that had happened to him. But she ached to be in his arms, to hear his comforting voice in her ear, feel his mouth against hers. They'd barely discovered each other and now he was so far away.

"Only if you tell me everything," she said, hands on her hips.

"All right. Everything, Heather. Sure you want that?"

She nodded. She had to know where Ross was and what was at stake. When she'd be with him again. It was the only way she'd survive this place a second time.

"Everything, Zakhart," she demanded, glaring at him.

The sound of wings thumped against the silence. Heather glanced up as Halea descended from the dark sky. And landed beside Zakhart.

"You needed more help?" she asked, glancing around. Her soft, copper eyes widened when her gaze met Heather's and she gasped. "Heather! You've come back? Oh, no! This is terrible!"

Heather started to respond when a smile curved across the pale angel's face. "Oh...Ross, right?" Halea replied.

Heather couldn't deny it. She nodded.

"He saved me from Death. It's my turn to save him."

"That's...good," said Halea.

"Time to go," said Zakhart. "Before the hunting packs turn out."

Zakhart lifted Heather into his arms. "All right, let's carry them toward the forest, see what Razasha's searchlight found. We won't set any of you down until we've found a safe place for you."

"A base of operations," Heather corrected him as Razasha gathered Zoe into her arms.

Halea picked up Knox.

Zakhart raised an eyebrow at Heather. "Base of operations?"

"Gotta have a base of operations to raise an army, Zakhart."

"An army?" Knox gasped. "What the hell? You were serious, weren't you?"

"If we have any chance of getting out of this place," said Heather, "then we'll need an army. It's the only way now, Knox. We're going to war."

Her gut told her that Mulciber was behind this and she'd need an army to rescue Ross. She'd let Zakhart explain that as soon as they got to safety. For now, they needed a safe place to gather other souls.

"I did two tours in Afghanistan," Knox replied and settled back against Halea. "Fifteen months each. I'll do one more here if I have to, but not until I have some answers. I've got a lot of questions."

Halea rose into the air, Knox in her arms as they flew toward the trees in the distance.

Get in line, Heather thought with a snarl. Right now, all she had was questions and no answers. And an ache in her chest that wouldn't stop.

Where was Ross? Who changed the Between and why? Who was trying to take over a place of infinite despair? A place where people went when they'd given up on everything.

three

. . .

ZAKHART HELD HEATHER CLOSE, the air smelling dirty and burned as they left the grasslands behind. Beyond the horizon, poppies crouched like smoke stacks, belching out thick swaths of dust that fell like snow through the poppy fields that looked like ashes across the landscape. Darkening it. Choking it with clouds of grey dust.

Heather covered her mouth, a cough rattling through her chest as she inhaled grit. So much of the grasslands had disappeared, gouged out by tight furrows of ashen soil where poppies sprouted like dandelions.

"Don't worry," said Zakhart. "The poppy dust won't harm you. It only changes into the final sleep after the sand runners gather it."

"Good to know," said Heather as a flash of light peeked out from her grey sleeves.

Startled, she pulled up her sleeves, staring at the strange coils of light tangled around her wrists. Like glowing bracelets.

"Zakhart? What are these things?" she asked, holding up her right arm to show him the writhing strands of gold light. "I've never seen them before."

The pale angel glanced at them and smiled, his gaze shifting back to the thin, broken forest ahead (or what was left of it). His grip around her tightened.

"They're from the Spiral, Heather," he said, nodding at the horizon. "They'll lead you back to it when it's time."

Heather ran her fingers over the thin bracelets of light, their presence oddly comforting.

"When I find Ross," she replied.

Zakhart stiffened.

That frightened her. He'd been so tight-lipped about what had happened to Ross. So vague that she feared the worst. A fate she hadn't been able to imagine.

"Heather, look at the forest as I fly over it. Tell me what you see."

Zakhart turned in a wide circle, banking low against a swift wind. He floated on an updraft and soared just above the trees as the forest floor took shape. Small, black mounds dotted the ground among mostly saplings and young trees. He flew in deeper, toward the taller, older trees that stretched long branches into a thin canopy, protecting the forest floor and blocking the sky. Dozens of black mounds dotted the ground, dissipating as the forest got thicker and darker.

"The older trees can still protect us," said Heather.

"Agreed."

"But it's so dark down there. Not a light to be seen. So much devastation."

It made her stomach ache.

Zakhart nodded.

Her chest tightened. She missed those amber lights twinkling in the dark. Lanterns the lost souls had carried under Avana's direction. She sighed. Where she'd first met Ross Shepherd. Those lights—and Ross—had once guided her and others to the safety of the great tree.

Gone now. All of it.

"Something used our escape through the Spiral as an opportunity, didn't it?" she asked, studying his pumpkin-orange eyes, trying to gauge his reaction. "It was a diversion. And it allowed them to set all of...this in motion."

"Yes, they did. I knew you'd figure that out, Heather." He was smiling.

Her eyes were drawn back to the black mounds sprinkled across the landscape.

"What are these black mounds? I've never seen them before. Were they part of the attack on the great tree?"

"Yes." Zakhart sucked in a breath, a troubled expression shadowing his pearly complexion.

"Mulciber," she said with a low growl.

His eyes widened and he stared at her. "How'd you know that?"

"Come on, Zakhart, he's a demon! He was not happy when we led half his slaves out of there. And he attacked Ross, singling him out from everyone." Heather stared at the mounds of black dirt. "There were tons of workers inside that cave, Zakhart, working what they called the coal fields. And so many tunnels." She let out a gasp, everything clicking into place. "Zakhart...they've been digging tunnels underneath the entire Between, haven't they?"

Sighing, Zakhart bowed his head and nodded.

"That's how they attacked the great tree, isn't it?" Heather cried. "They probably killed its roots slowly, hollowing out the ground beneath it until it fell through. Capturing all the souls inside!"

She curled her hands into fists, anger seething through her. Why had she and Ross dismissed the demons' danger so quickly?

"They've got Ross, don't they?" she demanded.

Zakhart pointed. "Look, this is the tree I wanted you to see," he said, flying into a small ring of thick-trunked trees. They were half the size of the great tree, but there were five hearty trees, sturdy like oaks.

"Tell me!" she shouted, struggling against his hold.

He ignored her, landing beside the tallest, widest tree in the small grove. He let her go and turned to the tree, patting its rugged bark. "I think we can defend ourselves from here, don't you?" he asked.

"Zakhart! Tell me!"

"Not here," Zakhart hissed, his eyes taking on a strange glow.

Halea circled above them, setting down in the small ring of trees. A moment later, Razasha landed. They set Zoe and Knox down beside Heather. Knox and Zoe moved closer to her, gazes still frightened and confused. Zoe clung to Knox.

Heather reached out and squeezed their hands, knowing how terrified they must feel. This place was bad enough, but with no haven, they were like rabbits running from owls and hawks. Except they didn't know the paths and trails.

"This is a good spot, Zakhart," Razasha cried as she flitted around the circle of trees, touching each trunk. "This place is perfect. We can rebuild here."

"Are you sure?" Halea asked, glancing at the dark forest and the strange scritching sounds rising above the screech of soulstalkers.

She pulled her wings tighter around her.

The sounds made Heather's skin crawl.

"What do you mean, Halea?" Razasha asked, her doe-eyed expression filling with concern. She laid her hand on Halea's arm, but the other pale angel moved away.

"This place doesn't feel right. I don't think it'll be safe. Razasha, reason with him, please. It's not safe."

Razasha turned to Zakhart and chimed soft soprano tones at him. She turned to Halea, toned again, and then trilled a long chorus. Halea joined her, laying down a repeating, alto harmony that lifted the sound, the notes entangled and the little clearing filled with a warm, comforting haze.

As beautiful as it was, they were arguing. Heather saw Zakhart's intense expression.

Zakhart thumped his fist against the bark of the largest tree.

"This is the one," he announced in a firm voice. "I've chosen this one. We'll convert it into a haven."

Halea's gaze darkened and she turned away, arms against her chest, wings shaking. With anger.

Zakhart gave her a moment until the melodies dissipated.

"How long will it take to change it?" he asked in a soft voice.

Razasha glanced at Halea who shrugged. "Not long. We'll get started."

She nodded at Halea. The two of them clasped hands around the big tree, closing their eyes and lifting their faces to the soot-grey sky.

A puddle of white light bubbled up from the soil, collecting around the tree's base. It eddied around Razasha's feet, swirling toward Halea until it deepened, rising to their ankles.

The pale angels lifted their arms and the watery, gold light danced at their fingertips, flowing up through the ragged channels in the bark toward limbs and leaves. Extending them. At their feet, the puddle widened, deepened as it spread across the ground. Toward the other four trees in the grove.

One by one, the ring of trees lit with the watery gold light, the glow spreading up their trunks, to limbs, into leaves as puddles collected at their bases. Bark turned into a hard shell, fresh new leaves sprouting from stronger, wider limbs, roots anchoring deeper, wider into the darkening soil. The rich, loamy smell of fertile soil hung in the air, reminding Heather of opening bags of rich, black potting soil for her mom's salsa garden every spring.

Shiny red, grapefruit-sized heirloom tomatoes. Sweet, fist-sized Walla Walla onions. Green, waxy jalapenos and lacy stalks of bright, sharp-smelling cilantro. Her mouth watered just thinking about Mom's salsa. She thought of Hannah's mom now, planting delicate pink English roses that filled the backyard with their heady, spring scent. She remembered Hannah's dad sprinkling the fragrant, loose petals across Hannah's mom's pillow once.

Heather had cared a lot for them and Grandpa Jimmy, but she loved her first mom and dad. It was sad leaving Emily and Dan. Hannah had just turned eighteen, but Heather didn't feel like she'd lived all eighteen of those years. She'd felt like an imposter much of the time, like she hadn't belonged there, something that had troubled her long before Zakhart showed up. Even though she hadn't understood why she felt that way. Until Zakhart reminded her.

"Zakhart, how many moms and dads do I have now?" she asked.

He studied her face a moment. "Just one mom and one dad." He brushed his hand across her cheek. "You're troubled."

"I wasn't supposed to be there, in that life, was I?"

He frowned. "What do you mean?"

"I was never supposed to become Hannah Girard-Davies, was I?" she asked. "Hannah had a friend, Rebecca Ross. Her twin brother, Rick died in a car accident. He should have graduated with her and Hannah. Everyone called him Ross. Too many coincidences, wouldn't you say?"

Zakhart cupped her chin in his hand. "No. You're right. You were supposed to begin again. A new life. Like Ross. But when Death snatched Ross out of the Spiral, everything changed. See, Hannah had a fatal heart condition. She'd been born with it."

"I know," Heather replied. "I had to keep medication with me all the time, take all these crazy blood tests. I had a huge scar on my chest from two open heart surgeries." She laid her hand to her chest, the once almost-familiar scar gone now.

"Hannah's life should have ended at fourteen," said Zakhart, crossing his arms as he watched the pools of light collecting on the forest floor.

Razasha and Halea stood motionless now as the streams of light did their work.

"Her heart fell into a fatal rhythm and they rushed her to the hospital," Zakhart continued. "Hannah coded and for fifteen minutes, the hospital struggled to bring her back."

Heather nodded. "That's when I arrived, wasn't it?"

The pale angel nodded, a solemn look on his face. "Yes. When Death opened the hole in the physical world, we struggled to fill it quickly. Imagine the awkward exchange I had with Death as I passed her in the ER. You in my arms, Hannah Girard-Davies in hers."

Heather rolled her eyes. "Oh, snap! How embarrassing, Death—we're wearing the exact same soul. Who knew?"

"I had no other choice that day, Heather," Zakhart replied, bristling, annoyance in his pumpkin-orange eyes. "When you came back as Hannah, they rushed you into emergency heart surgery which saved Hannah's life. But I placed you in Hannah's body for two reasons. One, it was a convenient but good match, I won't lie. Two, placing your soul in her body gave her family a reprieve. Gave them a little more time with their daughter. But more importantly, it was a short life. Like the one I chose for Ross."

"Don't get cranky. I was just kidding," said Heather, patting his arm. "What do you mean you gave her family a reprieve?"

"You were right about Rick Ross," Zakhart continued, his annoyance fading. "I was ready to put Ross into Rick Ross' life as the teenager lay dying in the ER. I wanted to give that family a reprieve, too, but I couldn't. I had to let Rick Ross' life go because I also had to watch Death carry Rick Ross and Ross Shepherd away, knowing the two of you would never meet now."

Heather fought back the tears welling her eyes and turned away, walking toward Razasha and Halea.

Was it all over now? Was Ross lost to her forever?

She folded her arms against her chest, her head spinning with too much information and too much grief. She missed Ross so much.

A hand touched her shoulder. Zakhart.

"I only wanted you and Ross to have a little time together in the physical world before letting your souls go on again. Like they should."

He was right. They both chose to end their lives. Getting a second chance was more than she'd deserved, but she'd been so grateful for it. So had Ross. She never expected to live a long, full life after throwing hers away. But she was glad to know that Hannah would have left them sooner if she hadn't stepped into that life. She'd done a little good there.

"This is just so confusing, Zakhart," she said, her voice cracking. "I miss Ross so much. Why can't you tell me where he is?"

"We'll do our best to find him, Heather," said Zakhart. "I promise."

The pale angel wrapped his arms around her, holding her tighter as Razasha and Halea stepped back from the massive oak, the light illuminating its branches fading now.

"Too many ears, Heather," Zakhart whispered in her ear. "Trust me. When it's safe."

Heather cast an uneasy glance around the clearing, unsure what Zakhart meant about too many ears. She'd trusted him with her life before. She'd trust him with Ross now.

"Razasha, Halea, how are things progressing?" Zakhart called.

"The trees will absorb the rest of this light into their roots over the next few days," said Razasha, rubbing her forehead.

Halea looked weak, shoulders slumped, cream-colored wings drooping, coppery orange eyes shadowed. She leaned against Razasha's shoulder and closed her eyes.

Knox and Zoe rose from the ground and moved over to the angels and Heather. Knox looked grumpy, angry, arms crossed, mouth pressed into a grimace. Zoe just looked scared.

"Good work, Razasha, Halea," said Zakhart, letting Heather go. "Halea, you should rest."

Halea nodded, trilling an alto chord. She closed her eyes, pulled her wings tight around her like a cocoon, and floated above the ground. Heather smiled. She'd never seen angels rest before.

Knox squinted. "What exactly does all of that mean?" he asked.

Razasha nudged him toward the tree. "Go and see, Knox."

The oak tree had grown taller and wider than the other four. A heavy, arched door appeared, stepping stones leading up to it. The wink of amber light from two lanterns hung on both sides of the door. Large, rectangular windows began to appear in the tree trunk, flickers of light piercing the encroaching darkness.

"It's beautiful, Razasha and Halea." Heather moved toward the door.

Knox and Zoe followed close.

Heather turned the doorknob and the door creaked open. With Knox and Zoe behind her, she stepped inside.

Into a large, empty room with light, honey-colored wood walls and floors. A large, winding staircase coiled up through the middle of the tree, reminding her of the former great tree. It was larger with a staircase on either side. She almost expected to see that familiar, blue sofa flanking the fireplace, where Ester and Matthew were curled up, drinking wine in each other's arms. Or the big, square meal table that stood near the fireplace. She'd have even welcomed Avana's smoky presence flitting through the room, the other smoke people drifting silently up the stairs.

Oops. The overstuffed blue sofa appeared beside a roaring fireplace made of smooth river rocks that stretched to the wooden ceiling. It covered half the wall, a large picture window looking out onto the forest beside it. She expected to smell the scent of woodsmoke as the flames crackled against a charred stack of logs. But all she smelled was warm sawdust and freshly tilled soil.

Might as well use the sofa. It looked comfortable. Heather sat down and sank into the cushions.

"It—it's nice," Zoe replied, tiptoeing through the well-lit space, to the other side of the tree, the ambient gold light radiating from the air. "Feels safe."

Zakhart, Razasha, and Halea entered the new tree, looking pleased with their creation. Halea still looked tired.

Heather wanted to bound up those stairs to the very top, expecting to find Ross lying on a red flannel comforter as he stared out the window and hid from Avana. She bit her lip, refusing to give up on him.

Zoe gasped and let out a squeak.

"What's wrong?" Heather asked, rushing to her.

A smile brightened Zoe's face as she pointed toward the opposite side of the tree. "Another fireplace!"

The crackle of wood and flicker of flames dancing across the honey-colored wood floor made Heather turn around. She smiled. Zoe had conjured another fireplace. Across the room. Made of red brick with a polished walnut mantle. She hoped it brought the girl comfort. She seemed so small and frail against Knox's tall, brawny frame. In the fluttering glow of firelight, he looked at least six foot three, maybe taller. He towered over Zoe's slight, five-foot-four height.

"Where'd that come from?" Knox replied, hurrying over to stand in front of the flames and then turned toward the sofa and fireplace that Heather had called up. "And those!"

Smiling, Knox held out his hands and warmed his fingers in the cold flames of Zoe's fireplace.

"I don't know," Zoe cried. "I was just thinking about the big, brick fireplace at home. And here it is! It looks just like the fireplace I grew up with! See, Dad always built these huge fires every night and we roasted marshmallows and made s'mores. Alberta gets so cold."

Zoe rushed over to stand by Knox. She reached out and ran her fingers across the rough red bricks, eyes brightening as she stared into the flames. Was she remembering something from her life? Zoe held out her hands, warming them.

Heather couldn't help but feel protective of the slight, shaky young teen. She was younger than she looked and she'd been through something terrible. It hung on her features, flickering in the dark parts of her hazel eyes, and clung to her thin body, weighing on every bone of her slumped shoulders. When she'd settled a bit, Heather would try to help Zoe in any way she could. She looked like she could use a friend. And protection. Those soulstalkers would swallow her whole at their first opportunity.

"Zoe, look on the table over there," Heather replied, pointing at the stack of graham crackers beside a bowl of fluffy, white marshmallows and thick, milky sticks of chocolate that she had conjured for the teen.

Zoe squealed and rushed toward the treats. "S'mores! I'm so hungry."

"I'd rather have a thick steak," Knox said with a growl, crossing his arms. "Sizzling over the fire."

A sputtering hiss filled the quiet space and Knox turned toward the sound. A metal grill plate stood above the flames in the river rock fireplace, balancing a thick steak that cooked slowly over the cold flames.

Knox backed away from the fire, eyes wide, as Zoe grabbed a metal stick and popped a marshmallow on the end. She held it over the fire, ignoring Knox who looked spooked now.

"Everything we think of—just appears!"

He shuffled away from the fireplace, pressing his back to the wall, watching the room. Every muscle in his arms and legs, tightened as he dropped into a crouch.

"What kind of voodoo is this?"

"Voodoo that will save your sanity, Knox," Heather replied. "The pale angels infused this gift of conjuring into the tree, to help us adjust while we're here. It's a comfort, Knox."

"I don't want to be comfortable here," he snapped. "I want out!"

Zakhart walked toward Knox.

The former soldier whirled around, blue eyes feral, hand scrambling for something at his side. The pale angel whispered something Heather couldn't hear and touched Knox's forehead. Knox let out a sigh and his body slumped against the wall.

Zakhart caught him, steering him over to the couch.

Knox snarled, jerking out of Zakhart's hands. He kicked the sofa and plopped down beside Heather.

Was she like this when she first got here? Knox seemed like a man of action. He didn't want to wait for anything. Made up his mind in a snap and wanted to dive in and take charge. She chuckled. He was the opposite of Ross who was thoughtful and contemplates every move.

"Great, now you're laughing at me."

He sank back against the cushion, his muscled arms tense, his face taut, blue eyes haunted with the fireplace's ethereal light. He seemed like he was running from something. That, she understood.

"Yeah, sorry. I just see myself in your reaction."

She leaned back into the cushions, wondering where Ester and Matthew were now. And Thraecius. She hoped they were with Juliana now.

"I was a little like you when I got here, Knox. I didn't want to pretend to eat and sleep. I wanted out. Look, you're not going to locate the Spiral tonight, so—"

"Spiral? What Spiral?"

Heather cringed, wanting to kick herself for mentioning the Spiral. Knox was already wound up like an overstretched rubber band. And things weren't this bad when she was here before. Back then, there'd been a path to the Spiral. There weren't dozens and dozens of soulstalkers hunting in packs and a demon uprising in the making. Back then, the great tree had always been here like an anchor.

Everything was different now. And so were the rules.

And right now, Knox would never understand that finding that path started within him. It wasn't a physical place yet. If he didn't get this quickly, he'd be sleeping in the poppy fields by tomorrow. And they were everywhere now, not far to the north like before.

She grabbed his arm and he recoiled, jerking back, fist cocked, rage in his wild eyes.

"Knox!" she shouted, not letting go. "I'm not the enemy, okay?"

He stared at her like he'd rip her head off. She held her ground, holding his gaze until something pushed through the rage. His face contorted, pain rushing in to fill up the rage. He smashed his eyes closed, his breath slowing.

She waited until his eyes opened. "Listen to me, Knox. Listen carefully."

He nodded, hard blue gaze softening.

"I get it. You're a big, brave soldier. You eat bullets for breakfast and belch hand grenades, I get it, but you'd better find some fear quick here. If you don't, you'll lose this last chance to make things right again. You got me?"

He stared unblinking, eyes brightening, a smile playing on his lips. He moved closer, reaching toward her face, fingers brushing her cheek in a gentle caress.

"God, you're beautiful," he whispered, leaning in for a kiss.

Heather held him back. "Knox! Listen!"

He ran his fingers down her arm. "So hot. And dangerous. You might be hiding a knife in your sleeve. Or spring one of those ninja moves on me like you dropped on those flying bastards."

His breath was hot, eyes on fire. She'd never felt lonelier than she did at this moment.

Oh, Ross...where are you?

She leaned forward, a hand on Knox's chest. He was beautiful. She tilted her head toward his mouth. Brushing her mouth across his lips.

"You can try and romance me all you want," she said, her voice husky and inviting, "but I won't tell you where the Spiral is. I won't help you kill yourself again, Knox."

"Aw, dammit!" Knox shouted as she pulled away. "Come on, Heather. I need information."

She settled back against the sofa and turned toward him. "Knox, there *is* a way out, but it's not a place you can just go to and escape. There's no physical exit in the Between. You've got to get that through your head or it's over."

Knox squeezed his eyes closed and hit the couch cushion with his fist. "Dammit! So we're all trapped here? Is that what you're saying? Forever?"

"Not trapped and not forever," Heather said. "Delayed." She

waited for those words to settle. "Knox, you've got to understand some things first. Things about you. Like why you killed yourself. Why you want to keep living. Only when you understand those things will you have any hope of leaving here."

"C'mon, Heather, tell me how to leave. Show me how to get to this Spiral."

She sighed. He'd deflected every word she'd said.

"Knox, it's not a place."

He sat up, excitement in his eyes. "Fine, I'll go alone. Head out and scan the perimeter, identify hostiles, and check for egress routes. Sight encampments and assess threat level."

"Do that and you'll be sleeping with the poppies by tomorrow, Knox," Heather said, sighing.

God, his head was as thick as the bark of these oak trees!

She grabbed him by the shoulders, shaking him hard. "Forever, Knox! Do you understand what forever is yet?"

He just stared, muscles rock hard, unmovable as stripped screws.

"You should be getting a good picture of it about now," Heather continued. "Stop trying to be a hero! You can't just run in and snipe everybody, toss a few grenades, and own the place. You don't even know who or what you're fighting yet. Turn off the Xbox and wait for the squadron."

"God, you're an arrogant bitch." He glared at her, pulling away. "And I thought Afghanistan was the worst my life could get. Boy, was I wrong about that."

Knox snapped up from the couch and moved over to the fireplace to retrieve his steak. Heather covered her mouth, trying to hide her smile. She wondered how many bites he'd take before he realized that steak had no taste.

"Who put you in charge anyway?" he muttered, dragging over a wooden chair from the meal table.

He stabbed the steak with a fork he'd grabbed off the meal table, the one Heather had remembered from the great tree.

She chuckled, watching him cool down while Zoe built s'mores by the other fire. Zoe seemed content, ignoring their argument.

"Technically, Zakhart did when he made me step out in front of that bus."

"Heather!" Zakhart frowned, embarrassment reddening his face. "I did no such thing! Only you could make that decision—"

She smiled at the pale angel. "That was a joke, Zakhart."

He let out a breath and leaned against the wall, looking relieved. "I knew that."

Heather sank into the couch cushions. "But seriously, Knox, no one's in charge. You're free to head out that door any time you'd like. But I'm glad we got to talk before you lose your mind and go out to play with the soulstalkers. Was nice knowing you."

He snorted at her and pushed a bite of steak into his mouth, tilting the wooden chair back against the tree wall so his feet dangled above the floor.

"Ever see combat, little girl? Be fresh out of high school and forced to make life-and-death decisions? Every. Single. Day? Ever stand next to your best friend one minute and see him blown to bits by an IED? Ever see your whole unit dropped one-by-one by a sniper while you fight to get a clear shot?"

She recognized Knox's anger now. He'd seen a lot of terrible things in combat.

"No, Knox," said Heather. "I'm sorry that you have though."

He poked his chest with his thumb. "Well, I saw all of that. And I'm an old man at twenty-four, Heather. I've walked through minefields and carried my buddies through a hailstorm of bullets."

His face was a mask of sweat, his blue eyes haunted by things no one should ever have to see. His hands shook as he gripped the fork and plate.

"I've watched a terrified kid stumble into camp with a bomb strapped to his chest, begging us not to shoot him while the bomb's trigger ticks down—a bomb that will kill all of us if it detonates. So, I think I can handle myself against those flying pricks." His eyes narrowed. "And you."

"When I first came here," said Heather, watching him shovel in the imaginary steak while warming himself in front of the cold hearth fire. "I wanted things to happen immediately. I didn't want to wait or pretend I was still alive. I wanted out of here now. When no one wanted to help me, I walked out that door, pissed off, and refusing to listen to anyone. Ran right into a hunting party of soulstalkers. They'd have carried me off to the poppy fields, too, if someone hadn't stopped them."

She winced. Ross. He'd protected her from the moment she arrived in the Between. Her stomach twisted into a knot.

Where was he tonight? Were they torturing him?

She couldn't take the thoughts of Mulciber pounding horrible images against his head, torturing him with awful pictures of Jessie's death until he couldn't think straight. Until he just wanted to die all over again to escape it.

Knox's face went pale, his anger dissipating. He ate more steak, watching her, his eyes looking far away. Deep in thought. She was relieved. He needed to just take some time to sit and think. About everything.

"I'm sorry about all those terrible things that happened to you, Knox."

He just shrugged. "You have no idea what you're talking about."

Heather rose from the couch and wandered over to the river rock fireplace. She grabbed a chair and carried it over, sitting down across from him.

"I mean that," she insisted. "I know you've seen things I can't even imagine. I wasn't trying to belittle you or make light of what you went through. I was just trying to get through to you about this place and how dangerous it is. I'm trying to apologize."

He looked up, staring at her through long, feathery lashes, teeth grinding, jaw clamped tight. He flicked the fork back and forth across the empty plate in front of him and wiped his mouth with his sleeve.

Still trying to be such a hardass. She'd better keep her distance for now.

"Fair enough," she replied, pulling herself out of the chair.

Knox grabbed her wrist.

"Wait," he said.

She didn't move, her gaze on his hand clamped around her wrist, bending the light bracelets under the crush of his fingers. And waited for him to speak.

Knox angled his tall body out of the chair, unfolding his legs as he got to his feet, setting the chair upright. Still gripping her wrist.

"Apology accepted," he said, not looking at her. "I'm not...used to people trying to help me. My whole life, people have tried to control me. My dad. Boot camp. The government." He sighed, running his fingers through that sexy tangle of curly dark hair. "When I came home, I finally got the chance to make my own decisions, but...I just—couldn't shake the memories. The fear."

He let go of her wrist, sadness and despair in his eyes as the wooden chair banged against the tree wall. He paced, restless now. His gaze never left the door, the pale angels by the window...his back.

Fear? That was the last thing she'd expected him to say.

Heather took Knox's hand and led him to the couch. She sat him down, conjured a beer, and handed him the cold bottle.

Grinning, he took it, twisted off the cap, and guzzled it.

"I love a woman who knows how to conjure a cold beer," he said with a snort.

It wasn't real, but he'd figure that out soon enough.

Heather dropped down beside him, folding her legs beneath her as she watched him drink, waiting for the right moment to get him to talk.

She let the illusion take hold before she spoke.

"Tell me about these memories, this fear."

A horrified gleam flickered in Knox's eyes as he clutched the bottle in both hands, fingers worrying against the bottle's slick, sweating surface.

"Just like that? Have a beer and bare your soul?" He shook his head, eyes sharpening. "Unless you were there, unless you lived through that constant state of hyper-alert, you can't understand," he said, almost angry that she'd even try.

"You're right, I can't understand what you went through unless I've seen combat," Heather replied, patting his forearm. "I just want to help you understand that pain, Knox. The fear."

She choked up, remembering that long ago night on the Bainbridge Island beach, her life trickling away as the tide came in.

He took a long pull off the bottle, wiping his mouth on his sleeve.

"Once you live like that, every moment on full alert, constant patrols that determined whether you survived the night with no switchover to whatever the hell normal used to be. You just can't reset that clock. Can't roll back to default."

"I can't even imagine that," she said in a quiet voice. "What I can understand is that bottomless despair. That three A.M. hopelessness that turns everything to shit, makes everything you ever cared about feel hollow and empty. Makes it easier to just toss it all in the trash like a bunch of empty beer bottles." She sucked in a breath, her bottom lip trembling. "I've been there. I couldn't even handle normal, Knox, much less get through what you went through in Afghanistan. No, I took a fatal dose of Molly, trying to turn it all off, to stop it all from mocking me one more time. And I died alone, not a single person nearby to even care that I was gone."

Her face was wet with tears and she let them cascade down her cheeks like a cool, cleansing spring rain washing the mud off her tires.

Knox's hard expression softened. He reached out and covered her hand with his, gripping it. The warmth startled her, made that ache in her chest intensify, her tears saltier as she tasted bitter regret on her lips.

Why hadn't she held on tighter to Ross? Wrapped herself around him, keeping him far away from Death? Why!

"Were you scared?" he asked.

She nodded. "Terrified."

"Why?"

"I didn't know what was about to happen to me."

"Yeah, I get that. I was in a constant state of alert. Every time I turned a corner or walked into a building, my insides would ball up, terrified of what was around the corner."

His body stiffened, hands gripping the folds of his clothes.

"For nearly three years, my world was surreal, like living on a movie set. Explosions, gunfire—buddies dying. Seconds of chaos then calm. You live in a state of hyper-alert. You have to be ready to defend yourself and your buddies. Every. Single. Moment. You have to expect that everything might turn to shit in an instant and anyone you see might try to kill you."

Heather kept quiet and still, trying not to break the spell as he opened up to her.

"The world always melts suddenly into a firefight, IEDs exploding...or it freezes into frames that tick forward so slow and I can't touch the remote. A little kid. Handing my buddy a box. I run toward him. Trying to get to him in time. With every step, I'm a second too late. I see his face. Ten steps, twelve steps too late. I see that look, that he knows he's fucked up. That he can't take it back. That it's gonna blow up in his face. And it goes up, takin' my buddy with it. But all I can do is stare. Just stare. And die inside."

Knox was sweating, fingers turning white as he strangled the bottle in his fists.

"I walk into the dentist's office and sit down in the waiting room. Already, I'm counting the people in the room, numbering the exits, the obstacles between me and the door. Mother and daughter six feet to my left. Old guy with a cane ten feet in front of me, standing at the window. Is that cane a rifle? Closed door on my right. Who's behind it? How many hostiles? How many weapons?"

His eyes were glassy now, fingers still twisting around the empty beer bottle.

"I watch every twitch, every gesture, listen for every sound, every change of emotion, my hand floating at my side, ready to pull my weapon because I know that cane's gonna be a rifle leveled at my head. My palms are drenched in sweat and my heart pounds so hard against my chest I think it's gonna explode. The kid lets out a screech and I jump, startled, and reach for the gun in my holster I'm not wearing, my blood boiling because I was startled, caught off guard. Everything inside me screams to go on the attack. Because that's what I was trained to do. That's how I survived three years in Afghanistan, but somehow, that last shred of the person I was before I signed on to be a man—a soldier—holds back the rage that wants to take out whatever's piercing my brain with that shrill spike."

A tear slipped down his face and he swiped it away.

"And now I realize it's a five-year-old kid and his mother and I hate myself for wanting to destroy everything in the room. My shirt's drenched and stinking now and I'm shaking like an alcoholic fresh out of the drunk tank. So I cancel your appointment and skulk home to my apartment where I can slam enough beer and shots to mute the fear and deaden the pain. The next day, it starts over again."

Knox could barely hold onto the emotions ripping him up inside. Heather put her arms around him.

The first sob tore free and he buried his face in her hair, shaking violently now.

The beer bottle hit the floor and rolled away, scraping its way along the wood floor until it hit the fireplace and broke.

"That cycle was killing me," he said, his voice strained. "And I didn't want to snap and hurt some innocent. I'm not worth that risk."

"Of course, you matter," she cried, holding him tighter. "Just as much as anyone. Everyone. You're suffering. It's not your fault."

"The bridge," he cried, his chest heaving now. "It was the only to stop it. To cut the fuse, let it burn out before it detonated into a bloodbath. Every night, I dreamed about shooting up the nearby mall, Heather. Or mowing down everyone I saw in the grocery store."

"Knox," she said in a soothing tone, "They were just dreams. Dreams! You didn't shoot innocents."

"But I could have," he sputtered, tears choking his voice. "I would have. I had to jump. It was the only way to save the innocents, Heather. Secure the perimeter. The only way."

She held him, stroking his hair as hard, as wracking sobs shook through him. The flood of emotion drained him and he sat up, listless, and covered his eyes with his hand.

"You're not alone now, Knox," she said, brushing a curl out of his eyes. "We need to pull together now. There are lots of people out there just like us. We need to find them and bring them here." She gestured at Zoe still eating s'mores. "To protect the innocents. There are a lot of them out there like Zoe. When we've got enough of a group to fight back, we've got to find out what's caused the destruction out there. And try to stop it." And find Ross. "I'm counting on you to be in that group, Knox."

"Of course," he said, his voice thin and tired. "It's what I do."

She smiled and conjured a blanket that she laid across Knox whose eyes were closing. "We're going to have to trust each other, Knox."

Knox sighed. "Not very good at that."

Heather let him fall asleep. She cast a worried glance at Zakhart. The pale angel nodded at him. Razasha and Halea were cocooned in their wings, floating above the floor now. Zakhart nodded toward the stairs. He wanted to talk to her in private.

She rose from the couch and climbed the stairs to the tree's highest level, waiting for Zakhart.

four

. . .

THE NEW TREE was so empty and quiet that it made Heather anxious. She'd conjured lanterns around the room that cast streams of warm light through the space and filled it with the sound of rainfall to dampen the silence. In the corner of the empty room, she imagined a small brass bed with thick, soft pillows and a downy, lavender comforter.

She crawled into the center of the bed and hugged a pillow to her chest, wanting to follow the bracelets back to the Spiral and leave this place behind forever.

But the memory of Ross' arms enfolding her in a warm, safe embrace, the press of his lips burning through her, making her ache all over.

For Ross, she'd hold on. For him, she'd see this through.

She tried to focus on the light and the calm and the conjured sound of soft rain as she watched the stairway for Zakhart's shadow.

The pale angel was acting strange. She wanted to know why.

Why wouldn't Zachary talk about Ross, tell her what happened, and how she could save Ross? Why wouldn't the pale angel feel free to talk in front of everyone? Zoe and Knox didn't know Ross, so they wouldn't even understand the conversation. Razasha and Halea knew Ross well, knew everything she and Ross had shared in the Between. Exploring the pathways, fighting off soulstalkers, stumbling onto the poppy fields.

Who else was listening?

Maybe Zakhart was just afraid to talk in front of the new souls because he didn't know how they'd react. Especially Knox who might run headfirst into disaster without enough information. Maybe he didn't want to traumatize Zoe more. The teenager could barely function right now.

One more horror story might just send her into the poppy fields.

At last, the whisper of wings rasped against wood, patter of footsteps on the stairs. She looked up. Zakhart stood in the doorway, his face drawn, worry bright in his intense, pumpkin-orange eyes.

Whatever it was, it was bad.

Even when Death had found her and Ross, Zakhart hadn't looked this beaten down and discouraged. He was always ready with a hopeful word, but right now, she doubted the pale angel could summon a single upbeat thought.

He crept inside and conjured a door into her nook, closing it behind him. For a long time, he stood by the door, eyes closed, arms outstretched.

"What's wrong?"

He shushed her with a finger against his lips, still holding this strange pose like he was waiting for something.

Heather drummed her fingers against the comforter, staring out the window into the dark, wasting landscape. Below, in the ring of trees, the soil had a faint glow, a pearlescent sheen to it almost like ice. By tomorrow, any visible trace of the light would be gone though, hidden in the ground and within the bark. She'd feel safer when it had all soaked into the dirt so she could go search for the other souls.

The pale angel was beside her when she turned back around, startling her.

She opened her mouth to speak, but he pressed a finger to his lips again, shaking his head. Then he held his arms out and she slid off the bed to stand in front of him, nodding her understanding. Wrapping her tight in his arms, Zakhart slipped through the wall of the tree and flew into the night.

The cold wind bit into her flesh as Zakhart rose through the darkness at breakneck speeds, surging past bare tree branches, climbing higher in the indigo sky.

All around them, soulstalkers circled and banked low over the dark grasses that threaded through the sweeping swaths of grey poppies. But to them, Zakhart was just another shadow creature carrying his prey. The soulstalkers chirred and screeched, their tinny, shrill voices piercing the quiet, making her skin crawl.

"Where are we going?"

He shook his head, still maintaining his silence.

Heather went along with it, keeping quiet as he slipped low toward sparse treetops, all that remained of the dense forest she and Ross had once explored, searching for the Spiral. That rich, old-growth forest had shrunk drastically, most of the big, mature oaks dead and dying. All through the forest, bald spots and burned-out stumps smoldered against the ashen ground. Hundreds of spindly saplings broke through the grey soil, already wilting. Without intervention, they would never reach maturity.

It made her sick to see the devastation.

The soil looked ghastly, pallid, and exhausted. Nothing could grow here now. Not unless the pale angels infused it with healing light. She looked closely at the scattering of saplings and her stomach twisted into a hard, aching knot.

They weren't saplings. They were poppies.

Sprouting at the edges of the dying forest. Up from the ashes of once-healthy trees.

"The trees!" she cried.

Zakhart tapped his index finger to his lips and shook his head.

Just south of the ring of trees, the soil still had a rich, dark color, like coffee grounds and trees still grew there, the poppy stalks absent. Along a clear, rushing stream, darkness hung syrupy and thick.

Where the heartlilies bloomed.

Heather remembered those ghostly orange blossoms and how they'd helped her save Ross from the poppy's deadly sleep.

Zakhart winked at her.

It was no accident that the new soul tree was near the heartlilies. He'd made his choice of trees look random, but she knew otherwise now. She didn't know why, but he wanted the new soul tree close to the heartlilies. Did these blooming plants somehow keep the soil clear of darkness and absorb the poppies' grey poison?

The pale angel climbed high in the dark sky again as he soared past the forest's edge. Where the plains stretched into sloping hills toward the distant mountains. Here, it was painfully evident how far the forest's edge had shrunk from the golden plains. A swath of broken dead trees, like a tornado had splintered them, gouged out a barren ring of earth around the entire forest.

Ahead, a small outcropping of rocks rose around the edges of the hilly terrain and Zakhart veered toward them, zipping through a tight corridor of rock walls that skirted the plains. It was a tight squeeze, but he shimmied through the cliffside's stony chutes and dropped through a deep crevice. Into darkness.

She closed her eyes, her stomach lurching at the disorientation.

He turned left then careened right and finally glided to a stop. In the darkness, the air smelled stale, but it was warmer than the Between's windy plains.

A soft white glow hugged his frame, illuminating the small cave with dim light. Again, he motioned her silent as he reached around his neck and untangled a thin, silver thread. It sparkled in the darkness.

Between both hands, he pulled the silver thread as tightly as he could. It hissed as the tension built until the thread snapped, splintering like glass, and collapsed into crackling shards all over the cave floor.

Zakhart summoned a pearl of white light that rolled around in his hand. He tossed it into the shards. With a flash, the shards ignited and burned away, leaving scorch marks on the rock.

"Now, it's safe," he said.

"What *was* that?" Heather asked, staring at him in confusion. "Zakhart, I have no idea what's going on. Everything in the Between has gone crazy."

Zakhart propped his hands on his hips, eyes narrowing. "You're right about that, Heather," he said, his voice sounding tired. "The realms have always been stable. Never in my life span have I ever witnessed such instability! Or sudden changes of this magnitude—unless it was ordained from above. So many archangels don't know what's happening here, Heather."

Her eyes widened. "What was that thing you destroyed?" she asked.

"I'm not exactly sure," he said, shaking his head. He kicked at the blackened debris that crunched under his feet. "I found it sticking out of the ground beside the tree. I put it in a satchel before Razasha and Halea converted the tree. Later, I heard musical notes coming from my satchel. When I opened it, the strand was flickering as every note and harmony I'd spoken was playing back. I spoke a few more phrases which lit up the strand with pulsing light. Then moments later, it repeated those phrases back to me, along with everything I'd spoken previously."

A recording device? Who needed something like that in the Between? And why?

"Where'd you find it?" she asked.

"Wound around the base of the new soul tree," he said, anger in his voice. "Someone or something was listening to everything. And it doesn't take a big stretch of the imagination to figure out who's listening."

"Mulciber," said Heather.

"Of course," Zakhart replied. "We already know that he's sent his demons out of the Veils and onto the Between's landscape. But how did this fiber get into the clearing? Into the new tree? I didn't know until a little while ago which tree I would select to replace the great tree. So...who put that thing there?"

Heather leaned against the rocky wall, folding her arms against her chest. Besides Heather, there had only been Knox, Zoe, and three pale angels at the tree site. Maybe the demons had already placed those silver strands everywhere and anywhere they'd seen pale angels and lost souls? Or...she shuddered...they'd planted them throughout the entire forest?

"The demons haven't been a huge threat until now," said Heather, remembering their almost benign presence before. "I know how dangerous they are, but they never seemed very interested in lost souls other than slave labor to keep their caverns warm. What would they gain, Zakhart? They can't harm people unless they're invited in. Can they?"

"I felt the same way, Heather, but because they're demons, I always considered them too dangerous and gave them a wide berth," said Zakhart. "Until I saw the imbalances."

"Imbalances?" Heather asked, frowning.

"Recently, the numbers of lost souls finding their way to the Between have grown." Zakhart flexed his wings and began to pace.

"You mean suicides," said Heather, feeling the weight of that word against her chest.

The memory still hurt.

Zakhart nodded. "Over time, there have been an alarming number of lost souls staying on in the Between instead of going on through the Spiral like they were intended to do."

She remembered how crowded the great tree had been and the dozens and dozens of lantern lights combing the grasses for new arrivals to the Between. Helping others find the great tree's safety. She smiled at the memory of Ross finding her in the tall grass, his sandy-haired, boy-next-door good looks. Golden hazel eyes brighter than the lanterns as he led her out.

"Being hunted by Death, demons, and soulstalkers made the

great tree a lot more inviting than coming out here and losing everything all over again, Zakhart," said Heather.

"You're right," said Zakhart, nodding. "It's become almost impossible to search for the Spiral. I think you already know that things were at their worst when you first arrived, Heather, but you and Ross turned that around. You set people back on track, convincing a great number of souls to risk that search again. The Between was not meant to hold so many souls for this long. It was to be temporary. It was never meant to be a permanent existence. And don't even get me started on the Red City."

Heather stared into the darkness, her head spinning with Zakhart's revelations.

"The great tree was so crowded when I got here, but despite Ross and me trying to get people out, too many of them still stayed behind. Although, a big chunk of Mulciber's slave labor did follow us out of the Demon Veils."

"True, true," said Zakhart, hands behind his back, wings twitching as he kept up his pacing. "The number of lost souls in limbo grew dramatically after you left, so I was sent back to locate and help them. Or find out what to do. I searched everywhere, but I couldn't find these lost souls. Not even in the Red City."

"They weren't at the great tree?" Heather asked. "Did soulstalkers get them?"

Zakhart sighed. "They weren't in the Red City, so I'd expected to find them with Avana. The great tree was very crowded, but not like it should have been with so many souls. The poppy fields weren't any fuller than they were before. But the number of fields had doubled. That's when I also noticed the increase in soulstalkers."

Heather laid her hand on Zakhart's sleeve. "I thought they'd been sent here from elsewhere. Like they were fallen angels or something."

The pale angel's clear tenor laugh jingled through the cave-like wind chimes.

"They may share their shape with men and wings with angels, but they are not angels—or men." He puffed his chest out, looking almost indignant. "They're almost animals, Heather. Full of hunger and a need to hunt. The Maker created them out of dusk and shadows and taught them to hunt souls. Just for the Between—and Death. They were only needed here. Only to keep the balance of shadow and Spiral in check. And to deliver souls that have completely given up to their final sleep. Like the sand runners that protect the poppy fields, collect poppy dust, and keep the souls of the lost asleep until Death collects them. Nothing more."

"Do they answer to Death?" Heather asked.

"No." Zakhart's response was sharp, clipped. "Death answers to another realm. She's a relic from the Beginning. Before there were angels of death to take on that responsibility. But only the Maker can destroy her. She is bound here to the Between and works strictly alone. But with this imbalance at hand, she may be ordered to clean house. Right the balance."

Heather turned. "Clean house? What does that mean?"

Zakhart nodded and resumed his pacing. "The Between can't handle this many lost souls for this length of time, Heather. Souls that refuse to move on and hide away, pretending they're still living. As the number of lost souls rises, so does the number of soulstalkers and sand runners. The sand runners plant more poppies and the soulstalkers harvest more souls."

Were the poppy fields overflowing with souls now? Heather shuddered. Was Ross lying in one right now—beyond her reach? And beyond help? Like so many other souls that she couldn't save.

"Who controls the soulstalkers and sand runners?" Heather asked.

For a moment, Zakhart looked startled. "I'm not exactly certain, Heather. I think that Death controls them."

"Does she also create them?"

Zakhart shook his head. "No, that's controlled by the Between itself." He motioned toward the grasslands, looking anxious. "When the balance here is restored, the shadow creatures will return to the shadows—and their numbers will adjust. With all of these new poppy fields, they should be full of sleeping souls. The number of fields adjusts like the number of shadow creatures. But most of the fields are empty now. Where are all the souls, Heather? The numbers don't add up."

His words were chilling. If Zakhart had seen the poppy fields so empty, then where *were* all the souls? What had the demons done to them? Heather gritted her teeth. And why wasn't someone higher up this ethereal chain trying to stop them?

"Why aren't your superiors doing something to help?" Heather demanded.

Zakhart shook his head. "Wish I knew," he said, his voice a lament. "There has been a war and many betrayals. But I've heard rumors that Hell no longer has a king. Leaving all those demons to govern themselves. So, why have the demons here decided to leave the Veils for the Between's surface?"

"Tunnels, Zakhart!" Heather cried and gripped his robe sleeves. "There are mounds of dirt everywhere! I saw them from the air. The demons are digging tunnels all through the Between, but why, Zakhart? Why?"

Zakhart winced, bowing his head. "To attack the great tree."

"But why?" Heather asked, her tone shrill. "They can't force a lost soul to do anything. Can they?"

His face tightened, shadows marring his pearly complexion as he looked away, hands on his hips.

She stepped toward him, fear trembling through the pit of her stomach. "Can they, Zakhart? Before, everyone said they couldn't do anything unless invited in...is that still true?"

The pale angel let out an exasperated sigh and turned toward her now.

"Not force—in almost all cases. But they can trick souls into letting them inside. And they can destroy the one safe place in the Between where souls hide. Pick them off one by one. Lure them into the false safety of the Veils." He motioned at Heather. "You went into the Veils, Heather, you tell me. Dangling cherished memories in front of someone lost, frightened, and alone would tempt anyone to seek that safety. That comfort. But the real question is—what do the demons gain by collecting all of the souls into those caves and tunnels? To do what?"

That's the piece that Heather didn't understand either. What were the demons doing in those tunnels? And what exactly was this Mechanism that they kept in motion? That required them to mine coal for it to work. Or whatever that coal really was.

She didn't believe Mulciber's line about keeping the tunnels warm for creatures that needed the hot, arid temperatures of Hell to survive.

"That's the first question we need to answer," said Heather.

A dull, throbbing pain ached in her chest, where her heart had fallen still. For a moment, it staggered her.

She grabbed hold of the wall to steady herself, her thoughts spiraling back to the memory of those Demon Veils. Of her mother. Of the life she left behind. Where Mulciber had entangled her in her deepest, most intense feelings and memories.

Until Ross pulled her out of it.

Yet when she and Ross had left with all those souls in tow, Mulciber used that same diversion to attack Ross. Why Ross? The demon had already weakened her. She'd been easy prey, so why turn to Ross instead?

Why had Mulciber been so interested in Ross?

Then she knew, the pain like a knife blade plunging into her chest, the dread and grief pooling in her throat.

Mulciber planned to replace Thraecius. With Ross.

"That's where he's been taken, isn't he, Zakhart? The Demon Veils."

"What do you mean?" the pale angel asked.

She grabbed Zakhart's arm and spun him around, forcing him to look her in the eyes.

"Zakhart. Stop trying to protect me. Tell me what's happened to Ross." Her eyes stung and she scrunched her face, fighting back tears. "I have to know. That's the whole reason I agreed to return here."

She let out a sharp breath, the memory of a second life lost hanging in her throat. It felt so careless, so reckless to just walk away from another perfectly good life and cause so many innocent people pain and grief so she could return here.

Just to rebalance the ratio of lost souls to soulstalkers and demons?

No, that didn't make sense. Zakhart didn't need her for that. That was for the angels to do. Not souls. No, Zakhart had specifically told her Ross was in danger.

Selfish or not, she hadn't come back to save the world. She'd only come back to save Ross.

Zakhart wouldn't have let her casually end another life and cause pain for so many people just to save Ross. Would he? No, there had been something bigger here to stop, something deeper and more sinister than she realized.

Saving Ross was only part of it.

She looked deep into the pale angel's eyes. Zakhart's pain was evident. He was struggling with something dark that he wasn't telling her and she wouldn't let up until he told her everything.

About Ross. About the Between. Everything.

"Zakhart, I walked away from a good life. I had family and friends. I had a future. It was the whole point of entering the Spiral. Yet, I just threw it all away to come back to my worst nightmare, knowing I might not get out this time because my heart hasn't been right since I left without Ross."

The pale angel stared at his hands, turning them over and over, still avoiding her gaze.

Suddenly, Heather was terrified. Was Ross lost now, his soul beyond saving? She swallowed a breath.

Had she just made the second-worst decision of her life?

She'd always trusted Zakhart. Had he steered her wrong this time? Had he convinced her to give up her last chance at redemption to save Ross when Zakhart knew all along that Ross couldn't be saved?

Would she ever see her mom again? Or Ross?

"I gave up everything, Zakhart!" She shook him. "Everything! On the chance to save Ross. You know that!"

"Heather, I—"

"No!" she growled, pushing him against the stone wall. "You *knew* I'd follow you back to save him! You *knew* I'd give up everything I'd gained to find him. If there wasn't even the slimmest hope of rescuing him, why would you let me throw everything away like this, Zakhart? Why?" Her lip curled into a snarl and she glared at him. "If you used my broken heart to lure me here for some other reason, I'll never forgive you."

"Heather!" He took her by the shoulders, his pumpkin-orange eyes watery now. "Is that what you think? That I tricked you into coming back here?"

She shrugged, feeling confused. "I don't know what to think. Every time I've asked about Ross, you change the subject or delay telling me anything. Later, it's always later. But I *need* to know where he is, Zakhart. I need to know how to save him."

Her eyes brimmed with tears, anxiety trembling through her.

"Every moment, I wonder if he's being tortured by demons or torn apart by soulstalkers. Is he still running for his life from Death's scythe and sand runners?" Her voice broke and she swallowed a breath, her voice tight and small now. "Trying to find me, thinking I was pulled out of the Spiral, too."

Zakhart enfolded her in his wings and put his arms around her. She pulled away, still glaring at him.

She didn't want to be held. She wanted answers. Now.

"All right, Heather. I should have told you sooner, but I can't stall the information any longer. You have to know what's happened."

"Tell me!" she demanded, kicking the rock wall. "I can't stand it any longer!"

"He's under Mulciber's control," Zakhart blurted out.

Heather froze, the horrible news tearing through her like a knife blade. She'd feared that he'd been captured by the demons all this time, but she'd never dreamed that he was being controlled by them. By Mulciber. Doing that monster's bidding. No longer making his own decisions or able to escape into the Spiral. Or even back to the safety of a soul tree.

She pressed her hands to her face as an angry shout bubbled up.

It was much worse than she'd imagined. Mulciber had hurt Ross so badly that night in the Demon Veils, punishing him with images of Jessie, forcing him to believe that Jessie's suicide was all his fault. Mulciber had been the reason Jessie ended up in the poppy fields, but he made Ross believe it was his fault.

Heather felt her body sinking. Zakhart grabbed hold of her and slid down the rocky wall with her to the cold, hard ground.

"No...oh, Ross—no!"

"I don't know exactly where he is and I don't know why Mulciber took control of him," Zakhart continued, holding her against his chest. "I've seen demons influence and persuade souls here, like Thraecius, but I've never seen them take physical control before. And I don't know what he plans to do to Ross. The one thing I do know is that, as long as Ross' soul survives, there's still a chance to rescue him, Heather."

She gritted her teeth, balling her hands into fists. "I'm going into those caves," she said with a growl, struggling to stand, but Zakhart held her against the wall.

"Heather!" he shouted, forcing her to look at him. "You won't be able to just walk into the Veils and break through their influence this time. We'll have to dismantle whatever physical bonds they've used to imprison him. Because, I assure you, he's been imprisoned by them. It will take a lot more of us working together to even get close to Mulciber again. And a lot more of us to free Ross."

"No!" she shouted. "I have to save him, Zakhart, I—"

Zakhart shook her again. "Heather! Ross has seen the Spiral! That's why they're holding him."

The revelation ached through her chest. Zakhart was right. If Mulciber controlled the Spiral, he'd control the Between—and any lost soul seeking that exit. That demon wouldn't let Ross go without a fight. Heather beat the ground with her fists, feeling more helpless than she'd ever felt before.

"I'm sorry I couldn't tell you any of this before now," said Zakhart, his face flushed. "I didn't know who or what might be listening, so I couldn't say anything. I don't want Mulciber to know that we're aware he's shackled Ross into his control. This little cave is one of the few safe places I know of in the Between right now—besides where the heartlilies bloom—so I had to bring you here and explain everything. But I give you my word, Heather, I will do everything in my power to help you save Ross. I won't let you give up that new life in vain."

"What can I do?" she asked finally, feeling so broken. "It seems impossible to even get close to Ross now. Much less free him."

"We keep to our plan. We gather all the lost souls we can find and bring them to the new tree. While I work on quietly removing those listening strands."

"What then?" she asked.

"We raise an army." Zakhart grinned. "You said it yourself. It's the last thing Mulciber's expecting, Heather."

Raise an army. That had been her plan when she got here—before she found herself alone in the Between. With two newly arrived souls. Zoe was no help. Knox would be invaluable—if he got past his issues. A big if.

She didn't know anything about fighting or combat. Much less strategy and planning. The thought made her head spin. But if that's what it took to save Ross, then she'd throw everything she had at it.

"When it gets lighter, I'll start searching for other souls," said Heather, her voice sounding weary.

But she wouldn't let defeat creep into her head. There was still a chance to save Ross. And dammit, she'd take it.

Zakhart frowned, shaking his head. "Not alone. Take Knox with you. And make sure you follow Razasha's light cords."

"Knox has way too many problems right now," she said, wiping the tears from her face with the hem of her silky grey top. "He won't be much help right now. What about getting help from the Red City?"

"Heavens, no!" Zakhart shouted, eyes wide. "You're not ready for the Red City yet," he said, gripping her shoulders a moment and then letting her go. "We have enough souls scattered in these forests to rescue Ross. Besides, searching for survivors of that attack on the great tree just might help Knox with his problems. Take his mind off them long enough to help other people. Let him do what he does best."

Heather shrugged. "He was a soldier. This kind of thing is second nature to him. Might keep him calm and focused. Okay, you're probably right about that." She sighed. "Sorry, I'm not thinking straight right now."

The pale angel brushed the hair out of her eyes and gathered her into his arms. "I know. The news about Ross has to be weighing on you right now. Come on, let's get back to the new tree. You need to sleep."

She shook her head as he took to the air, working his way through the tight curves of the crevice until he was out of the cave and soaring high in the Between's dark sky.

"I'm dead," she said in a weary voice, holding tight to his waist. "I don't need sleep."

"Humor me," Zakhart whispered. "And rest."

Heather nodded. She couldn't think anymore right now. She just wanted to crawl under that downy comforter she'd conjured and hide for a while, away from those horrible *what-ifs* that had been torturing her since Zakhart first touched her forehead on Bainbridge Island.

five

HEATHER DIDN'T REMEMBER the flight across the Between, coming back to the new soul tree, or Zakhart returning her to the small nook she'd conjured. When she opened her eyes again, lantern lights flickered softly through the small room, the lavender comforter warm, soft patter of rain carrying her back to dark, rainy mornings in the Pacific Northwest.

For a moment, she forgot where she was, who she was, as she rubbed her eyes and glanced around the bare, unfamiliar room.

As her eyes adjusted, she remembered that moment on the beach near the ferry terminal and later, that horrible step into the busy Seattle street. In front of that bus.

Her stomach sank, knowing those memories weren't just more nightmares she could brush away with a long, hot shower. Or tell her mom over buttered English muffins and peach jam. Or even mention to Hannah's mom over chocolate scones and Irish Breakfast tea. It was a nightmare she could only put behind her after she'd freed Ross.

Her chest ached, remembering how vicious and cruel Thraecius had been under Mulciber's influence and how difficult it had been to get him to remember his former self. But he'd chosen to be there. Ross hadn't.

Ross was an unwilling participant. Wasn't he?

Had Mulciber wrapped Ross in some kind of soul chain that the demon held in his leathery fist, binding Ross to do Mulciber's bidding? Whether he wanted to or not. Or had he gone willingly like Thraecius? Had he just given up when Death snatched him out of the Spiral? Had he fallen into Mulciber's hands by choice? After losing Jessie. She winced. And her.

Heather felt sick inside. And the not knowing made her want to hurl.

She scrambled out of bed and crept downstairs. Zoe sat in front of the fireplace, wrapped in a fuzzy pink blanket, a soft pillow under her head. The young teen clutched a pink stuffed unicorn to her chest.

Wait...how did Zoe get that personal item in the Between? She'd tried to conjure Charles the bear dozens of times. Other things from her past. But none of them had ever appeared.

She'd ask Zakhart about that when she got a chance.

Heather tiptoed past Zoe toward the blue sofa. Knox sat in the center of the couch, head tilted back, snoring, a beer bottle in his hand. Six more bottles lay on the wooden floor at his feet. This soul tree's illusion power seemed much more intense than the one in the great tree. Even she'd fallen into its influence, willingly, wanting only to forget everything for a little while. And Knox had fallen into these illusions with both feet.

His handsome face had a permanent beard shadow along his jawline. And those long, thick lashes framed his hypnotic blue eyes. Taller and more muscular than Ross, he was such a contrast to Ross' patient, introspective demeanor, lean body, and sandy blond hair. Knox always seemed like his short fuse was lit and burning toward an explosion. Acting first, analyzing (and apologizing) afterward. Ross was calm. Patient. Slow to anger.

Heather fell somewhere between those two aspects.

Her love for Ross had started as a pale flicker, a spark that became a flame that burned hotter and whiter until it was a forest fire. She loved his gentle soul, his quiet strength. The intensity of his love. He hadn't been afraid to show his vulnerabilities and she loved him for that.

But she couldn't deny the sudden burst of attraction she felt for Knox, a former soldier tortured by his past and too proud to reach out for help. Spilling his guts to her earlier had probably taken every last bit of pride he had left.

Why her? He'd been tight with that terrified teen, Zoe who was probably too young to understand it all. Knox had two beautiful, caring pale angels that had done their best to comfort him. And Zakhart whose heart was as big as the heavens. He was the easiest person to talk to she'd ever met. Yet Knox had picked her, the one screaming at soulstalkers, kicking them, throwing rocks, and ripping feathers out of their wings.

Why did she feel this stupid attraction? She loved Ross.

"Hey," said Knox in a raspy voice, those light blue eyes piercing as he sat up and stretched, rubbing his hands through those tangled, sexy curls that softened the hard, distant expression on his face.

"How you feeling, Knox?" she asked in a quiet voice and motioned toward the other fireplace across the room. "Zoe's still asleep."

He nodded, yawning, those lush, dark lashes fluttering, and stood up, knocking over a couple of beer bottles.

"Damn," he whispered. "Sorry."

Zoe stirred, sitting up in her tangle of pink blankets, unicorn in her arms. She pushed black hair out of her hazel eyes and smiled.

"Good morning," she replied. "Is it morning? I can't tell."

"It's hard to judge when the sky lightens here," said Heather with a shrug. "It's never really like daylight, but it does get darker. I always called that the nighttime here."

Zoe wandered over to the couch, blanket around her shoulders, and sat at the far end, legs crossed, unicorn in her lap. She didn't seem so shaky and frightened now. In the light, her heart-shaped face looked fresh and flawless, her waifish frame more like a porcelain doll. She was only a couple of inches shorter, but she looked much smaller than Heather's five-foot-six height. And Zoe looked like a size zero to Heather's size six, feet tiny compared to Heather's size eight.

Heather reached out and laid her hand on Zoe's shoulder, squeezing. She felt protective of the teen who had seemed so lost and almost paralyzed with fear.

"Zoe, how old are you?" she asked, sitting down between her and Knox.

Zoe picked up the unicorn, brushing her thin fingers through its soft pink mane. Heather still wanted to know how Zoe had summoned a personal possession.

"Seventeen," said Zoe, looking down. "I mean, I would have been. It was two days before my birthday when I—" Her gaze snapped up to Heather and then flicked to Knox before she clamped her mouth shut.

Knox's face tensed and he turned his body toward Zoe, leg pressed against Heather's now. His proximity sent a shiver through Heather.

"That's rough, kid," he said, his deep voice reverberating through Heather.

"What happened?" Heather asked and then regretted her question.

It was none of her business and it was probably the most private, painful moment in this teen's life. Why should Zoe share anything with her? She was a stranger. She had no right to pry, but she asked anyway. She couldn't help Zoe if she didn't know what had happened to her.

"I'm sorry," Heather added, holding up her hand. "You really don't have to talk about it if you don't want to. Please don't feel like you have to tell us." She shrugged, twisting the fabric of her sleeve between her fingers. "It's just that, well—the only way to leave this place is to overcome what brought you here. So, I just wanted to help if I could."

Zoe nodded, a shy smile rising briefly on her face. "It's okay. I'm here. It's not like I can hide what I did."

"Hey, I'm here because I couldn't hack it either, kid," Knox replied. He nudged Heather. "Not sure about Heather here, but I just couldn't live with the pain. It sorta helps to talk about it. Now, that you can't change what you did." He poked Heather's shoulder with his fist. "Talking to Heather helped me a lot yesterday."

Heather turned to gaze at Knox. His eyes looked peaceful, boyish, a smile playing on his lips.

"Thanks," he whispered.

Gone was that tough guy façade he'd put up like a shield yesterday. He seemed open and cooperative today.

"Anytime, Knox," she said, patting his arm, and turned back to Zoe. "Zoe, what year was it? When you...um—left?"

"It was 2023," said Zoe with a shrug, fiddling with the unicorn's wispy mane. "None of this was a big deal. See, there were these four girls in school. They were pretty and popular. The main one, Sharla, got a Range Rover for her sixteenth birthday, see, so all she did was look down on everybody else for what they drove. Her dad made a ton of money in the oil fields, so he bought his kids whatever they wanted. They built this huge house in Grande Prairie, see, and all Sharla did was brag about it. Her dad and older sister are really nice. Sharla was just mean."

Heather glanced at Knox. His eyes were glazing.

"So, four girls in school? Were they bullying you?"

Zoe nodded. "At first, they weren't so bad. I just tried to stay out of their way. My folks did okay, so we weren't poor. My brother had an old Buick SUV he was gonna trade, but I was saving money to buy it from him. He'd let me drive it to school sometimes. He's a senior, see."

"Sharla and the others were making fun of what you drove,

weren't they?" Heather asked, steering Zoe back on track. She could feel Knox drifting out of the conversation fast.

"Yeah, see, they kept posting pictures of the Buick online and making it look all busted up and rusty. Then they started posting pictures of me, saying all these terrible things."

Her eyes glistened in the firelight, turning glassy with tears. She pulled in a breath, fingers plucking at and twisting the unicorn's soft, cotton candy mane.

"See, they started pasting them in the hallways and on my locker. All the kids would laugh at me and call me names. Then one of the girls, Sophie, waited for me after school in the parking lot. She hit me in the head and jumped on me, broke my nose. Had to get stitches in my forehead."

Tears ran down her cheeks now.

"Did you tell your folks, kid?" Knox asked.

She nodded. "I did. They called the school. And see, Sharla, Sophie, Olivia, and Brooke all got in trouble. That's why Sophie beat me up. I begged my mother not to make me go back to school, but…I had to go back." She swallowed a hard breath, tears welling in her eyes. "They got hold of my cell number. Started texting me horrible messages, telling me I should just kill myself. Every day, calling me ugly and stupid. They made a picture of a wooden plank and pasted my head on top of it, saying I had the figure of a two-by-four and the personality of dirt."

Her voice choked up. She smashed her eyes closed, biting her lip as she tore bits of hair out of the unicorn's mane.

Heather got up and sat down beside her, sliding her arm around the teenager's shoulders. Zoe was shaking now.

"See, I tried to ignore them like my mother said, take the higher ground—whatever that meant. But it was every day, Heather. Every day! They found out when my birthday was and…" A sob bubbled up, her shoulders heaving. "See, three days before my birthday, they left a pile of wooden planks in the yard with my face on them. They had a bunch of dirt and topsoil delivered to the yard with a sign that said Happy Birthday, Zoe! Eat Dirt! They posted all of these online. Everybody was texting me about it, laughing, making fun. I was humiliated."

Heather hugged her, holding her close as tears ran in rivers down her face. "Then what happened?" Heather asked in a quiet voice.

Knox was sitting in front of Zoe now, a hand on her arm, stroking, pain in his face.

"Sunday night, I took a shower and cleaned my room. I put notes on all my favorite things, asking that they be given to my cousins, including Cassie my unicorn. I asked that they give her to my best friend, Ava." She patted the pink unicorn on the head, sighing. "She looked kinda like this one."

Zoe looked past them now, drifting back to the last moments of her life. Heather recognized that faraway reflection mixing with relief and anguish. Grief. She held Zoe tighter.

"Then I left my parents a long note about how sorry I was that I wouldn't be there for my birthday. Or any more birthdays." The tears ached through her voice. "And I asked that they take care of my dog, Toby...and I...I told them I'd see them again someday." She shook her head, staring at Heather with pleading hazel eyes. "But I won't now, will I? Because I..." She wiped her sleeve across her face, sobs working free now. "See, then I took a belt from my closet and..."

She squeezed her eyes closed again and collapsed over the unicorn, sobs trembling through her thin body.

Heather held Zoe as a wave of anguish and regret broke free. Knox laid his hand on Zoe's back, rubbing her shoulders.

"I'm so sorry, kid," he said, pain in his voice. "Nobody could take that much bullying every day. It's not your fault."

"Knox is right," Heather said above Zoe's sobs. "Those girls tormented you. Everybody has their breaking point. I wish you could have outlasted them. Gotten back at them by becoming a beautiful woman with an amazing life. I'm so sorry you didn't get that chance."

Heather had been bullied in school, but nothing like what Zoe went through. When her mom first got sick and she'd gotten the devastating news that it was stage four breast cancer, some people were just cruel, including some of her friends. Like Carly. So many were insensitive, expecting Heather to just get over her mother's death. Or keep it to herself. They didn't try to understand that her mom had been her best friend, that she was all the family that Heather had.

Her dad lived far away in Boston with a new wife and two young boys. For so many years, he'd all but forgotten about his only daughter back in Washington State. She realized now that, it took a few years of living, of experience, for her high school friends to learn about compassion. For others, it took a lot longer and for some people, they never learned compassion. They either couldn't see past their self-centeredness to be kind to other people or they just didn't care about others.

Now, after touching two physical lifetimes, she no longer blamed her father for abandoning her. She realized now that he'd just gotten tangled up in a new life that had required more of his attention, not intending to widen the distance between them.

She thought about the day they'd found her body on that Bainbridge Island beach and called him in Boston. How did he feel that day, flying back to Seattle, knowing his only daughter was dead? How had it felt to drive to the morgue and identify his oldest child when he hadn't seen her in two years? It had to have been a horrible moment for him and she wished she could have spared him that.

Finally, Zoe stopped crying and Heather let her go. The young girl sank back into the cushions, the pink unicorn in her arms.

Knox gripped Zoe's hand in his. "Kid, I don't know whether or not you'll see your folks again. I don't anything about where we are or why we're here. All I do know is I wasn't expecting this and there's gotta be some reason for it. And why we still have some sort of consciousness."

Heather smiled. "It's a second chance, Knox. It's a chance to see your parents again, Zoe."

"How?" Zoe asked in a hushed voice. "What do I do to go back to them?"

Knox watched Heather closely now, his eyes filled with hope, something she hadn't seen on his face before. But Zoe's question filled her with trepidation. Before, the first time she'd come to the Between, she hadn't understood anything about second chances and what her personal quest had been. She gave everything she had to find the Spiral, not understanding for a long time that she had to find it inside herself before she could find its physical location. She wasn't even sure she could explain that to Knox and Zoe.

But this time, things were different.

Any time she liked, she could return to the Spiral and leave. But she'd leave her heart behind, broken, and in pieces. Ross meant so much to her. Deep down though, she knew that Zakhart and Razasha had other reasons for convincing her to return. The pale angels knew she wouldn't have returned for any other reason.

She thought back to the moment that she and Ross touched the Spiral, everything so jumbled and confused. Ross had gone into the Spiral first. Of that, she was certain because he'd pulled her into the Spiral. When Death grabbed hold of her legs, Heather fought harder than she'd ever fought in her life.

How had Ross managed to get between her and Death? Letting her escape into the rebirth spiral. If Ross had been Death's prisoner, how had he ended up with the demons?

Had the pale angels somehow given Ross over to the demons? Zakhart, Razasha, and Halea had been there. Zakhart had glossed over that part, but she needed to know more about that moment. Was there more that he wasn't telling her?

Regardless of how it happened. Her heart understood that Ross had sacrificed himself to get her to safety. Her eyes burned with tears.

"So, you gonna spill it, Heather?" Knox asked, gaze unblinking.

Zoe and Knox were both staring at her, expecting her to give them the answers they needed. They expected her to explain how they could escape this place forever. Was it the same for them as it had been for her? Was making themselves whole again, finding the strength not to let go again of what they needed to accomplish? She'd start with that.

"Spill what?" she asked, grimacing.

Knox gestured toward the door. "Where the exit is? This Spiral you didn't want me to know about yet."

She stared at him in surprise. He was still fixated on the Spiral with her telling him that he couldn't just go there and leave this place. She understood, but she didn't know how to make him understand that it wasn't that simple. That she wasn't keeping anything from them.

She'd have to be more careful what she said around him.

Heather rose from the couch. "I didn't want you to know yet because right now, both of you think it's just a matter of following a path to a certain location and walking through it." She propped her hands on her hips. "Now, I want you both to listen very carefully. If you don't, you'll be done. Do you understand that?"

Knox folded his arms against his chest and sat back on the couch, still listening. Zoe hadn't moved, her gaze moving from Heather to Knox.

"The Spiral isn't a door," said Heather. "It isn't an exit where you can just enter and leave this place. It isn't a place for you yet. Neither one of you can even see it right now."

Knox's eyes narrowed, looking confused, a *you've got to be kidding me* expression on his face.

"Yeah, it's true," she snapped, motioning toward the door. "If you go running around out there, you can look forever and you'll never find it. I could take you to the exact spot and you won't be able to see or touch it."

"That's bullshit!" Knox shouted, jumping up from the couch.

He paced in front of her now.

"You just don't want us to know where it is. Admit it!" He pointed a finger at Heather. "You just want to keep us here to help you find somebody who got left behind."

"What?" Heather cried.

He poked his chest with his thumb. "I heard you whispering to that angel guy outside before they made this tree into a fort or whatever the hell it is now. I heard you talking about some dude named Ross."

"What about Ross?" she snapped, moving toward him. "You have no idea what's happening here, Knox, so don't go making assumptions and accusations when you have zero information."

"Then talk!" He leaned toward her. "Tell me what the hell that was about!" He laid his hands against his face, rubbing them across his eyes. "This whole place makes no sense! I don't like secrets. And I don't like people whispering things and hiding information."

Heather grabbed hold of his arms, staring into his steady blue eyes.

"Okay, you want to know what we were saying? You want to know about this big secret I'm hiding from you?"

He nodded, glaring.

Heather sat him down on the couch and crouched in front of him.

"All right, Knox, you listening? Ross saved me when I came here. He rescued me from a soulstalker that tried to carry me off the moment I woke up here. He told me about the Spiral and he kept me hoping and trying to find it because it was supposed to be the way out. Neither one of us realized that we couldn't even see it until we'd dealt with the mistakes we made in our lives."

"Mistakes?" he asked, raising an eyebrow.

"Yes, Knox—mistakes." She straightened up, taking him by the shoulders. "You're here because you gave up. You killed yourself."

He gritted his teeth, blue eyes darkening. "No shit, Heather. You think I don't know that?"

"So, if you know that, why do you think you can just find a door and walk away from it? That act is why you're here in the first place."

He went quiet, the anger softening now.

"That's why you're here, why I'm here, why Zoe's here. The

Between is that last chance. We can fix why we did it by finding reasons to live again and being strong enough to follow through with them."

Nodding, he cast a glance at Zoe whose eyes were wide.

"Okay, that makes a little sense, I guess. So we fix ourselves and go back?"

Heather shook her head. "You can't go back to your old lives. They're gone now because you gave them up." She cringed, hearing Zakhart in her voice now. "You can go on, to a new life through the Spiral, but the life you left is gone forever. Do you understand that, Knox?"

"Gone," he muttered, staring at the floor now. "Forever?"

"Forever," she replied. "But you can't enter into a new life until your soul is whole again. Until you've fixed yourself, you'll never be able to see the Spiral. The way out again."

Knox let out a hiss and laid his hand over his mouth. "Wow..."

"It's a lot to take in, I know," Heather said, the anger and frustration leaving her voice. "That's why I didn't want you to know about the Spiral right away."

Finally, he looked up at her. "What happened to Ross?" he asked in a quiet voice.

She inhaled sharply, the ache in her chest returning. "Ross and I found the Spiral, but Death found us first. She prowls the Between, looking for lost souls to collect. Because we cheated death. She was hunting us. Ross and I entered the Spiral, but Death grabbed hold of me. He—" Her voice cracked, her throat tightening with grief. She held her breath a moment, trying to push the pain away. "He—put himself between Death and me...letting me go on through."

Knox was on his feet now, hands gently holding her. "God... Heather, I'm sorry. Is he—gone now?"

She shook her head, swallowing the swell of emotion until she could respond. "The demons have him now. I—I don't know how but they've...enslaved him."

"Wait a minute," Knox replied, eyes squinting. "Demons? There are demons here?"

"Lots of them," she replied. "They were always underground before though, keeping to themselves—or so I thought."

"You've seen them?" he asked.

She nodded emphatically. "According to Zakhart, they're coming out of their caves and showing up all over the Between now. The pale angels don't know why either. That's what I was whispering to Zakhart before. I was demanding that he tell me what happened to Ross. That's the reason I'm back here, to find and rescue Ross."

Knox's eyes widened and he stared at her in amazement. "You were free? You were back in the world, living your life again, and you...you killed yourself to come back here?"

Sighing, Heather bowed her head. "I'm not proud of it. Zakhart appeared to me, touched my forehead, and my previous life came flooding back to me. I didn't remember that Ross hadn't gotten through the Spiral. I didn't remember anything from before until Zakhart came to me. But I had this terrible ache in my chest. That had never left. When Zakhart touched my forehead, I understood that ache. And when I found out what happened to Ross, I had to come back and save him. I had to."

"He must mean an awful damned lot to you."

She nodded.

Knox let her go.

"Zakhart told me that there'd been a demon uprising and that too many lost souls weren't moving through the Spiral. The overgrowth of shadow creatures was creating a dangerous imbalance." She didn't tell him about the missing souls yet. What he was already hearing was overwhelming enough without hearing that, too. "He believes that my search for Ross and the growing imbalance are connected. And that I can help him fix the imbalance which will also lead me to Ross."

Knox studied her face for a few moments, standing so close.

"What was Razasha talking about? Some cord of light she'd released?"

"That was to find the people who'd been in the great tree that got destroyed," said Heather. "I need to find them and bring them here to safety. I'll need their help to face all those demons. I sure can't face them alone."

To her surprise, Knox smiled and stood up straighter, throwing out his chest.

"If there's gonna be a fight, then count me in, Heather." He grinned. "I'm not good for much, but being a soldier is all I know."

"You'd help me?" she asked.

He nodded. "Looks like nobody's gettin' out of here without a fight. I'll go out there and help you find these people. And I'll help you figure out a way to fight these demons." He laughed. "Start a spirit boot camp and turn all of you into soldiers. If I don't, I won't be leaving any time soon either."

"Oh, Knox! Thank you!"

Heather threw her arms around him, hugging him hard. His arms were tight around her, his face pressed against hers. Her breath caught, his body so warm, the buttery smell of his skin, a hint of soap clinging to his hair. She closed her eyes, breathing him in, missing that physical presence.

Missing Ross.

She let go, face flushed as she took a step back.

Knox was grinning now. "When do we start?" he asked.

"How about now?"

"Let's go," he said, grabbing her arm and pulling her toward the door. "Zoe, we'll be back in a while. Stay here, okay?"

Zoe nodded as he pulled open the door, leading Heather outside, toward the shrinking forest.

six

. . .

SHADOWS LOOPED and dipped across the grey sky. Feathers rustled. Chirring trills echoed through the long, silvery green grass that grew along a path that edged the dying forest. The indigo sky had lightened to a soft grey. Wind blew through the trees, bare branches clattering above the distant flutter of wings.

Heather froze, crouching.

Knox hunkered beside her, his gaze intense as he looked around the area at every angle. A hint of fear burned in his vivid blue eyes, but his body moved with the rhythm and training of a soldier. He slid around her and took the lead, hand raised, ready to direct her forward. She stuck close, feeling safe as he took command.

Something screeched behind her.

She turned.

Brush scraped against the wind. A flash of black. Diving into the foliage. Wings beating bushes.

Heather winced. Soulstalkers. Searching for prey.

Knox met her apprehensive gaze when she turned back toward her and motioned ahead. She crept forward as Knox motioned for her to stick close as he hovered beside Razasha's cord of light that burned like a fuse in the twilight. Heather could almost imagine a rifle at Knox's back and fatigues on his lean, muscled frame. A T-shirt that hugged his pecs, broad shoulders, and muscled stomach.

The cord of gold light coiled around a tree and veered left, skirting the forest's edge. But the pack of soulstalkers hunting nearby made her nervous. They were too close and another pack searched through the sea of grass not ten feet to her right. She was shocked by how many prowled the forest when the Between's skies were at their lightest. So many shadow creatures. And they'd grown bolder. The forest was much more dangerous now than it had ever been before.

They had to be careful.

Knox motioned her quiet as he stepped around some brush and slipped past a pack of soulstalkers tearing through the brush on the left. With careful steps, Knox was deliberate but fearless as the light coil led them farther into the sea of grasses. The wind blew a cloud of grey dust through the fluttering grasslands.

She put a hand over her eyes as she looked out across the crisp blades, seeing three large poppies swaying in the wind. The huge blooms spread their massive, fan-shaped petals wide, releasing deadly dust. If they got too close, they'd be affected by them. But at this distance, the dust was little more than an annoyance.

Heather tapped Knox on the shoulder and pointed at the huge poppies.

"Danger, don't get too close," she whispered and motioned for him to keep moving.

His eyes widened and he nodded, slipping back from the edge of the grasslands and poppy fields as he moved off the trail, behind a line of brush.

Heather followed.

Something hissed. A blur of black!

Everything went dark and she hit the ground.

A shrill screech bit into her eardrums, deafening her. She tried to cover her ears, but she couldn't move.

Claws raked across her arms, blackness over her eyes.

She kicked out, writhing against the dark and being unable to move. She felt confused and disoriented.

"Heather!"

Tinny, hollow sounds clipped the silence, sounding far away and muffled.

A human voice screamed. Feet shuffling. Dull thumping—a screech!

Struggling, Heather rocked her body back and forth until she freed her left arm. She gasped when she felt feathers against her face.

Soulstalker!

Pulling the black mass of feathers toward her face, she bit deep.

It shuddered, pulling away.

And she was falling!

For a while, everything just stopped until she opened her eyes, staring up at Knox's smiling face. He sat beside her, his face framed by the forest. He was bruised, a cut on his lip, cheekbone red and swollen, a bundle of black feathers clutched in his fists.

"You okay?" he asked, nudging her gently.

He tossed away the feathers and they floated around her, drifting past the cord of light, and landing on the dirt path like fallen leaves.

"What happened?" she asked.

She tried to sit up, but he pressed her shoulder back toward the ground.

"Easy there. Give it a bit more time before you sit up. You took quite a fall."

Heather frowned. "Fall?"

Knox nodded. "Yeah, we got hit by a bunch of soulstalkers."

"How many's a bunch?" she asked.

"Six, I think," he said, sounding unconcerned as he helped her slowly sit up.

He kept an arm around her back, to keep her from falling backward.

"Six? Are you sure?"

Her head throbbed. She pressed her palm to her forehead, tilting her head down, feeling light-headed.

"Yep," Knox muttered and pointed to the ground.

Black feathers littered the forest floor, a thick, inky black substance clinging to the bushes and pooling along the dirt path.

Did soulstalkers have blood?

"What is that?" she asked.

He shrugged, a smirk on his lips, knuckles of both hands bruised and scuffed, coated with the black stuff.

"Don't know. I just started bustin' 'em up when the first one grabbed you. It knocked you in the head and picked you up as the rest of them went after me." Anger flushed his face. He gritted his teeth, eyes narrowing. "It almost flew off with you, but I ripped the bastard right out of the sky and body-slammed it into the ground. All of them were on me then, but I just started takin' them down one by one. This sticky stuff spurted from their wings and their skin."

"You took on six soulstalkers by yourself?" Heather asked, eyes wide.

Knox nodded. "The first six anyway, but the commotion attracted another group of those things. If it wasn't for these two, I think they'd have carried us both off." He pointed behind her.

Heather turned. Lamarr Diallo sat near her, his warm brown eyes looking tired but relieved, mahogany skin scratched from the soulstalkers.

"Lamarr!"

With Knox's help, she stumbled to her feet and rushed over to hug the excited young man with short, cropped dark hair.

"I thought you escaped this place, girl," he said, hugging her, his South African accent as smooth as she remembered. "Where'd you come from?"

Sitting beside Lamarr was a woman she didn't recognize.

Her fine blond hair trickled out of a blue ribbon tied at her nape, curling into wispy ringlets around her face. She seemed a little shy. Her silk grey clothes were smeared with that black stickiness, a tan shawl draped around her shoulders. She was about Heather's height, a little curvy with rounded hips and a tiny waist. Her oval, sun-washed face was freckled, features delicate—almost fragile—dark blue eyes looking sad. She looked a little younger than Heather.

"Long story, Lamarr," she said and nodded toward the woman. "Who's your friend?"

"Heather," said Lamarr, holding out his hand toward Heather. "This is Cora Abernathy. Cora, this is Heather Billot."

Cora hadn't spoken yet and Heather could see the hurt in her eyes. Like everyone in the Between, she carried around a painful past. And Lamarr seemed a bit protective of her. He'd always hung out with Barb Galki before and Heather wondered if something had happened to her.

Heather let Lamarr go and turned to Cora. "Thanks, Cora," she said in a soft voice. "I'm so glad you and Lamarr made it out of the great tree when the demons attacked."

The young woman shuddered and bowed her head, eyes downcast. "It was horrible," she replied. "Darkness and demons everywhere. I'm so thankful that I found Lamarr in the forest." She looked up, a shy smile on her face, her musical voice soft with a Southern accent.

"It reminded me of the night you first arrived at the great tree, Heather," said Lamarr.

"It did?" Heather said, surprised. "Why's that?"

"Because," said Lamarr, glancing up at the soot-grey sky. "You turned the great tree upside down that night. And every night after that. You gave me hope for the first time, Heather. You showed me there was another chance waiting out there for me."

"You helped me, too, Lamarr," said Heather.

Seeing how the other souls at the great tree had given up and lost themselves in illusions had kept her fighting to escape.

And so had Ross.

Cora sighed, her hand pressing against the left side of her face. "Hearing Lamarr's stories about you gave me the courage to try.

Especially when Lamarr said that you and Ross had rushed into the night headed for the Spiral."

Heather turned toward Lamarr who shrugged. "I told her about the Spiral. And how you and Ross had gotten out. Never dreamed you'd return here, Heather."

Smiling, Cora let go of her face and motioned toward the forest. "I was so excited! For the first time! I was so sure the two of you had escaped. You were both free! And that filled me with so much hope." Her face fell, the smile disappearing. "But I can't lie, Heather. It's devastating to see you back here. What happened?"

Lamarr nodded, brushing the dust off the silky, grey folds of his clothing. "Yeah, what's up with that, Heather? You and Ross got out. You were both free. What happened?"

"I did get out," she said. "I had a new life. I was happy. But I had to come back."

"Why?" Lamarr asked, frowning. He waved his hands in the air, that ever-present lighthearted smile still lighting his face. "What could have possibly brought you back to this place?"

His gentle South African accent soothed her agitation. She folded her arms against her chest, her gaze trailing north toward the mountains.

"Ross."

"Ross?" Cora cried. "What do you mean? I thought he escaped with you."

Heather shook her head, gritting her teeth to keep her eyes from welling with tears. "Death pulled him out of the Spiral after I got through. He sacrificed himself to make sure I got out. So, I had to come back for him. I had to." She turned her gaze to Lamarr and pasted on a smile. "And now, I can help the rest of you get out."

Cora let out a gasp, her hands covering her mouth. "You'll help us escape, too?"

Heather nodded and Cora threw her arms around her.

"I will, but I'll need your help to find Ross. I'm not leaving here without him."

Lamarr looked worried now. "Where is Ross?"

"Does this have anything to do with the great tree being destroyed?" Cora asked, looking confused.

"It's definitely connected," said Lamarr, motioning at the torrent of black feathers covering the ground. "That attack was planned, Cora."

Nodding, Cora folded her arms against her chest and poked the feathers with the toe of her shoe.

"It had to be," said Cora. "Those demons tried to capture all of us during that attack, but it sounds like maybe they targeted this Ross."

"You may be right, Cora," said Lamarr, staring at the feathers eddying around their feet, caught by the wind blowing off the grasslands. "Everyone was cheering and excited when Heather and Ross led Ester and Matthew and the others into the darkness to leave this place. Even Avana looked happy. Maybe the demons wanted to make an example out of Ross? Because he'd found the spiral."

Cora shuffled over to Lamarr, gesturing at the forest. "Maybe? I remember others talking about the Spiral after that, planning out how they'd go to the clearing soon and follow the path. The one that Ross and Heather had blazed." She grinned. "You and Ross were our heroes, Heather. You'd both shown everyone in the Between that it was possible to get out."

Lamarr's eyes darkened and he clasped his hands together. "That's when the whole tree shuddered, like something had slammed into it."

"Like a cannonball hit it," Cora added.

"The tree began to shake apart and then it—just dropped," said Lamarr, motioning toward the forest as his voice got louder, his words faster, "It knocked people to the floor and off the staircase. The tree heaved a loud groan, like it was breaking apart, and sank deep into the ground!"

Cora sighed. "It was horrible, Heather. Everything went completely dark. People were screaming and struggling to escape. That's when the demons appeared."

"So it was demons?" Heather stared at Cora, terrified for Ross now.

Cora nodded, shivering as Lamarr put his arm around her shoulder.

"So many demons," Cora replied in a small voice. "They were everywhere, pushing people deeper into the darkness, shouting at us, blocking us from climbing out of the tree."

"Where were they taking you?" Heather asked.

A cold chill danced down her spine. The demons were herding the souls somewhere? Into the Veils? The coal fields? Those dark pits where she'd first found Thraecius cracking his whip at workers that loaded carts with shiny black rock. Had they been herded into that foreboding room with the Mechanism where workers toiled at wheels and levers? Endlessly tending that monstrosity. Forever. What did that machine even do?

Cora shook her head. "I don't know. It was chaos!"

"It was so dark," said Lamarr as he paced through the black feathers littering the ground. "People were screaming, demons shoving us in all directions. Avana was shouting over them, white smoke from all the smoke people clogging everything. Barb and Javier grabbed Cora and me, pushing us upward, back toward the tree. Barb kept telling everyone to listen to Avana and head back to the great tree."

"We did," said Cora, tying the bow tighter in her hair. "Lamarr and Barb smashed through a lot of demons to get us back into the tree. The four of us climbed up the staircase and shimmied out one of the upper floor windows."

"And we all ran like scared rabbits into the forest," said Lamarr, motioning toward the trees. "Some of the others followed us out. Avana and some of the smoke people did, too." His eyes darkened and he stared at his feet now, shaking his head. "But most of them disappeared into the tunnel with the demons. I don't know where they went. Or what happened to them."

Heather reached out and pulled Lamarr into another hug. "Don't you worry, Lamarr. Knox and I are trying to locate every lost soul we can. The pale angels have built a new soul tree. A new sanctuary to protect us."

Relief welled in Lamarr's eyes. He exchanged an excited glance with Cora. "There's a safe place to go to? Really?"

"Yes," said Heather. "Knox and I just came from there. It's harder to find than the great tree. Knox and I are rounding up everyone we can find and taking them to the new tree. We have a plan."

Knox clapped a hand on Lamarr's back. "You and Cora are a welcome addition, believe me. We need people who can fight because we're going to tangle with those damned demons again."

"What are you planning, Heather?" Lamarr asked, stepping closer.

"I'm raising an army, Lamarr," she replied. "That's what it's going to take to free Ross."

"Free Ross?" Lamarr asked, squinting.

Heather nodded, her chest heavy at the thought. She was terrified of what the demons had already done to him. And what they planned to do to him—and the other souls.

"The demons have him now," she said in a quiet voice, unable to hide her desperation and fear. "Along with a lot of other innocent souls. I don't know what they want with all these souls. Or why they've singled Ross out for some twisted purpose. We need to figure out what they want with these souls and where they've taken them. This is the Between, not Hell."

"Then what do we do?" Cora asked.

"Then we go in and bust some heads," Knox announced, eyes narrowing as he rubbed his fist against his shirt, trying to wipe away the sticky soulstalker blood. "Free these people before it's too late."

"If we don't," Heather continued, "the demons will overrun the Between and it will collapse under the weight."

Cora's face turned pale and she pressed her hand to her mouth. "What happens to us if that happens?"

Something crackled behind Heather. She turned at the sound.

"We would all cease to exist," said the familiar, precise voice, white smoky vapor trailing through the air.

Heather smiled. Avana!

The smoke woman coalesced into solid form, a slender body with alabaster skin, thick white hair, and ice-blue eyes usually filled with condescension. But Avana looked humbled. Frightened.

"Avana! You're safe!" Heather shouted, rushing toward her.

Her icy expression melted and she smiled at Heather, reaching out to gently touch her face with a quick caress.

"Heather. I'd heard whispers that you were here again. I thought they were stories, but it's true. You're back." Avana tossed her thick white mane of hair, surprise mixing with relief in those glacial eyes. "Why would you return here? You were free. You could have put this place behind you forever. Why?"

"Ross didn't make it through the Spiral," said Heather.

Heather expected that look of disgust to harden her features. She'd always thought of Ross as a coward even though he'd worked his heart out to save as many people in the great Tree as he could. But nothing he did had ever been enough to please Avana. But this time, sadness touched her eyes, melting through that wintry expression.

"I know," she said in a half-whisper and bowed her head. "He paid a heavy price when he set himself between you and Death, Heather. It was noble and brave. The demons punish him daily for his transgressions."

Heather smashed her eyes closed, face contorting. "Oh, Ross," she moaned. "Forgive me."

"Heather, no," Avana cried, her voice sharp. "Don't you dare give in to guilt and despair. We need your strength now more than ever." Her hands snapped to her hips and she glared. "It will be instrumental in rescuing the souls in the demons' hands."

Heather looked up, surprised by Avana's words.

"That's right," said Avana. "Many of them were taken by the demons—like Ross. And we're going to rescue them. The pale angels entrusted those souls to the great tree and the demons stole them from my watch. We're going to get them back. And save Ross from being their example. Set the Between back on course, the way it's always been, helping lost souls back into the cycle of living."

"We're with you, Avana," said Lamarr.

Cora nodded.

Heather wanted to rage. She balled her hands into fists, pressing them against her thighs. Those demons were making an example out of Ross. Where? How? He was in more danger than she'd first thought. And she was terrified for him.

Knox hit his hand with his fist. "Just tell me whose heads need cracking," he said with a growl.

Cora stared at Knox in horror, recoiling. She took a step back from him, moving behind Lamarr.

"That's going to be up to Heather," Avana replied.

Heather had never seen her so interested and involved before.

"In all my time in the Between," said Avana as she turned to smoke again, coiling around them in swirls of mist. "She's the only person I've ever seen who could unite others onto one path. Besides, this fight is personal. I don't take kindly to demons invading my tree, destroying it, and kidnapping everyone inside."

"Avana, Heather says there's a new tree!" Cora replied.

"Is that true?" Avana turned back into her solid form and fixed Heather with her ice-blue gaze.

Heather nodded. "Knox and I will take you there. Then he and I will go looking for others."

Avana clasped her hands together, leaping into the air as her physical form disintegrated into swirls of smoke again, turning and twirling around Cora and then Lamarr.

"I know Barb and Javier are still out there," Lamarr replied. "And some others I saw. I just hope we have enough people to fight back against the demons."

"Maybe not enough for an open confrontation," Knox replied, stepping closer to the group. "But enough for a sneak attack like they made on that first tree."

Lamarr sighed and rubbed his eyes. "Too bad none of us knows how to fight demons. Do we throw punches or hand grenades?"

"Oh, I hope it's hand grenades," Knox replied with a snort. "But I'll settle for a punch to their stupid demon faces."

"I've never—thrown a punch as you call it," Cora said with a shrug. "I used to use Pa's rifle when he and Teddy went off to war, protecting Mama and the farm from wolves. But I never killed one." Her Southern drawl slipped out as she spoke.

"When did you, um—" Heather couldn't quite bring herself to say those words.

"Kill myself?" she asked.

Heather nodded.

Cora's sweet, innocent expression melted into a dark, faraway expression. She looked out across the sea of grass, lost in the past.

"September second. I remember it like yesterday. The fires burned for hours that night. The silence was terrifying, streets filled with blue coats. Yankees. Burnin' everything I ever loved." She shuddered, hugging her arms against her chest. "They took my Pa at Chickamauga. Teddy at Jonesborough. He was only sixteen, his whole life ahead of him. I brought him back to the farm as Atlanta burned. I'd just buried him when—" Her face contorted and she covered it, turning away. "When them Yanks came to the farm."

"The Civil War?" Heather asked. "What year did you die?"

"Cora?" Lamarr touched her shoulder, but Cora pulled away.

"It was 1864. I was barely eighteen, laying my brother in the grave beside Pa's...when they came." She winced as if she'd heard a horrible noise and crouched by the brush, hands over her ears. "I could hear Mama's scream from the house. I wish I could scrub away the sound. I got Pa's rifle from the barn. I could hear their laughin' and carryin' on, Mama sobbing as I tore a cartridge and loaded it, tampin' it all down like Papa taught me. I crept to the door, counting the voices. Three soldiers. Mama underneath them."

"Oh, Cora," Heather said and dropped down beside her, a hand on her arm. "What'd you do?"

"I kicked the door open and pointed the rifle at the nearest blue coat, firing. The explosion was deafening. It blew a hole clean through him. The others were scramblin' for their weapons when I slammed the rifle into the second one's head, dropping him on the floor. I threw down the rifle and lunged for one of theirs. He was a step too fast. He cocked it back and smashed it into my head. When I came to, he was rolling off me. I—I was bleeding, my dress in shreds. Mama was lying beside me, her eyes frozen on the ceiling. Her chest not moving. The blue coat leered at me, sliding a knife out of his boot. He grabbed my hair and jerked my head back. But I pounded an iron skillet into his head. He dropped like a sack of potatoes, the knife falling to the floor. I stabbed it right into his heart and watched him stop breathing."

Heather put her arms around Cora, holding her close.

"Mama was gone. After I set the house on fire, I buried her beside Pa. Then I slit my wrists with the Yank's knife and curled up in the grass beside Mama's grave and watched the moon fade from the sky."

Knox knelt in front of Cora, his eyes watery as he gently reached out to her. She flinched, dodging his hand. Knox could barely talk at first, but finally, his words slipped out.

"The hardest thing about war is the innocents in the crossfire. No shelter, no egress when it's happening on their doorstep. While the machines on both sides pump out kill orders to people like me."

Cora stepped behind Heather, peering around her shoulder at Knox. "Are you a soldier? Yank or Reb?"

"Neither. I'm an American soldier—I mean, I was," Knox replied, keeping his distance.

Cora's eyes widened, bottom lip quivering. She flicked a wispy lock of blond hair out of her eyes, watching him carefully.

Knox cleared his throat, voice raspy. "We're trained to obey orders and most of us go in wearing our white hats, trying to save the world. We think everything will be black and white. Bad guys and bad things will be clearly marked and targets cleanly separated from the cities and residential areas. From innocents." He swallowed a ragged breath. "But it's ugly and messy, filled with a constant string of life-or-death decisions and unexpected consequences. And collateral damage. But sometimes, there are horrible pieces of human excrement that use combat to do monstrous things to people."

Cora stepped back from Heather, arms folded against her chest as she put marked distance between her and Knox, moving behind Lamarr again. She stared at Knox with inquisitive eyes, the afterglow of that horrible night fading from her dark blue eyes.

"Were you in combat?" Cora asked finally.

Knox nodded. "I was. And I saw a lot of terrible things during my tours in Afghanistan. Eventually, they brought me here, not because I did them. Because I—I couldn't stop them. And I can't erase them from my head. I'm sorry about what happened to you, Cora."

Heather couldn't help but admire the curly-haired soldier. She'd expected him to be numb to people like Cora, but he'd surprised her with his honesty and compassion. She was impressed.

"Afghan—um, where?" Cora asked, grimacing.

He laughed. "It's a country far away from here. Near Russia."

"Russia?" Cora gasped. "Have you been to Russia?"

"I have, as a kid," his face brightened with a crooked smile. "My dad took us a lot of places. Wanted us to see the world like he had."

Cora had stopped shaking, but she kept a wary gaze on Knox.

Heather stepped toward Knox, laying her hand on his arm. "As you just heard, Knox has a lot of combat experience," she said and Lamarr nodded, looking relieved. "He has a lot of knowledge and he can teach us."

"What?" Knox replied, his mouth falling open. He waved her off, stepping back. "Heather, I spent two tours in Afghanistan, but I'm no drill instructor."

"And we're not soldiers, so it's a good match. Knox, you've seen these creatures in action. You can see that we need all the training we can get. We have to learn how to fight the soulstalkers—and the demons—or we won't last long with so many prowling the Between now. Zakhart and the other pale angels will help us, too." Heather took hold of his hand, a hot spark shooting across her skin. "Please, Knox? Will you train us?"

He shook his head and tried to pull away, but Lamarr was beside him now, hope shining in his face. Cora was behind Lamarr, watching him from a safe distance. She looked frightened, apprehensive.

Knox glanced at them, then Heather, and back again. Drawing in a deep breath, he crossed his arms against his chest.

"All right," he said with a sigh. "I'll do it. If there's enough people to train. I'm not going to lead five people against a horde of demons. You got that, Heather?"

"Deal," said Heather, nodding. "Looks like I'll need to raise an army for you to train."

Avana's smoky form trailed around Heather's head and fluttered into a foggy haze in front of her, turning solid. The smoke woman reached out, icy eyes turning misty, a smile on her alabaster face.

"I can help with that," Avana announced. "There are souls scattered all over the Between right now, scared and lost. They've been there since the great tree collapsed. In my ethereal form, I can travel unseen through forest and grasslands." She laid a hand against her chest. "Please, let me locate them and bring them to the new tree. For now, it's the best way I can help you."

Heather nodded, surprised by Avana's offer. "Sure, that would be a huge help," she replied. "Where are the rest of your people?"

"They're all in hiding," she answered. "I'll call them first. Then we'll split up, find the other souls, and follow the pale angels' light cords back again."

"Thank you, Avana." She bowed her head. "I can't tell you how much I appreciate your help."

Heather turned toward the forest and motioned everyone onto the path.

"Let's get everyone back to safety first. Then Knox and I will help Avana search for others."

Knox sighed. "Don't know what I just got myself into," he said, following Heather back toward the new soul tree.

"More trouble than you can possibly imagine," Heather replied. "But it's the only way any of us will reach the Spiral again."

"So," Knox began, squinting, "You're saying that if I help you raise and train this army, you'll lead me—and them—to this Spiral?"

Heather paced around him. "Not quite. You've got to help me go up against the demons, rescue the souls they're holding hostage."

His face turned pale, but he didn't flinch. "Okay, rescue hostages," he said, nodding. "No sweat."

She stopped pacing, turning to face him. She studied his face, those haunting blue eyes. At that moment, he looked like a lost, little boy, trying to stand as tall and as tough as he could manage, but underneath that determined mask, she saw his pain and the weariness that clung to his soul.

He was broken. She heard the little pieces rattling around inside, so much like her own heart. He was scared. That was clear. Scared of losing control, of loosening that ultra-tight grip he'd wrapped around his emotions. His anger crouched deep inside him, ready to savage his restraint. That's why he'd ended his life, to prevent him from snapping and killing a bunch of innocents as he called them.

Heather didn't know what Knox needed to figure out here, but something told her that maybe it was just to give himself a break. To see that he was a man who'd seen things that most people would never see—and shouldn't—in their lifetime. To know that witnessing those horrors and doing his job didn't make him a monster. To understand that his pain and anger were normal. They didn't make him a ticking time bomb. They made him human.

"If you help us with the demons—and finding Ross—I'll help you find the Spiral." She extended her hand. "Deal?"

His eyes lit up and he nodded. He reached out and shook her hand with a hard pump of his hand. He held onto her hand, one moment then two.

"Thank you," he whispered.

She smiled. "You're welcome."

He squeezed her hand and let go, turning away to look for soulstalkers. Heather turned toward the cord of light winding through the forest.

She plucked the cord and everyone fell silent as ripples of light drifted through the brush and trees. The dark skies had gone quiet, soulstalkers fluttering past, but keeping their distance.

Heather led Knox and the others down a winding path as it veered away from where the great tree once stood, twisting deeper into the sparse forest until the sound of a stream burbled nearby.

She turned toward the stream, following its bank toward the thick swath of blackness where heartlilies bloomed in complete darkness. Just before the darkness fell like a thick curtain, she turned onto an ashen path that led to a clearing and the ring of trees.

They'd be safe here for now. But they needed to fortify the circle and train themselves to fight. Only then could she even think about trying to find Ross? In the Demon Veils.

seven

· · ·

WHEN THE BETWEEN had darkened to dusk, shadow creatures grew bold, swarming the grasslands in packs as they hunted prey. Their screeches echoed across the forest, the sound like fingernails against a chalkboard.

Zoe huddled by the red brick fireplace beside Knox. Cora and Lamarr stood by the window. They looked nervous, worried. There had been no sign of Avana for what seemed like hours (there was no time in the Between).

Had Avana lost interest in the other souls and given up, hiding until the darkness had lightened again? And where were the pale angels? All three had disappeared, leaving them to fend for themselves right now.

Maybe that was good? It let her and the others get settled, and figure out what happened next before the pale angels returned with new information that might throw off everything again.

Heather paced through the room that began to change around her. Blue couch fading, furniture moving, changing before her eyes. The other fireplace disappeared.

She glanced over at Lamarr who shrugged. Cora pulled a tan shawl tighter around her shoulders, shaking her head.

"Not me, Heather," she replied.

Heather glanced at Knox and then Zoe.

"Wasn't me," Knox replied, elbows propped on his knees as he sat on a couch that kept changing form and color. "I couldn't care less how this place is laid out."

Zoe giggled, curling against him, head on his shoulder, pink unicorn in her lap. "That's better," she said, offering Heather a quirky smile. "You don't mind, do you?"

Heather shook her head. "No, it's fine, Zoe. Whatever makes you happy."

"Do you like the new sofa, Knox?" Zoe asked.

Knox gave her a half-hearted shrug, his gaze settling on Heather a moment then moving past her to Lamarr and Cora.

Zoe tugged on his sleeve. "Knox! Do you like it?" she repeated.

"Yeah, it's nice, kid," he muttered and gave Heather a weary glance.

At every chirr and screech, his body tensed, gaze taking in every detail in the room. Heather could almost see him mapping out the distance to each window, counting how many steps to the front door.

His breath quickened as Cora and Lamarr walked through the space, his gaze flicking from their movements to the door. And back to Heather. Every time a rug changed or the sofa faded into a new hue, Knox's gaze snapped toward it.

Zoe flounced up from the floor and wandered past Heather to sit at an ornate white and gold oval dining table that appeared by the door. With chairs that had curved arms and swirls of gold paint and pale blue accents. They looked like French antiques.

In moments, the dining table changed from round to square to rectangular, its size shrinking and growing. Benches scraped across the wood floors, a purple rug appearing underneath. A moment later the rug was turquoise. Two moments later, it was gone. Benches changed to chairs and back again.

Knox rubbed his face with his hands, sighing. His hands were starting to tremble as he dropped them to his sides, reaching for weapons that weren't there. His breath quickened, sweat glistening across his upper lip as he tried to take in all the changing details.

If that kid was going to change the room every time she got bored, Knox would go crazy. And so would Heather.

"Zoe," said Heather in a soft voice. She walked over and stood beside the bench that Zoe had plopped down on with her unicorn. "Some change is fine, but the constant changes are a little too much."

Her eyes darkened and she glared at Heather.

"But I like making things look pretty," she said and crossed her arms. "Other people like my changes."

Sixteen was a rough age. Heather remembered how every comment and every interaction felt like either the best thing ever or the end of the world. None of it compared to ending up in the Between and she didn't want Zoe to feel bullied here. But Knox was going to snap soon.

She'd try a different angle.

Heather smiled and dropped down on her haunches. "I do, too! This table is beautiful and the new couch looks much softer." She lowered her voice so only Zoe heard her. "But see, Knox over there was a combat soldier."

Zoe turned to stare at Knox. "He said he loved my changes," she said, pouting.

"I'm sure he does, Zoe, but if you look at him right now, you'll see how tense and shaken up he looks. He spent a very difficult time where every change, every move was a life-or-death decision for him."

"But he's not a soldier anymore," she replied in a shrill whisper.

Heather motioned her quiet. "He has something called Post Traumatic Stress Disorder. Ordinary things can trigger the memory of those life-or-death decisions. Flashbacks of combat. Everyday events get magnified, pushing him back into his training. Do you understand?"

"I guess so," said Zoe, eyes downcast, cheeks flushed.

"See, Knox feels comfortable when he's familiar with his surroundings, comfortable when he knows the people around him. He's already unnerved by the increase in soulstalkers and the new people in the tree. Sudden changes set him on edge and make him feel very uncomfortable. That's why we each have our own little nook, a place we're free to change as much as we like. Then we leave the main areas alone and ask everyone before making a chance."

Zoe glanced over at Knox and then back at Heather, her eyes misty, lips pressed into another pout.

"Poor Knox," she said in a soft voice. "I'm so sorry. I wasn't trying to hurt him. He's been so sweet to me, making sure I was safe and protected. I'd never hurt him."

Heather patted Zoe on the shoulder, trying to reassure her that no one was angry at her. "Hey, it's okay," she said, smiling. "You didn't know. We're all still trying to get to know each other."

The front door burst open.

Knox was on his feet, crouching, ready to take the offensive. Heather turned, setting herself, fearing a flock of soulstalkers bursting into the room. Or worse—demons.

Avana's alabaster face darkened, ice-blue eyes shining as she swept into the room in a trail of smoke. Behind her, dozens of lost souls surged inside, eyes filled with terror, chests heaving, hands shaking as they slammed the door closed behind them.

Something thumped against the door. A wild screech. Muffled voices. A scuffle.

Knox was behind Heather now, hands on the door. He opened it a crack, he and Heather peering outside.

Three soulstalkers swarmed two souls, not three feet from the door.

Knox shoved the door open, bolting outside. Heather was at his back.

He pulled the nearest soulstalker off a figure huddled on the ground and nearly cracked its body in half as he whipped it around by the wing, burying his fist into its pointy, almost bird-like face. It was male, its chest bare, legs covered in silky black pants, feet bare and taloned. Like its spindly clawed fingers.

It shrieked, the call shrill like a falcon's cry.

Behind them, something rustled.

Heather turned as a shadow passed over her.

Two more soulstalkers!

They swarmed Knox, dragging him backward.

Heather leaped at them, landing on one's back, her arm wrapped around its throat, squeezing as hard as she could.

Knox cried out in pain, the other two mauling him.

With her fist, Heather beat down the one she'd grabbed, choking tighter until it slumped to the ground. She hoped it was dead.

Again, Knox yelped. He let out a fierce shout, trying to shake free of them. They lifted him off the ground.

Heather leaped and grabbed another one. A female. Wrapping her legs around its waist, she buried her hands into its wild tangles of black hair and yanked as hard as he could.

The soulstalker swiped at her, but Heather was just out of reach of those taloned fingers. The soulstalker tumbled backward, smashing into the dirt.

Knox broke the other soulstalker's hold, beating it back with his fists, his face a raw mask of fury. A loud crack reverberated as he broke its wing, black feathers hanging at an odd angel.

The injured soulstalker chattered at the others as it stumbled backward, another soulstalker landing, lifting it into the air.

That left two.

Heather was at Knox's side, sliding her arm around his waist to get him on his feet. Together, they rushed the remaining soulstalkers.

To her right, the two souls moved toward the two soulstalkers' flank.

The last two soulstalkers screeched and took to the air, disappearing into the darkness that had settled over the forest.

And it was quiet again.

The two souls turned to face her and Heather couldn't hold back her grin. Barb and Javier! From the great tree.

"Barb! Javier!"

The tall woman and shorter man stumbled toward her and Knox who was still in defense mode. He motioned everyone toward the door as he crouched, watching in all directions for soulstalkers.

Heather shoved open the door, motioning Barb inside and then Javier.

Holding the door, Heather shouted at Knox who backed toward the tree, still watching the sky and the forest. Heather reached toward him. She gripped his arm and pulled him toward the door. He cast one last look at the dark forest and backed into the tree. Heather rushed inside behind him and slammed the door. He fell back against it, chest heaving.

Barb and Javier froze a moment, gazes flicking around the new soul tree, taking in the pale blue walls, honey-colored wood floor, and the round, burgundy rug in front of the roaring red brick hearth that had shifted to the right side of the room. Near the couch.

The familiar blue sofa had been moved against the wall and changed a billion colors until Zoe settled on an oversized beige sectional. And made the old blue couch disappear. To the left of the door was a dining room with a black feasting table and benches on both sides. That no one needed, but it was a comfort and reminded them of when they were human. Heather left it alone.

She sighed. But Zoe had changed everything—again—while she and Knox were outside just now. And now a huge flat panel television hung on the wall opposite the couch, screen dark.

Heather pointed at the flat panel. "Really, Zoe? Really? What do you plan to watch with no electricity?"

"Coz, I like streaming," Zoe replied. Giving her the eye-roll. Like every sixteen-year-old everywhere. Even here. "You *do* know what that is, don't you?"

"I do," Heather snapped. "Imagine that. Hell, I even had a

TikTok account. Now, stop being a condescending brat. And for the record, I'm twenty not eighty, Zoe."

"Wow, twenty? That's like...old."

Heather chewed the inside of her mouth. Okay. It was official. Zoe was getting on her last nerve. Wasn't it bad enough that there were hordes of soulstalkers carrying souls off and attacking them without dealing with this?

"It is—if you're like five, Zoe. Stop being a jerk." Heather turned her gaze to the flat panel and conjured a blank wall.

Zoe flounced over to the couch and flopped down, arms crossed, mouth pressed into a pout.

"Pouting?" Heather frowned. "Toddler much, Zoe?"

A flash of black caught her eye. She turned. The flat panel was back. Gritting her teeth, she conjured it away, blocking the wall with a tall bookcase filled with books.

"Heather?"

Heather turned at the familiar voice. Javier and Barb were behind her. Javier's eyes were wide, staring at her like she was a ghost.

"So glad you're safe, Javier!" She held out her arms. "I was hoping that you and Barb made it out of the great tree when it fell."

"But I—I watched you leave," Barb sputtered as she hugged Heather, holding her out at arm's length, and spun Heather around. "Is it really you? How did you end up back here? The pale angels said you'd gone through the Spiral. That you'd gotten out!"

Javier was at her shoulder, smiling. He kissed her cheek. "Good to see you, hija."

"Zakhart came to me," she said with a shrug. "Found me in the physical world again. He said things were bad and he needed my help, so I came back."

"Don't get me wrong, it's great to see you," Barb replied, pulling her into another quick hug. "But why would you...make the same mistake and come back here? I mean, did you have to—"

Heather nodded emphatically.

Barb's eyes widened, a shocked look spreading across her face. Knox kept quiet, taking in the conversation.

"I had to," said Heather in a tight voice. "Souls were being captured. The great tree was gone, demons everywhere." She stiffened. "And Ross. I'm so terrified for him, Barb."

A knowing expression darkened her long face, thin dark bangs framing her tired brown eyes, lines around her mouth deeper than Heather remembered.

"Ross...yeah—how terrible. I've heard the whispers, so many stories. I don't know what to believe."

"Sí, es muy malo," said Javier and patted her arm, a sad look in his eyes. "But it is true, Heather...verdad."

Heather gripped Barb's arms, her mouth dry, fear trembling through her now.

"Barb. Javier. What did you hear?"

She trusted Zakhart, but something inside told her that he was still holding back parts of the story. All the raw, painful details from her. Part of her didn't want to know, but she knew she couldn't avoid them any longer. She had to know to save Ross. Everything. The full story of what happened to him.

Barb bowed her head. "You know the demons have him now, right?" She stared into Heather's eyes, watching her reactions.

Heather nodded. "How'd that happen?"

"They stole him away when everything was in chaos," said Barb.

"Sí, Ross was—dazed," Javier added. "On the ground. At the clearing. So was La Muerte...Death. And—ángeles pálidos." He flapped his arms. "The pale ones. They fight for Ross." Javier shrugged. "Then he just—gone."

Heather's anger burned hot. Damned demons snatched Ross when Zakhart and the other pale angels were trying to stop Death from taking him.

"Thanks for explaining, Javier," said Heather in a quiet voice.

Barb closed her eyes, the lines on her forehead and around her eyes deeper than Heather remembered. No one aged in the Between, but Barb looked a bit more haggard, more worn down. Even Javier's square face and stocky build seemed more fragile now, the lines carved deeper around his mouth and into his chin.

How long after the great tree fell had they been hiding in the forest? How long had Ross been in demon hands?

Barb sighed, crossing her arms, looking sad. "He's switched sides," said Barb. "You know that, don't you?"

Javier nodded.

Switched sides? Slowly, the words sank into her fevered brain.

"No," Heather snapped, shaking her head. "No way. He would never do that."

"Some of the lost souls have seen him traveling with the demons," Barb continued. "Unfettered. Like he'd chosen to be with them or something. Like they trusted him."

Heather stumbled back from Barb, glaring. She was just like Avana, hating on Ross. None of these souls had ever appreciated his efforts, even when he'd tried to get them to follow the paths to the Spiral. The demons had probably forced Ross back into the Veils, taken over his willpower, memory by memory, until they had replaced Thraecius in the coal fields.

"Sí, Heather, we spent a lot of time in the forest. Several of us saw him—traveling with demons."

Javier sat down on the bench by the feasting table and leaned his tired body against the wall.

"Ahhh...es bueno."

"I don't understand," said Heather, her brain on fire with questions.

"It's good to be here—and not out there," Javier replied, closing his eyes, his head resting against the wall. "Was a long time in those trees."

"In the forest," said Barb.

"Sí, forest," Javier said with a weary smile.

He seemed relieved to be inside the new soul tree, away from the growing numbers of shadow things outside.

But their words cut right through Heather's heart. Was Ross helping the demons inside and outside the Veils? Something so much worse than being forced to work at the Mechanism or in the coal fields?

Was he actually helping them kidnap other souls?

She shook her head in disbelief. No! She refused to believe that.

Barb moved over to her, patting her shoulder. "I know you don't want to hear this, Heather." She sat down on the bench beside Javier. "But Avana saw him hunting with the soulstalkers."

"Hunting?"

She winced. Her heart was breaking. Avana was a windbag at times. Maybe she was spreading rumors for her amusement?

"He carry bags of...uh...dust. Pollen. For the sand runners." Javier's brown eyes turned sad. "It's too late for him now, hija," he said, his voice heavy.

Barb stretched her long legs. She was six feet tall and a head taller than Heather, but sitting on the bench, they were almost at eye level.

"No, you're wrong!" Heather shouted. "It's not too late! It can't be!"

"Heather, we may even have to fight him," said Barb. "*And* the demons to rescue the other souls taken hostage."

Her body wilted under that blow. She shook her head, backing away. That thought hadn't entered her mind. What if she had to face Ross like that? She turned away, hurrying to the beige sectional, hands over her ears at the roar of noise in the tree, that empty ache in her chest surging into her legs and arms.

Barb followed her over to the couch, Knox behind her. His blue eyes were a confused mix of hunger and concern, his lean body tensed like an over-wound spring.

"No worries, Heather," he said with a hungry grin. "I've got *your* back next time." He clenched his hands together in a strangling motion. "I'll drop him before he even makes eye contact with you."

Anger overcame despair. Heather snapped up from the couch,

shoving past Barb to grab Knox by the folds of his shirt. She shoved him against the wall, the room falling silent. She pointed a finger in Knox's face. The former soldier looked surprised and confused by her reaction.

"No one touches him! You hear me? No one!"

His eyes glimmered, a devious smile creeping onto his face. "What's the story, Heather? He an ex? Unrequited crush?"

"Stop it," Heather snapped through gritted teeth.

Knox's gaze moved from Barb to Heather, the playful tone leaving his voice. With a slow slide of his hands, he gripped Heather's forearms.

"Come on, Heather," he said. "Why you protecting a traitor? He's probably the reason that tree got stomped by the demons."

"Stop it!"

She jerked her arms free of his touch, wanting to smash her fist into his face. She glared at him and then turned and walked away. Before she punched him in his leering face.

Knox grinned, following. He enjoyed poking her with a sharp stick, not realizing she was seconds away from bitch-slapping him. Hard.

"Face it, Heather! Ross threw all of you under the bus and now, he's hunting you all down for demons! I say we make him our first target." He motioned at the dozens of souls gathering around them now. Zoe was at his elbow, a taunting smile on her face. "C'mon! What do the rest of you say?"

Whispers hissed through the room. "Destroy that demon-lover," said someone behind Heather.

She turned.

"Traitor," said someone else across the room.

She glanced around.

Was it Lamarr? Or Javier?

"Take him out before he gives us up to the demons, too," said another whisper. A female voice. Zoe?

She whirled around, facing Knox again with an unblinking stare.

"You heard the room," Knox replied a triumphant sneer on his face, blue eyes taunting as he put his hands on his hips. "We take out this Ross on sight." He snickered. "You put me in charge of this outfit, remember? That's my decision. End of discussion."

She glared at him as he turned toward the others a moment like he thought he was in charge.

No one knew the full story. She'd clear Ross' name. She'd save him from the demons—and Knox—before it was too late. And she may have to do it alone now.

Knox turned his smug face back to her, arms crossed, daring her to act. It was too much.

With a snarl, she slammed her fist into his mouth with a loud crack.

He yelped in pain, grabbing his face.

Barb gasped. Zoe cried out and tried to shove through the crowd to get to Knox, but Barb held her back.

Groaning, Knox doubled over as Heather walked away, clutching her hand to her chest. Pain snaked through every finger and knuckle of her right hand, sharp aches threading down into her wrist. She pulled in a breath, barely able to breathe. That hurt more than she ever dreamed it would. It never looked that way in the movies when people threw punches. If she'd been in a physical body, she'd have broken every bone in her hand. And her body when Knox recovered from the blow and retaliated.

Knox straightened to his full, six-foot-four height, clutching his swelling jaw, fury burning in his eyes. Something inside him snapped. He let out an enraged scream, eyes narrowed as he rushed at her, grabbing her around the waist. He pressed her against the wall with a hard thump.

Heather's skull smacked hard against the wall, pain shooting down her neck and into her ribcage. His arm shot across her chest like an iron bar, holding her against the wall, left hand clamped around her right wrist so she couldn't punch him again.

For a moment, everything turned black, voices whispering

around her. When the blurriness receded, she was still staring into Knox's wild, blue-eyed temper. She struggled against his hold, but couldn't break free. Shadows dampened the pale wildness of his wide-set eyes, hardening that droopy, puppy-eyed gaze into a feral glare, pupils swallowing any trace of gentle blue.

The monster had awoken.

Knox drew back, teeth bared, whole body taut like an over-stretched wire.

She sucked in a breath, bracing for impact.

"Go ahead!" she shouted. "Punch me back! But I won't let you touch him, Knox! None of you know what happened. Anyone who goes after Ross will go through me first. That's a promise." She met Knox's murderous stare, fist cocked over his right shoulder. "You may be in charge of training, Knox, but this is *my* army."

Fear trembled through every nerve and muscle, her body board-stiff, head held high, chin up, waiting for his fist to slam into her face.

She'd hit him first. She deserved it.

Knox's fist careened forward. Striking the wall with a loud crack. He screamed, an animal cry of frustration exploding from his lungs, and bowed his head, hands pressed against the wall on both sides of her face.

Heather's muscles went slack, her breathing slowing as she closed her eyes, shaking in the awkward silence. Finally, she opened her eyes and met his drained, blue gaze. Slowly, she laid her hands on his shoulders. He flinched but didn't shove her away.

"I'm sorry, Knox. I was out of line, I know that. You had every right to hit me in the mouth. But we don't have all the facts yet. Just a couple people claiming they saw something. I'm not running with a bunch of vigilantes who jump to conclusions and act without facts. So, if that's the plan, I'm out of here. I'll take my chances out there alone."

Knox exhaled sharply. He let go of the wall, looking drained. Gone was the fury burning like kerosene in his eyes. His face brightened, shadows receding as the corners of his bruised mouth quirked into a quick smile. He rubbed his jaw with the palm of his hand.

"That was some punch, Heather," he said finally.

Her face burned with shame. "I'm sorry. I don't know what came over me."

"Sounds like it was loyalty. And some deep feelings." He smirked, still rubbing his jaw. "Lucky man."

Heather laughed. "Ross saved me, Knox. More than once. He even put himself between me and Death, letting me escape through the Spiral while Death took him prisoner. He sacrificed everything for me. And I can't live with that. I've got to find him."

Knox frowned.

"When the pale angels were struggling against Death to rescue him, the demons must have slipped in and taken him prisoner." Heather continued. "I don't know what happened, what they did to him, but I know he wouldn't help them willingly. I have to go in there after him. Break their hold somehow." Despair burned in her stomach now. "It's the only way I'll know...if he can—be saved."

Knox brushed a lock of coppery brown hair out of her eyes. His touch was soft, tender now.

"That's a bad position to be in," he said, his voice dry and raspy. "I hope you won't...have to um—put him down, Heather."

"What? What do you mean?"

"Look, I don't know how any of this works, but maybe he's already dead? His soul, I mean. Maybe Death already took his soul and the demons just scavenged what was left? Maybe there's nothing left to rescue? Or maybe he made a bargain with the demons? His soul in exchange for yours."

A chill tore through her chest and she winced, a sharp pain cutting deep. Was Ross beyond rescue? All because he chose to save her instead of himself?

Her eyes stung with tears.

No! She balled her hands into fists, overwhelmed now, unable to even send those words tumbling through her brain. She swallowed the lump in the back of her throat, hands turning clammy, panic rising. Had she let Zakhart convince her to come back here under false pretenses? Dangling Ross in front of her so she'd return to help the Between? Knowing all along that he was lost?

The lump rose in her throat again, lodging tight in the back of her throat.

Maybe Zakhart brought her back to save his soul? A last compassionate act to set him free. Had she come back to rescue a corpse? She hurt all over now, the hopelessness drowning out everything. She fought back the tears filling her eyes, not wanting these people to see her cry. She owed Ross that release.

No, she owed him everything.

Horrified, she fled past Knox, shoving past the confused souls huddling in the new tree. She pounded up the stairs to the top and threw herself inside her little nook. She crawled onto the bed and wrapped herself in the thick lavender comforter, trying to forget these speculations, stories she couldn't face.

But what if everyone was right?

What if all she could do was set him free? She'd already given up everything to come back. Was it all for nothing? Or just too late for Ross? Why had Zakhart let her remember him and then take it all away like this?

She buried her face into the comforter, shoulders heaving, thin light of the Spiral's bracelets tempting her now. She didn't want to battle demons and train people to fight. She wanted out of here. Now. And she wanted any memory of this place—especially what she'd lost here—erased, all of the pieces permanently scrambled.

Oh, Ross—where are you?

eight

· · ·

THE HAND against Heather's shoulder startled her.

She jerked her head up from the comforter, staring at Knox through watery eyes, her cheeks hot with tears. He stood there looking contrite but concerned. She winced at the bruise swelling around his mouth, her face burning with embarrassment. All around his mouth was purple now, bottom lip swollen.

"Knox...I'm so sorry I hit you."

He offered her a sincere, crooked smile and sat down on the edge of the bed. "I was eggin' you on pretty hard. I thought you showed incredible restraint actually."

She smiled.

"I like what you've done with the place," he said with a chuckle, walking to the end of the bed. "A bed. Empty walls. Purple comforter. What do you call this decor? Early prison motif? Don't let Zoe get hold of it or you'll have fuzzy pink ponies everywhere."

She couldn't help the laugh that spilled out. Okay, it was pretty sparse compared to her first trip here. She'd conjured a double bed and put some color on the walls. Sage green? Mint? This time, the lavender comforter was all she had the energy to do.

Heather shrugged, sitting on the bed's edge, feet dangling. "It's a work in progress."

"Mine's pretty impressive," he said, stretching out across the bed. He laid back on one elbow, studying her expression. "Sort of early military inspection meets Genghis Khan. I'll show it to you sometime if you're interested."

"Sure," she replied. "Stop making me laugh."

He was quiet now, eyes alight, the silence between them lengthening.

"Anything I can do?" he asked finally. "Besides apologize again for nearly punching you in the face."

"That wasn't your fault," she replied. "I hit you first. You had every right to hit me back."

"Only for a nut shot," he said.

"Knox?" a thin voice called from the doorway.

Zoe stood in the doorway, peering around the threshold. Her grey, silken clothes hung on her thin body, making her look like a drowned street orphan as she cradled that pink unicorn in her arms, hazel gaze looking weepy as Knox glanced toward the doorway. She scowled at Heather through hooded lids, looking at her with an accusatory glare.

That's when Heather realized that Zoe was jealous. The teenager had claimed Knox as her own and didn't want to share him with anyone, especially Heather. And she was certain this was news to Knox who viewed her as a little girl, nothing more. He'd signed up with the army right out of high school and had done two tours in Afghanistan. Heather guessed he was about twenty-four or twenty-five.

"Yeah, kid?" he asked. "Somethin' wrong?"

Zoe glanced from Heather to Knox with an angry gaze. She looked timid, her bony frame looking so fragile like a stiff wind would carry her away. But angry. She'd grown quite attached to Knox. He'd saved her from soulstalkers...like Ross had saved Heather.

She sighed. It felt like a lifetime ago since she'd seen Ross, felt the rumble of his warm voice ache through her or the sizzle of his touch against her skin. The memory of the slow heat of attraction that had built between them burned through her now, making her ache all over. A slow burn that had reached flashpoint—just before everything unraveled again.

"Why were you and Heather fighting and shouting at each other like that?" Zoe demanded, her hazel eyes sad but angry.

That wasn't why she was here. She never let Knox out of her sight.

This teen was different. She was an impressionable sixteen-year-old who'd been bullied. To death. At that age, things never seemed subtle. Things were either on or off, lights were either red or green, and people were either friends or enemies. With nothing in between. But she acted even younger than that. More like a tween—or younger. Regardless, Knox was Zoe's hero. She relied on him, never getting very far from his side, never quite letting him out of her sight.

She was crushing hard on this hot, explosive soldier.

Heather understood. He was a powerful force. And he was incredibly hot, in that underwear model kind of way. Even she couldn't deny the hint of attraction she felt for him.

"It's kind of a long story, Zoe," said Knox, his gaze heavy, not leaving Heather's face. She felt it burning into her eyes.

Knox intrigued her, stirred awake the memory of when her heart had still beat in her chest. He unearthed the afterglow of warm blood that had once rushed through the now-empty tracts in her body. He had a strange way of drawing together all the shattered pieces of her broken heart and filing away the sharp edges.

But only Ross could put them back together again.

And then she went and exploded at the guy in front of Zoe. All those lost souls had just escaped from soulstalkers, nerves shot, and then they walked into a fistfight. That she'd started. Heather groaned. It hadn't been her best moment. Heather hoped Zoe wasn't traumatized over their fight. But she worried that Zoe's crush would lead to heartbreak. Being sixteen was hard.

She still remembered those days. They weren't that far off.

"I want to know." Zoe turned to Heather, glaring. Anger flushed her thin face, her voice sharp. "So why'd you hit him, Heather? He was just trying to protect the rest of us. Why would you treat him like that? It was so mean."

Knox cast a confused glance at Heather and then looked back at Zoe.

"I know what it looked like to you, Zoe, but believe me, it was all just a big misunderstanding," said Knox. "Heather and I are still friends. See? It was just a little disagreement and it's over now. Water under the bridge. Nothing to worry about."

"I apologized and told him how sorry I was, Zoe," said Heather. "He's forgiven me." She squinted at Knox. "Right?"

He laughed and pulled Heather into a hug. "Of course, I forgive you. I was the one out of line, Heather. I deserved that."

Zoe's eyes darkened, mouth falling open. "Knox! Your mouth!"

She rushed over to him, wedging her way between Knox and Heather.

Heather held in a chuckle and slid back, making room for Zoe who pressed thin fingers against the puffy bruise surrounding his lower lip. She cast another dagger-laden glare at Heather and turned back to Knox.

"Of course, you didn't deserve to be hit in the mouth!"

"It's complicated, kid. I was trying hard to push Heather's buttons, not Control-Alt-Delete, so that punch was half my fault. All's forgiven now." He stood up, steering Zoe to the doorway. "Now, Heather and I need to talk about training and how to deal with these demons. Okay?"

"Okay," she replied, unicorn dangling from her left hand. She stopped halfway to the door, grabbing hold of his sleeves. "Are you gonna talk about this guy named Ross? I hope we get to fight him!"

Heather bristled.

"No, Zoe," she snapped, her voice sharper than she'd intended.

"Ross' situation is very complicated and no one has any facts yet. We need to do a lot of investigating. Find out the truth."

She turned toward Heather. "But he's helping the demons kidnap people!"

Heather got to her feet, arms crossed, anger burning hot again. Everybody was an expert on things they knew nothing about. It made her furious.

"You're jumping to conclusions like everyone else, Zoe. You don't know a damned thing about this. Ross is a wonderful guy. He's not our enemy. He's in trouble and he desperately needs our help. Just like when you needed Knox to save you from soulstalkers."

"Heather's right, Zoe. Don't go jumpin' to conclusions." Knox stared at Heather for a moment, smirking. "Besides, any woman who can throw a punch like that is a woman I want to get to know better. One I'd trust with my life."

Heather was intrigued by the mysterious expression on Knox's face. Admiration? Fascination? The hint of a connection. Like there was a deep, personal secret between them, something he'd never told anyone else before and had suddenly shared with her. And he wanted the world to know he had, too.

Zoe crossed her arms, her hard eyes narrowing into an annoyed glare, studying Heather for a moment, clearly unimpressed. And popped the eye-roll.

"Whatever."

She turned to Knox now, ignoring Heather, jealousy building.

"Knox, I want to hear some of your war stories," she said, picking at the remnant splotches of hot pink nail polish that clung to her short, blunt fingernails. "Come down now and sit by the fireplace with me. Right now, okay?" She grabbed hold of his right arm, tugging him toward the doorway. "See, I haven't heard any of your stories and you're always talking about Afghanistan and being a soldier."

At this remark, Knox looked annoyed. Heather hadn't heard

Knox even mention telling war stories and from talking to him, he didn't seem interested in talking about those days.

He stopped in front of the doorway and slid his arm out of her grasp. "Sorry, Zoe, but that's not a place I tell stories about."

"Please, Knox," she insisted, taking hold of his arm again. "Tell me about where you grew up. About your family. Where you're from."

He gripped the girl by the shoulders, forcing her to look at him. "Zoe, listen," he said in a stern voice.

The teenager stopped fidgeting, at last meeting his gaze, a storm of emotions swirling in her eyes, the winds shifting her mood from annoyance to infatuation and back again. Was this Zoe's first crush? Had she died before she'd experienced her first crush? Heather felt sad now. Zoe having her first crush in the Between just sucked.

Thankfully, Knox seemed to realize that, too. His stern expression softened.

"After everything's settled down, we'll sit around the fire and I'll tell you about growing up in central Illinois. And my crazy Australian Shepherd, Gunner."

"Your dog?" Zoe asked.

Knox nodded. "Yep, he was my best bud. Had him since I was five years old. Unlike me, he lived a long life."

"Come on!" Zoe cried, tugging him toward the stairs.

He dug in and stopped her just shy of the first step.

"Zoe, *after* everything's settled down. That means much later."

Zoe's gaze fell to the floor. She looked crushed that he wouldn't drop everything and run down the stairs right now with her.

"Right now, Heather and I have a lot of things to discuss." He glanced back at Heather, his eyes sparkling. "We need to talk about this army we're building and how to train people. This is gonna take a lot of planning."

"Fine," Zoe snapped, turning her back on him.

She let out an exaggerated sigh and clamored down the stairs to the first floor.

Knox watched her go downstairs and disappear into the small group of souls milling around the fireplace before he walked back into Heather's nook.

Heather nodded toward the doorway, feet still dangling over the side of the bed. "Zoe's really crushin' hard on you, Knox. You know that, don't you?"

A door appeared in the threshold and closed suddenly, making her jump. She glanced over at Knox who was smiling.

"Sorry, couldn't help myself," he said and sat down beside her on the bed. "I conjured a closed door for you. Now, what were you saying?" With his index finger, he traced the curve of her forearm in a white-hot line that nearly took her breath.

"Zoe," she snapped, sliding away from his touch. "She's crushin' hard on you."

"What about you, Heather?" he asked in a soft, intoxicating voice, moving closer.

"Just don't break her heart, okay?"

"I won't," he replied. "She's just a kid. She's just starry-eyed because I saved her from those soulstalkers, that's all. And she likes my stories. She'll get bored with me in no time. Being dead is a really bad time to start a new relationship."

She chuckled at his joke, but it was true.

"Seriously, Heather, she was scared and needed someone to help her. But right now, I've got my own traumas to deal with and so does Zoe. I still haven't wrapped my brain around this place."

"Me, too," Heather sighed. "And I'm a repeat customer."

"So, no worries, I plan to keep my distance."

Knox stretched out on the bed, turning on his side, elbow propped, head against his palm. With his other hand, he reached out, fingers tracing the patterns in her silken sleeve.

"Look, Heather, I came up here for two reasons," he said, his voice suddenly serious. "One, to make sure you're all right. And two, to talk about what happens next." He glanced at the closed door and then lowered his voice. "By the way, that smoky chick sure talks a lot, doesn't she?"

Chuckling, Heather laid her arms in her lap. She angled her body around to face him. "Yes, she does, but why do *you* say that?"

He laughed. "She's down there right now, yelling at people, ordering them around, assigning jobs like she owns the place."

"She was the caretaker of the great tree. She and her people. I don't who or what they are really. Everyone just called them smoke people, so I did, too. They have this ethereal form that lets them turn into smoke and a physical form. They can shift back and forth instantly."

He frowned and glanced back at the door again. "Where'd they come from? Same place as those pale angels?"

Heather shrugged. "They've always just been here. No one knows where they came from. The first time I was here, Avana was arrogant and angry at everything. She was always disrespectful to the souls in the great tree like they were all lazy slackers. She treated Ross like something on her shoe and I never understood why. She and I argued quite a few times. She's changed her tune about him now though."

"Over Ross?" Knox asked.

Heather nodded. "Especially Ross. She always called him a coward and worthless like the rest. On the night I arrived, Ross fought off the soulstalkers that were trying to carry me off. Alone. He got me safely to the great tree. And he told me about the Spiral, asking if I would help him find it."

Knox shook his head. He folded his legs underneath him and sat facing Heather who shifted, crossing her long legs.

"Doesn't sound like a coward to me."

"Exactly!" Heather replied. "He and I walked into the Demon Veils and faced those demons alone. All to save Thraecius, a Roman gladiator who was under their control. Later, Ross went alone into the poppy fields to try and save his girlfriend."

"You?" Knox asked, pointing at her.

"No," Heather said, shaking her head. "His girlfriend, Jessie." She flicked coppery brown hair out of her face and stretched out her legs, arms propped behind her.

"You're not his girlfriend?" Knox asked, his body shifting closer, a smirk on his face now.

"No," she replied. "Jessie was from in his physical life."

Why was he smirking at her?

"So, there was nothing official between you two? No ring? No promises?"

Heather shook her head. There hadn't been time. His last words to her, inside the Spiral, still burned deep. *I loved you more than my own life.* She'd whispered those same words through the Spiral back to him, but she had no idea if he'd heard them.

"Not yet," said Heather. "He and his girlfriend in the physical world committed suicide together, but someone found them. Jessie died, but they got to Ross in time. For a year afterward, people blamed him and shamed him. On the first anniversary, he killed himself with a shotgun."

"God, that's awful, Heather," said Knox, screwing up his face.

It was? After everything Knox had seen? Maybe something was getting through to Knox after all?

She nodded. "But he hadn't been here when Jessie reached the Between. She ended up in the poppy fields. Ross always blamed himself for what happened to her. He went into the poppy fields, trying to save her, but she was too far gone. He couldn't save her and fell under the poppy dust's endless sleep. Zakhart and I carried him out. We used heartlily blossoms to bring him out of the sleep."

Knox was quiet for a moment and Heather saw the thoughts almost race across his eyes.

"So, how did you and Ross find the Spiral?" he asked finally.

"It was tough," she replied, pulling her knees up to her chest. "Zakhart told us we had to connect with other souls—and ourselves. We had to find our own will to live again. Only when we'd done that could we even see the Spiral, Knox. So, as long as you want to die and be isolated from the world, you won't be able to see the Spiral."

He gaped at her, brows furrowing, head shaking. "What do you mean? We all wanted to die. And we did. That's how we got here."

"True. But you have to want to live now, Knox. To live again. You have to fix the broken parts inside you. The dead stuff that made you seek out Death instead of Life. The Spiral is the turn of the cycle of life. Without it, there'd be no Between. No second chances. Does that make sense?"

He sat up and crossed his legs underneath him, looking so serious. His skin smelled warm like summer. Like sunscreen and sunbaked sand. Those pale blue eyes were so hypnotic in the soft light, so intense beneath that mop of chocolate brown curls.

"I guess it does," he said, shrugging, "but how do I just turn on my will to live? It's the reason I'm here." He looked down at the comforter, not meeting her gaze now. "Heather, I'm so broken inside. There's just too many tiny little pieces...I don't think I can ever put them all back together again."

He seemed so lost tonight, so defeated and confused. She understood how he felt. But when she first got here, she'd felt defiant, fearful of becoming like the complacent souls that pretended to live their lives, pretended to eat and sleep and be alive. Knox just seemed angry and in pain. She felt sorry for him. There was no way she could even comprehend the horrors he'd seen, the atrocities he'd witnessed. Those kinds of events messed people up. They left scars on their hearts and psyches. And they broke people into thousands of tiny little pieces. Like Knox.

How could he ever connect those pieces again? Was connecting with others enough or was he too far gone, too?

He avoided people, cut himself off from the world. He seemed to have lost that sense of being normal, like he'd closed the door on the innocent, idealistic young man that had gone off to war, knowing he was lost now. He came home disillusioned, traumatized, hating the lies he'd been told. The things he'd been forced to do and see. Things that would haunt him forever.

Those events had left him bitter and detached, a very dangerous emotional state. He'd stopped seeing people as individuals. They were just threat levels to him: potential threats, threats, and obstacles. Knox even said that was why he'd jumped off that bridge. He didn't want to end up on the news as the latest mall shooter.

"Do you really think you would have snapped, Knox?" she asked.

He nodded emphatically, staring at her with desperate eyes. He was pulling back the shutters, letting her peek inside now.

"You think you're a monster, don't you?"

His eyes grew misty. He bit his lip, nodding. "What else would you call someone who sees total strangers as prey? Kill or be killed."

She took his hand in hers. "Hero," she said, not looking away from his eyes.

His eyes lit with bitter blue flames. "No!" he shouted. "No. Don't you call me that." He struggled to his feet and paced the floor, hands clutching his head. His eyes were wild and he was choking back sobs.

Heather rose from the comforter and got between him as he lunged for the door. She held him back, her shoulders pressed against the door. He let out a feral growl, trying to pry her out of his way, but she planted her feet. She fought his strength, his rage, until she felt him give in. She could see him struggling not to hurt her. He screamed, shaking with rage as he slammed his hand against the wall and sank to his knees.

She slid down with him and with a slow, deliberate move, she put her arms around him.

"Hero," she said against his ear. "Because a monster wouldn't have hesitated to act on those feelings. A monster would have relished those thoughts and enjoyed acting on them. A monster wouldn't have even questioned its actions."

"No," he moaned, the intensity fading from his voice. "I'm a monster. A bomb with a short fuse." His voice was an aching whisper. "Even here. Why didn't I do the job right the first time?"

He fought so hard not to give in to his emotions, trying to tamp it all down beneath the surface, packing down the fire and anger that had become an active volcano. If he didn't release the pressure, he'd never leave this place.

"Knox, no!" she shouted, turning his face toward her. "You were a hero. You were so frightened of harming even one innocent that you leaped from a bridge to save them. You gave up your own life rather than risk hurting a single person."

Knox's face contorted. He looked so vulnerable now, so little-boy lost.

Heather couldn't stand it. She pulled him into her arms and held him. He needed to connect with someone. If he didn't, he'd never make it out of here. He'd be the perfect prey for the demons. Like Thraecius had been. She didn't need two people trapped in demon hands.

She needed Knox functional. Strong. She needed him to meet the proud, brave man inside him, the man that had been there all along. She needed him to train her—all of them—to fight. To help all of them become a force strong enough to challenge the Demon Veils and rescue all the kidnapped souls held there.

Why hadn't she and Ross paid more attention, helped more souls escape? Why didn't she go alone the first time and keep Ross safe?

"I hate what's inside me," Knox sputtered, teeth gritted, hands sliding tightly around her, holding onto her as his whole body shook with fear. "It feeds on my anger, on the combat memories—my fear. It whips it all up into this massive rage that just...just takes control over me. Blinds me! All I see is this red haze and it tears at me until all I want to do is release it!"

She ran her hand through his curly hair, fingers sliding down the nape of his neck to rub his stony shoulders, muscles like steel cables.

"It won't let me get close to anyone," he said with a moan.

"Why, Knox?" she whispered.

"If I get close, I'll let my guard down. I'll let the monster out." His teeth were chattering now and he trembled like he was freezing. "If it gets out, I can't pull it back again. I can't control it."

"But the only way to fight it, Knox, is to let it out. Then slay it once and for all."

"No!" He gripped her tighter now, smashing his lean, muscular body against her, his face pressed against her shoulder. "I can't let it escape. I can't!"

"Why?"

"Because...it'll kill everything I care about."

Heather sighed. "It already has, Knox. It took your life. Don't let it take your soul, too."

"Oh, God," he whispered, a moan escaping through his pinched lips. "It's true—isn't it?" He cursed under his breath. "I know you're right. But...Heather, I don't know how. I'm afraid I'll lose all control of it. How do I do that?"

Knox's monster had already taken everything from him. And it was trying to take his soul now. To get back the hero inside him, he had to slay it. It was the only way. He knew that now.

"Teach me to fight and I'll help you slay it," Heather said, laying her face against his soft, curly hair.

She felt him smile against her shoulder.

"Knox, if you don't, the demons will prey on that monster. And before you know it, you'll be doing their bidding. Just like Ross."

He let out a breath. "I hadn't even thought about that."

His anger floated away, his muscles going slack. He held her at arm's length, studying her face for a long moment of silence. He reached out, tracing his fingers across her cheek, the curve of her chin. His stormy blue eyes grew calm. She couldn't look away, the ache inside him so strong.

Knox leaned down to kiss her.

Heather pulled away, shaking her head.

"I—I can't, Knox," she said.

He sat back on his heels as he stared at the floor. "Ross...right.

Forgot about him. No crushes in the Between." Finally, he nodded, hands pressed together as he met her apologetic stare again.

The pale angels made her forget him once. She wouldn't let that happen again.

"He means so much to me," she said.

"A day late and a dollar short, as usual," he muttered. "It's okay. Thanks for giving a shit, Heather."

She took his hand in hers. "I do care, Knox. And I'll help you beat this. You have my word."

"You had my back out there against those soulstalkers," he said. "I've got yours, too. Be my wingman?"

She smiled. "Deal."

Shouts erupted beyond the closed door. Heather and Knox glanced at each other and rushed to the door. He yanked it open, letting a tangle of voices pierce the quiet of her nook. Shrieks and shouts carried up the staircase, mixing with chirrs and screeches.

Furniture scuffed across wood floors. Feet pounding. Dull thumps. Rustling.

Knox grabbed her arm and pulled her toward the stairs. Shadows and darkness swirled through the room below, flashes of light, as they ran down the stairs into chaos!

nine

· · ·

SOULSTALKERS SURGED through the soul tree, front door flung open. So many that Heather couldn't count them all.

More swarmed inside, tangling with Avana and the other souls, their dark, empty eyes gleaming in the dim light. Black wings beat the air, shadow creatures knocking souls to the floor and pinning them.

The lost souls fought back—hard—kicking soulstalkers off each other and scrambling to their feet. No matter how many times they hit the floor, they got back up and fought the soulstalkers.

The vicious creatures were fast, leering mouths baring pointy teeth as they chattered like angry blue jays, pursuing Avana and any soul in range. Wings spread. Claws out.

Herding them toward awaiting soulstalkers at the door.

The males wore only black pants, their black hair wild and hanging to their shoulders, bare arms and chests rippling with muscles as they worked as a team, mobbing terrified souls and driving them toward the open door.

The females wore torn black pants and thin, gauzy mid-drifts, exposing sculpted stomachs and muscular arms. They had longer, sharper black talons on their bony hands and feet, higher-pitched screeches, and wind-blown, black hair that hung past their shoulders.

In the corner, by the feasting table, five or six terrified souls huddled together, kicking and screaming as they fought against being dragged off.

Zoe was in the middle of the group, lying in a fetal position on the floor, face red and eyes filled with terror.

The others held onto the table with both hands, kicking soulstalkers, punching them as hard as they could.

But they were surrounded. Shadow creatures crowded them on both sides as they bunched deeper into the corner and under the table.

By the door, Barb and Javier worked in tandem, beating back several soulstalkers, fighting to slam the door shut.

Barb grabbed one and tossed it outside. Like a banty rooster, Javier tore through the hungry soulstalker pack, twisting wings, and throwing punches until he'd put several of the creatures on the floor.

Beside them, Cora manned the door. Terror in her eyes, blond hair loose from its ties, and hanging in wild curls, she tripped soulstalkers. Knocking them down.

Barb whistled shrilly, waving a hand in the air.

"Now, Cora!" she shouted.

Cora thrust open the door as Javier plucked a screeching soulstalker off the slippery wood floor. With Barb's help, he flung it out into the night. When the twitching thing had cleared the threshold, Cora slammed the door shut again, black feathers crunching in the door jamb. She grabbed a straight-backed wooden chair and wedged it under the doorknob to keep them from coming back inside.

Frantic thumping echoed through the tree, the wooden door trembling as things beat on it.

Avana faded to smoke form, circling the soulstalkers' heads with thick, smoky rings that blinded some, tripped others, and led others into collisions. She twirled and dived, weaving her way through the crowded room.

Other smoke people joined her, switching from solid to vapor as they goaded soulstalkers into chasing them.

"Wow, look at 'em go," Knox replied, a brief smile on his lips. "A lot of promise down there."

Heather nodded. "Let's join them," she said, smiling, and hurried down the stairs.

Knox was a step behind her.

To the left, by the fireplace, Lamarr and two others struggled against a big pack of soulstalkers. Getting beaten down fast.

Soulstalkers overwhelmed them, dropping all three souls to the ground. One of the creatures plucked free a black feather from its wing, unraveling it between taloned fingers. The shadowy, black cord floated in the air as the creature snatched it in its claws and wrapped Lamarr's hands and feet. It moved on to the next soul as Lamarr kicked and rolled, trying to get free.

Knox nodded toward Lamarr. He ducked under the wings of a soulstalker and sprinted toward the fireplace.

Heather followed close behind.

Knox knocked away two of the creatures, twisting out of a third's hold, and struggled toward the sectional where Lamarr and the others lay tied up. Heather counted six of the creatures as they turned as a group and attacked her and Knox.

Heather pivoted, sliding out of one's grasp, and grabbed hold of a wing. She spun the thing around, both hands tangling in its spiky black feathers.

"How's it feel on the other side, losers!" she shouted, dragging it across the room.

With a kick, she knocked it backward onto the floor. Barb pounced on it, slamming it against the floor, and dragged it toward the door.

Heather lunged at a second soulstalker that had thrown Lamarr over its shoulder.

Lamarr's tall, lanky frame hung limp over the creature's thick, muscular shoulder, its arm wrapped in a headlock around Lamarr's neck. Lamarr gasped for air and swung his arms in a wobbly circle, trying to score a hit, but the creature was just out of his reach.

The other soulstalkers swept up the remaining tied-up souls and the four of them tried to bolt for a window.

Knox threw himself into the pack, knocking all of them to the floor. He broke wings, twisted soulstalkers into choke holds, and delivered blow after blow. The four abandoned their captives, swarming Knox.

Knox was fast, his moves fluid as he dodged wings and claws, pounding them with well-aimed fists and delivering roundhouse kicks, spilling inky, black shadow blood across the floor and sofa.

Heather stood behind him, kicking and clawing at a soulstalker that had tried to blindside Knox with its powerful wings. She grabbed hold of the wing with both hands, stopping the soulstalker from slamming a fist into Knox's head. She pounded the wing with her fist and tore out a handful of feathers.

When it wheeled around, teeth bared and hissing, she went for its face, clawing and grabbing hold of its long, wiry hair.

She wasn't proud as she pulled out a hank of its hair.

It screeched, slicing at her with its talons, but she kicked it hard in the kneecaps. Whatever got the job done. It was messy, but it was all she had.

Knox was all symmetry and grace as he ducked under taloned swipes, slid under beating wings, and landed a kidney punch on one soulstalker. He kicked another one hard in the chest, staggering it.

With a sharp uppercut, Knox slammed his fist into another one's face, flattening the third one's chin, and laying it out cold and twitching on the wood floor.

Two more punches and two kicks brought down the other two creatures.

Knox swiveled left, trapping a deadly wing that tried to bust open his skull. Pivoting right, he ducked under another swipe of talons.

Catching its wing under his arm, Knox pounded the soulstalker's ribs with his foot until it dropped to its knees and collapsed.

In a short time, Knox had laid out all of the soulstalkers by the fireplace.

Heather ripped and tore at the shadowy cords binding the other souls until she'd shredded them enough for Javier, Lamarr, and the others to destroy. After they'd broken free, Lamarr, Javier, and the other souls helped Heather and Knox gather up soulstalkers and drag them to the door.

"Cora?" Heather called, nodding toward the door as she dragged a soulstalker toward it.

Lamarr and Knox were behind her, lugging more of the creatures.

"It would be my pleasure," she said in her soft Southern accent and slid the chair away from the doorknob.

Cora tugged open the door and Heather dragged the creature outside and hurried back in as Knox and Lamarr worked together to fling soulstalkers outside.

Six in this group.

Knox gave Cora a nod, and the blond woman slammed the door shut, replacing the chair. Then Knox pointed toward the dining table at the group of souls cowering underneath it, still kicking and biting at least four more soulstalkers.

By the door, Barb and Javier struggled to hold the door closed as four more shadow creatures tried to get inside and help their brethren.

Heather turned toward the table when the pounding began on the door. A loud, thunderous sound. The door shook, something heavy battering it.

"Knox! The door!"

He turned as the wooden door cracked apart and splintered, falling to pieces as seven more soulstalkers broke through it. They poured into the tree, even more behind them.

Like locusts, they swarmed the room, screeching, wings thumping in wild swipes, knocking people and furniture out of the way. The furious movement created a whirlwind that swept through the room, the sound deafening.

One of their wings hit Heather hard, knocking her back against the wall. Dazed, she struggled to get her balance, but another one surged past, spinning her around.

Arms grabbed her around the waist, dragging her across the floor. To the door.

Shadowy cord wound around her hands and she swatted it away, tearing at it with her fingers. Heather kicked her legs, twisting, and swiveling until she felt the door frame at her fingertips. She grabbed hold, stretching her legs as far as she could, hooking her feet into the other side.

"No! Let go!" she shouted.

"Heather!" Knox called, trying to get past the soulstalkers in his path.

A soulstalker tried to pry her hands free, but she clamped her hands tight against the wooden frame and held on with every bit of strength she had left.

If they got her outside, she was doomed.

Knox was a machine, tossing soulstalkers right and left as he and Javier fought their way to her. He ripped the soulstalker off her, kicking it out the door as Heather let go. Knox wrapped his arms around her waist, punting another soulstalker into the darkness.

Heather got to her feet as eight more soulstalkers poured into the tree. She backed away, Knox at her back as the creatures advanced on them.

"We're so outnumbered," Knox muttered.

"What do we do?" Heather cried, crouching, setting herself as the creatures rushed them.

She felt the brawny curve of Knox's back against her arm as she knocked a soulstalker away. Together, she and Knox turned in a circle, hammering another shadow creature into the floor.

Something glimmered near the door.

Heather glanced up as a brilliant burst of white light exploded through the room.

Heather shielded her eyes, her shoulder still pressed against Knox's back. He turned his face away from the light, eyes closed, arm covering his face.

Soulstalkers dropped to their knees, screeching in pain, and holding their eyes.

"What was that?" Heather cried, looking toward the door.

Above the shouts, a clear alto note floated through the room.

Wind moaned past the door frame as a haunting soprano aria filled the night. It hung in layers through the growing stillness, delicate and aching as ghosts fluttered through the darkness and spilled into the soul tree. Light gleamed at their fingertips.

Pale angels! A dozen!

Zakhart led the charge.

The pale angels swept the soulstalkers into a writhing ball of shadow and wings, rolling the fight outside, into the sky.

Razasha and Halea stood in the door frame, summoning a thick swath of gold light that became a humming barrier the soulstalkers couldn't cross.

Through the pulsing gold light, Heather watched as Zakhart led the pale angels against the massing flock of soulstalkers. Their wings had turned the sky pitch black, their shrieks piercing, and the constant chirring made her whole body vibrate.

The creatures flew at the pale angels, raking their robes with sharp talons, and pummeling them with powerful swipes of those dark wings.

Several pale angels fell out of the sky.

The soulstalkers rammed into other pale angels, robes and wings tangling as they locked together and sank like stones.

Every time they fell, the pale angels dusted themselves off and surged back into the sky to rejoin the fight. Heather winced as Zakhart fell out of the night sky. With a grunt, he brushed off his light-colored wings, the color of a sparrow's belly, and surged back into the sky to fight beside his clan. The pale angels were outnumbered, but their persistence was unfailing as one by one, they wore down the soulstalkers.

The piercing drone of shrieks and trills faded into the night as the Between fell silent. The soulstalkers were retreating!

Huge clumps of black feathers swirled around the soul tree's doorway like autumn leaves and littered the forest floor, lightened by only a handful of beige feathers.

Exhausted, the dozen or so pale angels staggered into the soul tree and collapsed onto chairs, on the sofa, and on the wooden floor still sticky with soulstalker blood. When the last angel was safely inside, Razasha waved her hand through the pulsing gold light, summoning another swath of watery gold light that created a warm glow.

Halea lifted both arms in the air, outstretched palms filling with pearlescent sparks. She held her hands on both sides of the door and outlined the frame with pearlescent white. The sparks surged along the path, burning like fuses that met at the bottom of the door frame. The light pulsed steadily as a new door appeared, thicker, stronger, reinforced with some sort of pale energy. Sealing the soul tree with some sort of sticky, protective force.

The two pale angels worked their way around the tree's interior, casting sparks that burned along a path outlining the windows as the fire burned across the walls. When they finished the main floor, Razasha and Halea flitted up the staircase, setting up their nets and lines of sparks on every floor.

"It's over," Zakhart said with a groan. "Is everyone all right? Everyone accounted for?"

Heather walked through the room, counting everyone. To her amazement, no one had been carried off. She was grateful for that.

"Everyone's here," she said, dropping down beside Zakhart on the couch.

In a few moments, Razasha returned down the stairs, her face grey and shadowed. She was unsteady as she moved to the couch and sat down heavily. The light illuminating her face and wings had faded a bit. She was exhausted.

Finally, Halea came down the stairs with staggered steps until she reached the sofa. She moved behind it to stand near Razasha, her wings folding softly against her shoulders, flattening Halea's beautiful, blue-black hair.

Razasha leaned back against the cushions, her face haggard as she adjusted her taupe-colored wings. Halea laid her hand on Razasha's shoulder, trilling a soft soprano note, the sound soothing, and squeezed, wings twitching. She hung over Razasha as if standing watch, her gaze flicking toward the door every few moments. Zakhart looked shaky and concerned.

The other angels were a calming presence in the room. They all looked to Zakhart for guidance now, waiting patiently for his orders.

"Where'd all those soulstalkers come from?" Heather asked, glancing at Razasha who sat at the other end of the sofa opposite Zakhart. Knox followed her to the couch, his steps slow and painful. He groaned, rubbing his left shoulder, and sat down beside Heather.

"I'm not sure," said Zakhart with a shake of his head, his thick white mane of hair wild. "I felt a disturbance in the Between's fabric. A deep, thrumming that shook the ground. I alerted the other angels. By the time we got here, they were swarming the tree like locusts. Enraged. Crazed. Like nothing I'd ever seen or felt before."

A trail of smoke fluttered through the air. For a moment, it hovered near the fireplace and shuddered, smoke scattering as Avana coalesced into human form. She waved her hands in the air as several smoky trails swirled past her, wrapping around her body in a thick, ropey line of mist that careened up the stairs.

More smoke people. Taking refuge upstairs. The pale angels remained, comforting the frightened and battered souls around them.

"Never in all my days here have I ever seen that many soulstalkers in one place!" Avana cried. "Or so vicious." She shivered and hugged her arms against her chest, her body glimmering with a pearly sheen. "That was terrifying."

"I'll say," said Lamarr, leaning against the wall by the fireplace. "Like Javier, they had me bundled up and ready to carry off. If Heather and Knox hadn't been here, I'd be sleeping with the poppies now."

"I couldn't overpower them by myself," Cora said and leaned against Lamarr, taking his hand in hers. "Thanks, Heather. Knox."

Knox gave her a sharp nod and returned his attention to Zakhart.

"Me, too," said a trembling voice from the floor.

Zoe peeked out from behind Cora's long tan skirt, unicorn pressed against her flushed face and wide-eyed, hazel stare.

Cora bent and put her arms around the slight teenager, helping her to her feet. She moved Zoe between her and Lamarr who put his arm around Zoe's shoulders. She leaned into him, huddling, a hand clutching Cora's arm.

"Something stirred them up," said Razasha, her voice like crystal. "They weren't hunting. They were—crazed, frantic. As we approached the tree, I felt strange vibrations in the darkness."

Like something had intentionally stirred them up, enraged them into attacking as a single force.

Heather stared at Zakhart. The pale angel looked unnerved as he exchanged glances with Razasha and Halea. Their eyes were wide, pupils nearly eclipsing coppery-orange irises. Halea couldn't stop watching the door. They were struggling to keep each other calm.

Around the room, the other nine or so pale angels seemed unusually quiet, coppery eyes either watching Zakhart or the door.

Like Halea.

Zakhart's wings twitched, feet tapping the floor, brow furrowed. Shadows bruised his alabaster complexion, hollowing his cheeks and dampening those pumpkin-orange eyes. He rubbed his forehead a moment then spoke to the other angels with a string of clear, tenor notes that quickly turned sharp and clipped. Razasha spoke, her voice a soprano harmony against his until Halea countered with a sudden discord that darkened the melody into a lament. The other angels joined in, supporting the melody in rich layers.

"I felt it, too, Razasha," Zakhart replied. "It was a tone I'd never heard in the Between before. Unnatural. Angry." His brow furrowed. "No, not a tone. It was a rhythm."

"Vibrations?" Knox asked, raising his eyebrows. "From what?"

"Wish I knew," said Zakhart. "It wasn't anything I'd felt before. And that's unnerving."

He cast a worried glance at Heather.

Zakhart was always informed and always in control. Right now, he seemed at a loss, something she rarely saw in the pale angel. He sang another note that became a three-part chord as Halea and Razasha spoke, too, the notes rolling up and down some perfect, major scale. Abruptly, the scale darkened to a fast-paced chorus that tumbled into a requiem as all the angels spoke at once.

It was beautiful and haunting, sending shivers through Heather as she listened. What were they saying? She wanted to understand their beautiful voices, the evocative tones, but all of it was just beyond her comprehension.

The room fell silent, the angel song fading. Heather couldn't interpret the notes, but this time, she didn't have to. The meaning was obvious as she looked at their faces, studied their eyes. Never had she seen such fear in the angels' eyes or heard such trepidation in their voices.

Something deep in the Between had broken. And unless they put it back together, the shadow creatures would overpower it. Heather had no idea what would happen, but the consequences seemed dire.

"Zakhart," Heather called to the pale angel.

He turned toward her, that hopeful mask falling into place, brightening the shadows hollowing his face. That was Zakhart, always portraying the best in everything, trying to keep everyone from worrying. But if she knew Zakhart, he also had some theories about those vibrations. Theories she could investigate.

"You're concerned, of course," he said. "I'm not sure if I can answer any questions you have, but I'll try. There's much we need to do."

Heather rose from the couch and stood in front of him, casting a glance at the dozens of souls huddled around the angels. Tomorrow, everyone was supposed to go out into the grasslands and forest and search for other lost souls. That wasn't going to happen now. It was just too dangerous.

"Zakhart, what is your gut telling you about what happened tonight?"

He waved her off, turning away. "Not yet, Heather. I need time to think."

She grabbed his shoulder turning him around. "Come on, Zakhart. Talk to me. I know you have at least one theory rattling around about what happened. Tell me."

"I always have lots of theories, Heather," he said, smiling as he rose to his feet, steepling his fingers as he paced. "Theories that require thorough investigation and careful study. They aren't anything I can properly formulate yet though." His eyes narrowed. "And certainly nothing that you can poke your little human nose into yet. What you can do though, is make sure the soul tree is secure. Let me and my clan investigate some things first."

Heather's stomach twisted into a knot. He was redirecting her attention to the soul tree. Things were bad. Whatever theories he had were much worse than she'd first thought.

Either he was trying to protect her heart or her soul.

Regardless, she had a few theories tumbling through her brain. Just thinking about them terrified her, but she needed to say them out loud and gauge Zakhart's reaction, find out if she was way off target or painfully close. Either way, she had to do something.

They might not survive another soulstalker attack like the one tonight.

"Everyone says that the demons took Ross."

Zakhart nodded, still pacing. "Unfortunately, that's true, Heather."

Not a flinch or flutter of eyelids.

"They also took a bunch of other souls, didn't they?" she said, following in behind him. "From the great tree? And not smoke people. Just lost souls, right?"

"They almost carried off a pale angel, too," said Halea.

A frown shadowed Zakhart's forehead and he gasped, turning to stare at her, his mouth open.

"What? When?"

Halea's wings twitched and she chewed her bottom lip.

"Halea? Tell me. Who was—"

The pale angel bowed her head, black hair tumbling off her shoulder as her wings fluttered.

Zakhart shook his head. "You?" His voice grew quiet. "Halea... why didn't you tell me?"

She cringed, her alabaster face scrunching up, arms crossing. "I— I don't know, I was afraid to tell you. And...I was ashamed."

She and Zakhart exchanged a frenzy of trills and discords until Halea's eyes grew misty. She bit her lip, her wings trembling, a creamy beige feather falling free.

"Please," said Zakhart finally, laying a hand on hers, his voice soft and comforting now. "Tell me what happened. Did they harm you?"

"No," said Haley in a hushed voice, pressing her arms against her chest. "I wasn't hurt. It was the night that the demons attacked the great tree." She looked distraught, eyes downcast. "Just after they took Ross. The demons immobilized me with their shadow strands, tying down my wings so I couldn't fly. Some of the captured souls helped me. They were bound like me, lying on the ground beside me as demons carried us off one by one."

Zakhart's eyes were wide. "How'd you get free?" he asked, his voice nearly a whisper.

"The souls and I worked on each other's shadowy cords, trying to free as many as we could. They freed my wings. Without the human souls, I wouldn't have escaped. For a while, I didn't move, working free as many of their shadow cords as I could, but there were just too many demons." Her voice cracked, her throat too tight to speak. She paused to clear her throat. "I was selfish. I sang the highest, sharpest note I could, dropping demons to their knees. It hurt the humans' ears, too. And I'm sorry for that. While the demons were incapacitated, I bolted, surging up and out of the blackness, not stopping until I reached the night sky."

"Not selfish, Halea," said Barb, leaning against the wall, hand propped on her hip. "Because of that note, Javier and I escaped."

Halea's face brightened. "You did?"

Javier nodded. He knelt before Halea, bowing his head. "Sí! The light...it saved me."

Barb nodded. "That note weakened the shadow bonds. They broke easily after that. I'm sure others escaped, too. We just need to find them now."

Zakhart was deep in thought, the possibilities flashing across his face. Heather could almost see him turning the facts over and over in his head. But he hadn't entered the Demon Veils with her and Ross. He didn't see what the demons were up to in there. It was time he had that information.

"Zakhart, we know that the demons have tunneled through the Between," said Heather, walking through the room as she talked.

Gasps and whispers filtered through the room. Avana looked horrified.

"Ever since I escaped through the Spiral, the demons have kept burrowing out of the Demon Veils, haven't they? Where none of us could see it."

"Yes," Zakhart replied, his tone sounding defeated.

Heather motioned toward the doorway. "When you brought me back here, I saw a bunch of black mounds scattered across the forest and in the grasslands. I didn't know what they were at first, but then I remembered the Demon Veils. When Ross and I entered the demon cave, we saw so many tunnels that the demons had dug. Or maybe the human souls they'd tricked into working for demons dug those tunnels?"

Zakhart stopped pacing and turned to stare at her. "Yes,

Heather," he said, sounding almost annoyed. "We talked about this, remember?"

Heather nodded. "At the time, I didn't understand why demons needed all those tunnels, but even then, they were digging under the places where souls took refuge, weren't they? Like the great tree. They had already planned an attack. They'd planned to destroy our safe place and capture all the souls inside."

Zakhart's expression darkened, his gaze far away as those wheels inside his head churned into motion. His face looked pinched now, his wings twitching, eyes narrowed.

"Given Halea's story, that had to be their plan," he replied. "But why didn't they attack you and Ross? They let both of you leave in peace. With half their captured souls."

Heather rubbed a hand across her face. "Ross and I went in there alone and rescued a bunch of the souls. We took away Thraecius, too. Took away their foreman. While their attack on the great tree took shape."

"Foreman?" Zakhart asked, frowning. "Foreman for what?"

"The coal fields," said Heather as she kept pacing. "And the Mechanism—whatever that is."

A surprised look softened Zakhart's features. He stared at her a moment, shaking his head in confusion. "Coalfields? Mechanism? They've built an infrastructure? Those demons don't belong here! They got here just like the pale angels did—through the Spiral. Us through the front door, them through the back door. They're trespassers huddling in caves. They were never part of the Between."

Heather shook her head. "Maybe so, but they are now. They've moved in and built a hidden fortress in the caves below the ground. And Thraecius was their...I don't know...foreman or something. He was in charge of keeping the other souls working and in line."

Zakhart frowned as he cast worried glances at Halea and Razasha. "Other souls are keeping the others in captivity?"

Heather nodded. "Thraecius ordered around throngs of souls in this big cavern, forcing them to mine and gather shiny black rocks."

"What shiny stones?" Zakhart looked unnerved now.

"I'm not sure," said Heather, unnerved by the fear rising in Zakhart's eyes. "But in the big room where the demons gathered, there was a huge machine. They called it the Mechanism. It billowed smoke and required constant attention from a bunch of souls who worked flywheels and flipped levers. Mulciber said it kept the demons warm in the Between."

Zakhart's mouth fell open, his eyes wide with terror.

"What's the matter, Zakhart?" she asked.

"Heather, there is no coal, no minerals, or fossil fuels in the Between. No gems and no need for heat because demons are only affected by extreme temperatures."

"Then what are those shiny rocks that they're mining?" Heather asked as Zakhart swallowed hard. "And what about that machine?"

Zakhart cast a horrified glance at Razasha. Halea gripped Razasha's shoulder, her eyes misty.

Something was terribly wrong here.

Heather cursed under her breath, wishing she'd told Zakhart more about the Demon Veils after she'd gone into the cave. Maybe it would have protected Ross?

Zakhart sucked in a breath, eyes pinched closed, shoulders sagging. Finally, he straightened to his full height, wings folded tightly against his back, and met Heather's confused stare.

"Whatever those demons have built," he began in a dark tone, "it's a danger to the souls of this realm. I don't know if it's a trap of some kind, a weapon, or something that defies my imagination, Heather. Nevertheless, they're capturing souls for some nefarious use. Processing their energy for fuel. Forcing them to toil endlessly to run or support it. In either case, tonight must have been their first time testing it. On the soulstalkers."

Knox was on his feet now. "Demons? Building a weapon? Or some sort of soul furnace?" His laugh was caustic. "Are you serious?"

"The vibrations!" Razasha cried.

She grabbed hold of Halea's arm, staring up at her, doe-eyed expression fearful, and whispered a soprano note or two. Halea nodded, gripping Razasha's hand in hers as the other angels rose from the chairs and couch and gathered around them. A quiet melody whispered between the whole clan, the notes turning dark and melancholy.

"Whatever they're doing, it's controlling the shadow creatures," Heather replied. "Soulstalkers. Sand runners. Anything else that's made of shadow. And those vibrations got them to attack us. It's just the first one, isn't it?" She held out her arms, the fear cold in her stomach now. "Zakhart...what can we do?"

Knox stepped toward Heather, his face a mixture of disbelief and fear. Heather already knew the answer to her question, it was already tearing through her gut. The demons had quietly hidden themselves below ground and built some sort of device to harm or capture souls. And when no one was looking, they activated it.

What did it do? What were they hoping to gain?

Somehow, she had to get inside the Veils again. Find out what they'd created. And why. Then destroy it.

Before, she and Ross had simply walked into the Veils without incident, but Heather doubted that anyone could just walk inside that cave now. If they did, they wouldn't be able to get out again. Why hadn't she realized what was happening? Why couldn't she have damaged all of those machines the first time? If she had, then maybe Ross wouldn't have been captured.

But with so many souls kidnapped and missing, especially after the assault on the great tree, shadow creatures outnumbered humans. Even if every soul from the great tree was here now, they'd still be no match for an organizing force of demons.

Using soulstalkers and other shadow creatures as weapons.

Somehow, she and the souls had to raise their numbers. Fast. And learn how to fight. Before the demons attacked again. Next time might destroy all the souls—and the tree.

Like it or not, someone had to slip into the Veils and find out what the souls were up against. It was the only way to know for sure how to fight back against the demons. And maybe locate Ross at the same time.

They had to rescue the trapped souls in the Demon Veils. And they needed every soul in the Between to fight those demons before it was too late.

Of all the souls in the soul tree, Heather knew she was the only one who'd been inside the Veils before. She knew the layout. She'd seen the main chamber and she knew how to get out again.

She had to be the one to go into Veils.

But she couldn't tell Zakhart about her plan. He was doing everything in his power to steer her into the safety of this fortified soul tree and keep her here. He'd stop her if she even mentioned venturing into the Veils. Especially alone.

When it got light, she'd get Knox to start training people to fight. And when they were all practicing, she'd slip away. Take a little walk to the forest clearing where all the paths converged. She'd follow the path into the Demon Veils and do a little spying. Try to uncover what they were up against. See what the demons had done since she'd left the first time.

She had to find out what all the lost souls were up against.

The hard part would be to slip away unseen. And keep her plans hidden from Zakhart and the other pale angels.

ten

. . .

THE NIGHT FADED, the sky lightening to a dull cement grey as Heather crept down the spiral staircase. Wood creaked, the air dry and smelling of straw as she gazed around the quiet room. A dozen souls huddled on the beige sectional, a dozen more curled up in front of the hearth fire that burned low, embers glowing through the ash. There was no heat, no fragrant smell of burning wood. But the sight of it brought comfort.

Cora and Lamarr sat together on the floor, a blanket over them. Zoe was curled up against Cora. A handful of souls sat around the feasting table: Barb and Javier along with the solid forms of Avana and other smoke people that Heather didn't recognize.

Pale angels remained in the soul tree, congregating in groups of two or three. Zakhart was in the corner near the fireplace. Razasha hovered beside him. Neither spoke as they stared into the hearth flames, looking lost and worried. Knox leaned against the wall, listening intently to the angels' conversations. His arms were folded against his chest, his head bowed. His face looked pinched, eyes narrowed, brow furrowed. He seemed troubled, but he was quiet, listening to Zakhart.

"I'll do my best, Zakhart," said Knox. "It's all I can promise."

"I'm sure it will be more than enough, Knox," Zakhart replied, nodding at the curly-haired soldier. "And I thank you for even attempting it."

"We're fortunate to have your expertise," said Razasha.

Her blond hair was radiant, coppery doe-eyed gaze so soft and innocent against Knox's wild blue eyes.

At last, a smile lit Knox's intense face. "This is as good a time as any to get started."

Razasha nodded, landing on the wooden floor that had changed to a pale maple hardwood, the walls made of plaster now. Painted a soft blue-grey. Razasha turned toward the door and held out her hand, summoning the sticky white light that coiled around the door frame.

Knox stepped away from the hearth, moving toward the door. When he saw Heather standing there, his lips quirked into a smile.

"Heather," he said, stepping close. "Was wondering where you were. I checked upstairs but couldn't find you."

She shrugged, glancing at her feet. "I've been walking the stairs and pacing through the nooks, counting souls. There are barely fifty souls in here. We're badly outnumbered."

"I know," he said, sighing as he glanced over his shoulder at Zakhart and the other pale angels, his voice falling to a sharp whisper. "They've asked me to train the others to fight shadows."

His shoulder was pressed against hers now, his mouth against her ear, his warm presence sending shivers through her.

"I don't think I can teach them the skills they need," he whispered. "They didn't cover how to fight demons and shadows in basic training."

Heather laughed. "Don't think there's any training available for that. But I watched this group fight yesterday and they did pretty well, considering. They banded together which impressed me."

Knox ran a hand through his dark curls. "Yeah, I couldn't help noticing that either. It gave me a little hope. We were actually winning until the sheer number of those bastards overwhelmed us."

"Wasn't a fair fight," Heather replied. "And it never will be because we're facing demons. But we've got to even the odds somehow. Give ourselves a fighting chance."

"Couldn't agree more," said Knox, nodding. "So, I'm gonna give this training thing a shot." He nudged her with his elbow. "You game?"

"Of course," she said. "I'll do whatever it takes. Just tell me what to do."

He was grinning now, staring into her eyes.

"You have the prettiest green eyes I've ever seen," he said in a soft voice, reaching out to brush a lock of brown hair out of her face.

"Thanks," said Heather and gave his forearm a gentle squeeze.

"Let's get started then," he said, walking toward the door.

Knox opened the door and stood on the threshold, turning around to face the room.

"All right, people!" he shouted, his voice filling the soul tree. "We've got a lot of work to do. On your feet and go outside to learn some combat basics."

Cora and Lamarr sat up, looking half-asleep as they pushed the blanket off their shoulders. Zoe didn't move until Cora shook her awake. The teenager got to her feet and watched Knox with sleepy eyes as Lamarr and Cora moved toward the door. Cora turned around and motioned for Zoe. She hesitated, but when Knox called her name, she bounded over to him.

"You gonna teach us to fight, Knox? Wish you'd been in Grande Prairie to teach me this stuff sooner." She made a bony fist and held it in the air. "I could have blacked Sharla's eye!"

Knox patted Zoe's black hair. "Wish I'd been there, too, kid. It might have helped you stand up to those bullies and kept you safe."

Zoe wrapped her arm in Knox's. He turned to Heather, extending his left hand to her. She nodded and gripped his hand, following him outside. The other souls filed out alongside Avana who led the smoke people out of the tree. Even the pale angels left the soul tree, including Zakhart.

Knox made everyone gather around him in a half circle and listen. Heather started toward the group, but he tugged her against him.

"Will you be my partner for this, Heather?" Knox asked, those pale blue eyes making her ache all over.

She nodded. "Sure."

He grinned and positioned her on his right side.

"All right, people, listen up! When you go up against the enemy here, it's gonna be a life-or-death struggle. I want to show you how you can be the winner in these fights, so watch and listen carefully. And I expect every one of you to practice these moves. Got it?"

Angels and souls murmured their agreement, the smoke people taking solid form behind the group. There were nearly two dozen of them which surprised Heather.

"Okay, so rule one," Knox continued as he stared around the clearing at all the souls gathered in front of the soul tree. "Maintain balance at all times. When you're in a stable position, you have a base of power to work from. You can defend and attack from that balanced stance. This means standing with knees bent and feet even with your shoulders. Like this."

He spread his feet apart so they were even with each shoulder. He bent his knees just slightly and brought his arms up, fists raised. Heather mimicked his stance, facing off from him.

"Okay, everyone, stand ready. Like this. Try it on, see how it feels."

People started to move and shift positions, but Knox seemed annoyed.

"Now! This isn't a parade, people! Move it!"

The souls and angels quickly got into position, imitating Knox's stance.

Knox studied Heather a moment, looking her up and down. "Looking good, Heather," he said with a smirk. "Okay, turn to the person on your right. That's your partner. Now, try exchanging punches. Move it!"

He walked through the group, correcting postures and repositioning people, working with them pair by pair. He sparred with each person in the groups of two, leaning out of swings and ducking under punches until the souls found their own comfort zones. Then he put everyone back together into a single group again, watching each soul's technique and correcting moves.

Heather found it amusing to watch pale angels throw punches at lost souls and smoke people, but she knew that things were bad in the Between—and about to get worse.

"Now, remember how it felt to throw those punches, dodge those blows," Knox shouted, moving back beside Heather. "It's supposed to feel comfortable. Balanced. Like you could initiate any move or action from that position. Exploit your enemy's weaknesses. Put your opponent off balance. Make 'em over-stretch to swing at you while you pivot in and out of your opponent's attack range. Got it?"

A couple of people nodded.

"Got it?" he shouted. "Don't make me guess. Tell me you got it. Loud and clear!"

Low shouts rumbled through the group.

"Like you mean it!" Knox roared.

"Got it!" the entire group shouted.

Their loud voices made the curly-haired soldier grin as he paced around the group.

"Excellent! Now, the next part's a little harder," he said, laying his hand against his chest, thumping the heel of his hand against his breastbone. "Because it's gotta come from here." He pressed two fingers to his forehead. "And here." He pointed at his heart. "Mental readiness is heart and mind control and it's just as important—maybe more important—as physical balance. You've gotta believe that you're in control and that you can defeat any enemy. Use your brain to trick opponents, feed on their insecurities, and convince them you're fierce and unbeatable."

He whirled around, throwing a punch toward Heather's stomach. She twisted her body to the side, stepping sidewise, and dodging the blow.

"Excellent, Heather," he said and turned back to the rest of the group. "See, Heather used position to turn her body out of the range of my attack. She also stepped out of the line of my attack, using quick moves to her advantage."

Knox bounced from left foot to right foot, ducking and bobbing, his body in constant motion. He spun around in a lightning-fast pivot and put Heather in a chokehold, dropping her on the ground.

"See how this stance improves speed and momentum? It lets you quickly turn the tables on your opponent."

He relaxed his arm around her head and knelt beside her, a hand against the side of her face.

"You okay?" Knox asked.

"Fine," said Heather.

When he turned his head toward the group, Heather grabbed his arm and used her feet to catapult him over her head, putting him flat on his back on the ground.

She leaned over him, grinning. "You okay?"

Everyone broke up laughing, including Knox who let out a belly laugh.

He nodded. "You're a quick study," he said.

"I've got a good teacher," she said with a smirk and helped him up from the ground.

"Okay, people," he said, motioning at the group. "Let's practice. Pair off with someone new and let's go!"

Zakhart ended up with Cora. Lamarr and Javier faced off, Halea sparring with Barb. Razasha moved over to Zoe and the two of them worked on their stances.

Knox motioned Heather to his side. "You can still spar with me."

"Sure thing," she said, raising her fists as she shifted her weight from left to right foot.

She did her best, but Knox was too fast for her. He put her on the ground several times, making her anger flare. After the fifth time, she was about to punch a tree out of frustration.

Scrambling to her feet, Heather set herself, crouching with fists raised. This time, she didn't wait for him to react. She launched herself at him, pivoting left then lunging at his waist. She wrapped her arms around his body, rushing forward in a crouch. Slamming him backward, against the ground, she threw her entire body on top of him and pinned him.

He stared up at her, blue eyes bright, a grin splayed across his oval face. He slid his arms around her.

"Nice work," he said. "You made that look easy, Heather."

She grinned, his muscled body pressing against hers. "Thanks."

Knox stared into her eyes. She watched the smile move through his eyes and into his face. With thumb and forefinger, he traced the curve of her cheekbones, the slope of her chin—shape of her lips. His touch was warm and comforting.

A shiver fluttered through her stomach, flushing her cheeks. It felt like a lifetime since someone had touched her. He brushed the backs of his fingers across her face and stroked brown hair out of her eyes.

Grinning, he rolled left until he had Heather on the ground beneath him. He stared into her eyes, silent as the other souls and angels around them grunted and shouted, feet thumping against the ground. He reached down and caressed her face. Stroked her hair.

"So beautiful," he whispered. "And so talented."

She couldn't look away, couldn't stop staring into the vivid blue pools of light in his eyes. They were clear and unwavering, no hint of the monster he insisted lurked there. In them, she saw the truth. A deep, aching wound that had festered, overcoming his will to live. Dark specks of midnight blue rage, rage over the death and combat he'd already seen in his short life. Sharp grey threads of disillusionment had torn his confidence to shreds. Shadows of the broken hero he'd become. Not because he was a soldier. Because he'd been so terrified of snapping and acting out his nightmares that he took his own life to protect others.

Knox was a genuine soul who tried so hard to hide his emotions, but they leaked out through his deep, wide-set eyes. Through the vivid calm of soft blue that had expressed his growing distress.

Those tangles of curly brown hair made him appear young and playful, but the circles shadowing his eyes reminded her that he'd seen some awful things. The deep lines around his mouth hadn't come from laughing and a carefree life. They'd come from brooding and shaking himself awake at three A. M. from the same awful nightmare.

The signs had all been there, the isolation, the fear, the pained expression begging for hope when he couldn't bring himself to say the words. It was a shame that he hadn't had a single soul around him who saw it. Or tried to help him. Like her own life. She'd taken her own life after being unable to stand the pain of losing her mom any longer. Or the loneliness that had gotten darker and deeper. In the end, she couldn't take staring into the void of her eyes in the mirror one more day.

The need to save him churned through her chest, a thick, burning ache that pushed her to reach out and caress his face. He was beautiful and fragile and so broken inside. She didn't know if she could help him put those pieces back together, but she'd be there to help him try.

He closed his eyes, pressing his face against her hand. Like he was losing himself in her touch.

"Knox," she whispered. "You've been through so much."

His eyes opened. He nodded, pressing his lips together.

"So many tragedies. So many people you helped. So many life and death decisions you had to make."

His jaw tightened, those light blue eyes intense, emotions churning as he bowed his head.

"Yet when you needed help," she said, fingers tangling in the curls around his face. "No one was there to carry you out of combat, were they?"

He swallowed hard, looking down at her. His eyes turned misty, regret heavy in his hooded lids as he sighed.

"No one understood when I came home from Afghanistan. Didn't know what to say, what to do. Honestly, who could blame them? How could they understand the magnitude of it all? Agonizing decisions they can't even comprehend."

"Like what?" Heather whispered.

"Like playing God." He stared into her eyes. "Ever had to decide who lives and who dies, Heather?"

She shook her head, reaching down to hold his hand.

"Never," she said.

"Seemed like every patrol got ambushed. IEDs lurked everywhere. Never could save everyone even though I tried my damnedest every single time."

He was shaking now.

"It's not your fault, Knox."

"So many patrols pinned us down there. Caught us in the crossfire. Forcing us to call for backup. Or call in an airstrike. God, every decision was the worst one I'd ever made until the next one."

"Tell me about that," Heather replied, squeezing his hand.

She cupped his face in her hand, stroking.

"Like crouching over your buddy, plugging his femoral artery with one hand and calling in an air strike with the other. For the rest of your unit that's pinned down on a ridge. Or having one grenade left and your unit's bein' flanked. Enemy's rushing you from the front. Someone's gonna die and there's nothing you can do to stop it. And you have to decide who's gonna live and who's gonna die that day. Those faces stay with you for a lifetime, Heather."

His face contorted, but Heather kept stroking his cheek.

"I wake up in the middle of the night with them staring at me. Shouting at me. Demanding I explain why I didn't choose them. They were instant decisions. I had to act right then or lose everybody.

I tried to make the best decision I could, but each one weighed so heavily on me."

"You did the best you could, Knox," Heather whispered. "Never forget that."

He slid off her and scrambled up from the ground. "Sorry, I should have kept that to myself," he muttered, his back to her as he watched the other souls sparring. "Nobody wants to hear these awful stories. Including me."

Heather got to her feet. She moved behind him and laid her hand on his right shoulder.

"That's not true, Knox," she said in a quiet voice. "If you don't talk about it, tell me what you went through over there, then I'll never understand what you're going through now."

He whirled around, his eyes blue flames. "Understand?" His laugh was caustic and he stared at her, the anger burning across his face as he poked his chest with his thumb. "You think you can understand even a shred of what I went through? Think you know what combat was like over there?" He waved his arms, leaning in close, wild eyes filled with rage. "Well, you don't! You can't! Unless you were there, it's just a gritty war movie you watched once. It doesn't mean a thing to you because you'll never feel it."

Heather shrank back from him, arms folded against her chest.

"Knox," she said, her voice steady but solemn. "I would never pretend to understand something so visceral and devastating." She took a step back from him, watching as the raw fury softened into quiet contemplation. "What I want to understand is your reaction. Unless I've been there, I could never empathize with you."

Knox propped his hands on his hips and watched Heather in silence. The muscles in his jaw twitched.

"All I can offer is sympathy for going through those horrors. Comfort against the pain that torments you. Someone to listen and tell you they care about what you went through. That they care about you."

He bit his lip, regret surging across his face.

"I'm not trying to force you to spill your guts or play mind games with you. You're troubled and hurting, Knox. I was just trying to help."

"I don't mean to sound ungrateful," he replied, his voice softer, raspy as he began to pace back in forth in front of the sparring souls and angels. "I—I couldn't talk about this to anyone when I was alive. I called one of those helplines from the bridge. Tried one last time to spill my guts to someone. Anyone. But I lost my nerve and hung up before someone answered. When my phone started ringing, I panicked. Threw it on the road and climbed over the railing. I needed to quiet the voices warring in my head. The memories. The pictures I couldn't fade to black. The water below looked so calm. So soothing. I just wanted to sink into the depths of it. Forget all of it. Before I hurt someone."

Heather kept her distance. "If you want to talk about it, I'm here, Knox. That's all I wanted to say."

"Heather, I—"

His voice trailed off into an awkward silence.

She turned away, moving toward Barb who'd stopped working with a stocky man Heather hadn't seen before. Avana had brought in a few more lost souls from the forest this morning before Heather came downstairs. The man had stopped practicing, looking bored. Barb looked irritated.

"Need a partner?" Heather asked, tapping Barb on the shoulder.

"Gladly," said Barb with a grin on her face.

She set herself, knees bent, fists raised, and Heather faced off with her.

"Let's see if I can do this."

Barb grinned then lunged at Heather.

Knox walked through the group, scrutinizing everyone's fighting stances. He seemed annoyed at the half-hearted efforts. Most of the souls had stopped trying, their attention drifting away from the fighting. And learning.

"Think about those flying bastards overrunning the tree again tonight," he said, correcting Zakhart's posture. "If you truly don't give a shit, it's really showing in the amount of effort you're putting into this."

"Come on, everyone!" Zakhart shouted as he stepped out of the group to stand beside Knox. "This is important."

His face flushed red as the pale angel rushed through the group, his wings unfurled to their full span, beating the air with hard thumps.

"We can't win like this!" Zakhart shouted. "We've got to try harder. Do you hear? Harder!"

Barb and Javier joined Zakhart in stirring up the others. The group stepped up their efforts, practicing the stances that Knox had taught them, throwing more punches, and trying new ways to dodge blows. Zakhart kept up his pep talk, making Knox smile now. He seemed pleased with the renewed effort.

After a while, Knox corrected someone's stance or showed them a pivot or twist and some other moves to increase an opponent's distance. But most of the souls seemed to have mastered the stances that Knox showed them.

"Don't forget to protect your face," he replied. "Keep those hands up, ready to block. Gotta guard those weak points."

A frown spilled across his face.

"Wait a minute," Knox replied, nudging Zakhart. "Guess I don't need to teach you guys that. No sense in protecting your jugular or other arteries. Can't bleed out if we're dead, can we? That will improve our mental readiness, knowing they can't kill us."

For a long time, Knox worked with the group, hammering home basic offensive tactics for hand-to-hand combat. He used Zakhart to demonstrate several different maneuvers, including surprise attacks, everything focused on neutralizing his opponent.

Zakhart was a good sport, following Knox's instructions. He was a good match for Knox. When Knox finished teaching maneuvers, Zakhart and Razasha stepped up, teaching Knox and the other souls a few angel tactics.

"Don't let the soulstalkers convince you that they're harder to fight because they can fly," said Zakhart, motioning at Razasha who took to the air, circling Zakhart's head. "Use their momentum to your advantage. And don't let them intimidate you. Don't chase them. Let them come to you."

Razasha took to the air and circled overhead twice as Zakhart crouched, waiting. The third time Razasha came at him, she was lower to the ground.

Zakhart lunged at her, locking his grip on her wrist and pulling her out of the air. He shoved her to the ground and threw his arms around her neck in a chokehold, letting her go after a couple of seconds.

Knox applauded Zakhart. He seemed surprised by how fierce the pale angels were in battle.

Razasha soared back into the sky again.

"Taunting them into a frenzy will get them to fly more recklessly. When they're off-balance like that, you can take them down easily. Try and maintain the stance that Knox taught you, to keep your body balanced. Remember, a well-timed hit can land you on top of them, effectively grounding them."

Zakhart motioned Razasha to the ground while he flew into the air. He let Razasha demonstrate a well-timed hit and how to taunt the soulstalkers into flying in erratic patterns.

"If you zig-zag back and forth," said Zakhart, "they'll attempt to follow."

Razasha ran back and forth, zigzagging her way through the clearing. Zakhart followed, his flight speed matching her strides.

"Get the soulstalkers into that erratic rhythm like this," said Zakhart, out of breath. "Then circle back around to deliver a well-timed blow."

Razasha led Zakhart into the zigzagging movements, moving back and forth in tighter and tighter turns. Without warning, Razasha whirled around, slamming him into the ground and immobilizing him.

"All right?" Zakhart asked, getting up from the ground. He brushed off his cream-colored silk robes. "Does that make sense?"

A few souls nodded.

"That looked painful," Knox said, wincing, and moved over to Zakhart. "Everyone pair off with a pale angel and try this." Knox patted Zakhart's shoulder. "I'll work with you."

Heather hung back to the edge of the clearing. Watching the other souls practice with the pale angels. Knox seemed in his element, keenly focused on stances and tactics like Zakhart.

With everyone distracted, it was a good time for her to investigate the Demon Veils.

Heather slipped away from the group and hurried toward the soul tree, watching souls pair off from a distance. She waited a moment to make sure they weren't calling for her and then hurried around the massive trunk. Disappearing into the forest.

It took a few minutes of getting lost near the black swath of darkness where the heartlilies bloomed to find the main trail that led to the Convergence—where the Endless Paths met. The trail to the Convergence began where the great tree once stood.

She kept off the trail, following it by ducking behind trees. Too many soulstalkers patrolled the skies now.

Heather scurried through the woods for a long time until up ahead, the familiar clearing that stood on the edge of the grasslands appeared. The Convergence of Endless Paths.

She gasped when she saw the pathways.

Dead trees surrounded the Convergence, forest floor grey and dry, clearing covered in ashen soil. The trees surrounding it were broken, burned husks. The air smelled like cold, dirty ash from a long-extinguished fire.

She traced the trail that should have led back to the great tree, but the remnants disappeared into tall, swaying grasses that hadn't been there before. Once, those grasses had framed the distant, northwest edge of the forest where the great tree stood. They had been far from the great tree.

Now, those grasses had consumed the former location of the great tree—and a good part of the forest—swallowing it up. Changing it into thick, reedy grasslands. Distant grey poppies raised their heavy charcoal heads to the grey sky, casting a chalky mist around them, obscuring the horizon.

Heather remembered the times that she'd traveled this path. But it was gone now, not even a trace of it.

Or Ross.

She hunched over and skirted around the dead trees, searching her brain for the memory of the Convergence path that led to the Demon Veils. She remembered when Zakhart had brought her and Ross here. She closed her eyes, summoning the memory.

The farthest path to the right. She could see Zakhart standing there, pointing at the farthest right path.

Ahead, in a clearing of sparse and dying trees, she found the Convergence. The Endless Paths had faded beneath a thick cover of blackened soil, but she saw traces of the wide ashen path.

Heather darted across the blackened soil and onto the right-most path. Ash scritched under her feet as she ran down the path. Last time, she'd been flown to the Demon cave. She'd have to do her best to get there on foot now.

Crouching, she followed the path along the edge of trees that ran along the right side.

She listened for soulstalkers. And for Death.

The forest abruptly thinned out, merging with the grasslands. Taking away all her cover. Spindly rushes of silvery green grass soon took over, making the ashen pathway difficult to see.

Heather kept her head down, feeling for the crunchy ash under her feet as she hurried through another dangerously open area into a pristine stand of trees. Untouched by flame or greyed with poppy rot.

The Between fanned out into patches of forest that intertwined with grasslands. Grasslands that hadn't encroached so far into the thick, dusky woods.

Shadows rushed across the grass. She froze, huddling deep into the thick grass.

Soulstalkers. In packs. Searching for prey.

Her mouth went dry, fingers cold as she waited for the soulstalkers to disappear on the horizon.

Only when the world was quiet did she move quickly down the path again, ash crunching. Her breath quickened. Her senses heightened.

The forest and grasses seemed to go on forever, but she kept to the path as it wound into hilly terrain, the ground softening.

Something screeched.

She froze in place, a chill raking her spine. And counted the shadows winging past. Three, four—five!

Excited, sharp trills reverberated around her, soulstalkers diving into the grass, scuffling, and then darting into the air again. Had they seen her or found a lost soul hiding there? Or were they just fishing for prey?

She waited until the shadows and screeches dissipated before she ran down the ashen path toward darker, mossy terrain. And more trees.

The ground turned swampy, hills and rocky outcroppings dotting the marshy landscape. It had a loamy, dead smell, like a fish tank that hadn't been cleaned in months. The swampy ground looked thick and spongy, broken tree trunks crusted and bright green with algae as she followed the ashen trail toward a rise of big grey rocks that broke through the swampy ground like bones through skin.

This place felt darkly familiar.

Her skin turned to gooseflesh at the memory of standing here beside Ross, holding his hand. His beautiful face was so tense and worried. For her.

That entire time, he'd been afraid of losing her to the Veils. Heather never dreamed that she'd lose him here. She missed the warm glow of his gold-hazel eyes, his loving touch, and his gentle, determined demeanor. His big hazel eyes were like embers on a cold winter night. She ached to feel his strong arms holding her, protecting her—loving her. She longed to run her fingers through his light, sandy blond hair. And breathe in his warm, buttery scent. She ached to feel his embrace and the sultry resonance of his voice as he whispered her name against her ear.

He only lived in her memory right now. Like her mother. And the lives she'd left behind. She couldn't lose him, too. Not after losing everything else.

Ahead, she saw it. The demon cave that led to the Demon Veils.

Oh, Ross, where are you?

So much time had passed since she'd left the Spiral and returned here. She felt time's swift current surging around her, flowing so fast. Months, even years had rushed past while this demon cave stood unchanged and hidden, marking time at these trapped souls' expense.

At Ross' expense.

Had he given up on everything by now? Maybe he'd forgotten her? Or were his memories of her constant torture to him? Like Jessie.

She dropped down behind a boulder and watched the cave's dark entrance, expecting a ton of demons clustered around it with more pouring in and out. The dark alcove looked quiet, empty, no sign of movement. Nothing stirred. Not even a leathery grey demon skulked around the dark tunnel's entrance.

Could she walk in there and have any chance of getting out again? Would Mulciber attack her on sight? Could she even get close to Ross now? Was he even inside there? Death could have already claimed him.

Her heart clenched. Maybe he was lying in the poppy fields and it was already too late.

Before, the demons hadn't been an overt threat. They'd let her come and go as she pleased, but so much had happened since the night that she and Ross had walked out together. She doubted they'd let her enter again like that. Maybe she could disguise herself? Blend in with others somehow?

Something moved out of the shadows from the cave entrance.

Heather turned her head toward the sound as it grew louder.

Rumble…squeak…rumble…squeak.

Out of the darkness, a metal cart thumped and rolled out of the cave. A lost soul, a man in sooty rags, pushed it outside and onto a small path that veered into the trees to her left. A second cart squeaked out of the darkness behind it, another lost soul—a woman—in matching dusty grey rags pushing it. Both carts brimmed with dirt and ash. The faces of both lost souls were smudged with dirt. A fine sheen of soot clung to their hair and clothes. In moments, the two carts disappeared behind some brush.

Heather darted across the marshy landscape and followed the two carts at a distance as they rolled into the forest.

Where were they going? What was in those carts?

Overhead, something screeched. A shadow scraped the ground.

Heather slid into the brush, crouching as the shadow passed. A moment later, three soulstalkers swooped out of the dusky sky, careening toward the two lost souls.

In an instant, the souls were on the ground, struggling, flailing. They seemed sluggish, every movement a struggle.

Heather leaped out of the brush and ran toward the nearest soulstalker.

She threw herself at it, tackling it to the hard ground. She pinned its wings, flattening her body against it, holding down its taloned hind feet. So it wouldn't tear her up.

The two lost souls stared at Heather, looking bewildered as they stopped thrashing. One soulstalker hefted the almost waifish woman off the ground and wrapped his arms around her. Lifting her into the air.

Heather snatched a rock off the ground and threw it as hard as she could. It slammed into the soulstalker's head.

The creature shrieked, grabbing its head as inky black gel dripped down the side of its face.

The woman tumbled to the ground.

"Fight!" Heather shouted. "Fight for your lives! Your souls!"

Heather plucked another rock from the ground and flung it at the other soulstalker, beaning it. It screamed in rage, whirling toward Heather as she kept the third one immobile on the ground with a knee against its wings.

Life returned to the man's brown eyes. He snapped out of his stupor and turned on the soulstalker trying to carry him off. He punched the creature in the gut, staggering it. It got up quickly, cracking him in the head with a blow of its wings.

The woman cried out, her face filled with fear as she clawed at the soulstalker's chest, biting and gouging until she grabbed a handful of feathers. She yanked hard, pulling them out with a snap. And clawed its face.

Heather sat on the third soulstalker and kept throwing rocks until the other two soulstalkers gave up and fumbled away from the two souls. With a leap, one of them soared into the sky. The other one beat its wings until it rose from the ground and disappeared on the horizon.

Only then did Heather let the third one up from the ground. It let out a desperate screech as the man and woman rushed at it and threw itself into the air, wings unfurling. It wobbled over the trees, branches scraping its bare chest as it lifted into the air.

"Thanks," said the man, extending his hand to her.

Heather shook it. "You're welcome. I'm Heather Billot, by the way."

"Ian," said the man, brushing off his tattered clothes. "Ian James." He pointed at the woman. "This is Gemma Bonetti. My fiancée. At least she was before we uh—" His gaze fell to his dirt-covered hands.

Ian was at least five foot ten, shorter than Ross. A bit older. His voice was smooth and pleasant with a British accent. His light brown hair was short and slicked back, no trace of a mustache or beard on his strong chin. He had sad brown eyes and a kind smile on his long face. Beside him, Gemma looked wary. She was a slight woman with soft auburn hair swept away from her face into a rolled pageboy style that framed her oval face. Despite the dust and grit, it almost gave her that 1940s Hollywood siren look. She was slightly taller than Heather (maybe five foot seven?) with big, round, slate-blue eyes that were wide-set. The soot smudges gave her eyes a smoky, intense look.

Gemma pursed her full, rosy lips. "How did I get out here?" she asked, rubbing her neck.

Her clear soprano voice was soft with a pronounced Italian accent that made her voice sound intriguing.

Heather remembered her long-ago Italian classes from high school. It was such a beautiful language, so lyrical. She'd only managed one Italian class in college before she'd... She balled her hands into fists.

Why was it still so hard to think about even now? Even now, she felt ashamed of her actions.

She'd tried to live with her pain for two years, live with the loss of her best friend in the whole world, her mom. Mom died on prom night, leaving a hole in Heather's heart that grew bigger and bigger until she just couldn't go on anymore. She'd been all alone. Struggling to make a life, but the emptiness just got bigger and lonelier.

Looking back, she wished that someone had cared enough to stop her, that she'd reached out one more time to someone. Anyone. Like Jimmy at the Orca Café.

Ian turned his hands over and over, looking puzzled. "What is this substance that we're hauling?" He picked up a handful and sniffed it. "It smells chalky and foul." He dropped the dirt and made a sour face at Gemma who nodded.

"I don't remember doing this—hauling this," said Gemma, brushing her hands together. "I was so far away from here." She motioned toward the horizon, a wistful look lighting her eyes. "I was not in this horrible place. We were at university, Ian. It was springtime in Paris." Her face lit with a smile. "Everything was in bloom as we walked from the Sorbonne, browsing the bookshops on rue de l'Odéon—"

Ian smiled. "On our way to Jardin du Luxembourg and then Montparnasse for drinks by the Seine."

Gemma moved toward Ian, sliding her arms around his waist. She stared into his eyes and leaned up to kiss him. "Ian and I met at the Sorbonne, Heather."

"Yes, university students in love," said Ian, putting his arms around her neck and kissing her.

"What year did you meet?" Heather asked.

Gemma pressed her cheek against Ian's. "Nineteen thirty-seven."

How long had they been here?

Maybe they were older when they died? "When did you uh, commit suicide?"

Gemma's gaze fell to the ground as she slumped against Ian who held her up. "June eighteenth, nineteen forty," she said in a tight-lipped voice. "Most of the city had fled. Ian and I tried to get out, but it was too late." She held onto Ian tighter.

"For days, Gemma, Thomas, and I huddled together in a closet in our flat with a jug of wine, two tins of biscuits, and three revolvers," Ian explained. "All around us, the Gestapo rounded people up and took them away. None of them ever returned to their flats."

"Then, in the middle of the night, I awoke to someone tearing through the flat," said Gemma. She was shaking now. "Ian and I held each other, Thomas beside us. We all readied our revolvers—should they...find us."

"The room went silent after a while," said Ian, letting go of Gemma. "We thought they'd gone on, that we were safe." He shook his head, leaning against one of the carts. "But we were so wrong. The closet door burst open, and five S.S. soldiers pointed rifles at us and shouted in German. As one of the soldiers reached into the closet for Gemma, we all fired our pistols." He sighed. "Ending up here." His brow furrowed and he glanced at Gemma, shaking his head. "But we weren't always here, were we? Hauling this ash?"

Gemma nodded. "Sì, we were in the forest for a long while. With lots of others."

"The great tree?" Heather asked.

"Yes, that was it," said Ian. "We finally left with a Roman fellow and dozens of other souls. Thraecius was his name."

Heather smiled. "Yes, I knew Thraecius. I helped him and his parents leave the Between. Through the Spiral."

"There's a way out?" Ian cried, taking a step toward Heather, his brown eyes widening. "Are you certain?"

Heather nodded. "I left through it, too, but I came back."

Ian's mouth gaped. "Dear God! What on earth for?"

"To rescue Ross."

Gemma slid her hand into Ian's again. "I think I understand why."

"You're both under the influence of the Veils," said Heather.

"She's right, Gemma," said Ian, tapping the handle of the cart. "This morning, I dreamed I was home in Brighton. I was on the beach, digging a bonfire for a family gathering."

Ian and Gemma stared at the dirt on their hands and finally at the carts they'd been pushing.

"I was home. Hauling sand out of the hole we were digging. And now I see this cart."

Gemma's eyes widened. "I was remembering the day we moved into our flat, Ian. Carrying cartloads of books and clothes. It never seemed to stop."

Heather shuddered, remembering how entangled in her own memories she'd become when she came here the first time. If Ross hadn't pulled her out, she might have ended up carting away those shiny rocks forever. That was how the demons got the human souls to labor for them.

"What is the stuff you're hauling?" Heather asked, pointing at the carts.

"Dirt," said Gemma, frowning. "I think."

"It must be from the tunnels," said Ian. "The digging never seems to stop. Ever. The sound is constant."

So, the demons were still digging tunnels all over the Between. Why? It couldn't just be to attack souls taking refuge in the forest. There had to be another purpose to these tunnels.

"Well, you're free now," said Heather and motioned over her shoulder, pointing toward the east. "If you head along this path, it'll take you to a large clearing. You'll see five paths to your right. Turn left away from all the paths, toward a small stream in the distance. Follow that stream and turn right when you reach the wall of darkness. You'll find a glowing ring of trees northeast of there. It's a safe place."

Gemma's eyes widened. "Is this a way out?"

Heather shook her head. "No, but it's a place where you'll be safe from the soulstalkers and the demons. The great tree was destroyed, but this soul tree is protected."

Gemma's gaze fell. She sighed, casting a look at her fiancé. "Ian, we need to leave this place. Please, can we go there?"

Glaring, Ian shook his head. He was angry and Gemma stepped back from him.

"Just like that?" he snapped, arms crossed. "How could you?"

She rolled her eyes. "Save myself? What a terrible thing for me to do!"

Ian sighed. "So, we should just exit this horrible place and leave Thomas to their mercy? Is that what you're proposing, my beloved, Gemma?"

Gemma paced around him, waving her arms. "You know it isn't something I do lightly, Ian. But we've got a real chance to get away from here. Let's take it!"

"No," Ian snapped. "I couldn't live with myself."

"Ian, I won't go without you," she said, her voice softer, shaky.

"Who's Thomas?" Heather asked.

Ian turned toward her, his brown eyes sad. "My younger brother.

He's still inside with the other human souls." He gave Heather a wary look, raising an eyebrow. "You're not trying to trap us, too, I hope."

Heather shook her head. "No, of course not! I'm a lost soul like you. I took my own life to come back here, remember?"

"If you help us rescue Thomas," said Ian, "We'll help you rescue your person."

"All right, deal," Heather said, nodding. "If you help me rescue Ross, I'll help you get Thomas out, too. And other souls who want out."

Ian gasped and exchanged a horrified look with Gemma.

"What's wrong?"

"I've heard that name before," said Gemma. "From the demons."

"He's been brainwashed, I think," said Ian. "Works for the demons now. You may have a fight on your hands for that one." He patted her shoulder. "Sorry, not what you hoped to hear, I'm sure."

Heather winced. "I won't leave the Between without him."

Gently, Ian touched Heather's arm. "Then try we shall, Heather."

"She'll stand out like a sore thumb looking like that," Gemma said to Ian.

"True," Ian replied. "We'll need to dirty you up a bit. Smudge up your face sprinkle and dirt in your hair. Then we'll all go in together."

"Let's do this," said Heather, picking up a handful of dirt and smearing it across her silky grey clothes. "But now that you're not under the demons' spell, you need to protect your mind against them. Block them out and keep blocking them out. Understand? And don't go near those Veils, no matter how homesick you feel."

Ian and Gemma nodded. "Now that we know, it should be easier," said Gemma. "I think."

With Gemma's help, Heather worked dirt through her long coppery brown hair and smudged it all over her arms, neck, and face. Gemma tore a couple of gashes into her clothes while Ian tossed handfuls of dirt at her shirt and pants.

"Could I push the cart?" Heather asked. "There's a chance that they might recognize me.

"Of course," said Ian. "Keep your head down and let us do the talking. We'll show you where we work and rest. And then we'll start looking for Thomas and Ross."

Gemma and Ian dumped the dirt out of the carts and turned them around toward the cave. Ian pushed the first one while Heather and Gemma pushed the second one, following Ian into the dark cave entrance.

eleven

· · ·

HEATHER'S STOMACH churned as the endless, dark tunnel snaked into the blackness toward a brassy gold light that appeared at the end. She focused her thoughts on Ross' bright, gold-hazel eyes and the pale angels, hoping to create a blockade in her brain that wouldn't let those demons bend her to their will. They'd grown a lot more powerful since she'd first been here.

As they rolled the carts closer to the entrance, Heather saw a line of carts filled with dirt, working their way past them in the darkness. Heather studied all their eyes as they passed each enslaved soul, the emptiness frightening her. After the fifth cart squeaked past, she realized that the vacant stare she'd first seen in Ian and Gemma's eyes was constant. Much deeper than she remembered.

Had they all been like this before? While hopelessly tangled in the Demon Veils?

No, the souls' expressions looked frozen. Empty. Permanent. And that terrified her.

Somehow, she'd pulled Ian and Gemma back from that abyss. It had taken soulstalkers carrying them off to shake them free of that empty numbness and nothing she'd done. And, in Ian's case, it was a misplaced rock. Because she'd accidentally hit him in the chest with it while aiming at soulstalkers.

They reached a rough-hewn, granite-like stone archway that opened into the familiar, well-lit cavern where she'd first seen the Mechanism. Her fingers turned cold, her mouth going dry. As her eyes adjusted, she was overwhelmed by the changes.

The Mechanism was huge! Three floors high now and three times its former size. It sprawled in the center of the cavern that had been carved out to make room for it. It looked like a massive engine with a bunch of shuddering and moving parts. A railing surrounded the huge, sprawling machine with floors above and below it now. It belched greasy black smoke, ticking and vibrating as something inside pumped and churned, filling the cavern with a deep, moaning thrum. That made Heather's skin crawl.

Above and below the Mechanism, floors, and rock had been carved into a circle around it with several doorways on the opposite wall. She counted at least five where there'd only been two or three cave-like holes before. The cavern was better lit and looked—constructed. Refined and industrialized—almost like a huge factory. The Mechanism's surface looked blackened and oily like it was in constant use.

What did it do? Did it produce something? Power something? Or destroy things?

Ian slowed his pace as he maneuvered his cart around the throngs of souls and demons rushing through the crowded space. Heather waited until he moved ahead before creeping forward.

Before, this dank, dusty cavern had been little more than a festering sewer of demons. A deep hole in the ground with stalactites and dark tunnels opening into small chambers and endless rocky walls. Navigating it had been easy. One tunnel led into the Veils, the other into a mining pit where souls toiled with pickaxes, hacking out shiny black rocks. The Mechanism had been a single story tall, skeletal with exposed parts requiring dozens of souls to constantly turn flywheels and flick levers.

Before, the demons seemed almost polite and laid back—in a way that had been frightening, luring human souls into the cavern through those sparkling Veils that brought her and every other soul back to their former lives through vivid memories and intense emotions, hopelessly entangling them. Once under the Veils' spell, it was easy to persuade souls to run the Mechanism. The Veils were like a spider's web and before, they had been the first thing souls saw when they entered the cavern.

By design.

Heather knew that too well. If Ross hadn't pulled her out, she might still be trapped in the Veils, reliving a life lost to her. Forever.

But now, the caverns, the Mechanism—the demons—had evolved. Heather couldn't see the top of the Mechanism that ran independently now, not requiring so much manual labor. It seemed to require frequent monitoring and adjustments though.

Why did the demons move the Veils out of the way? Their only way to lure humans into the caverns? And why had they developed this—this industrial complex in the middle of the Between? Maybe they had plenty of souls to do their bidding now that they'd upgraded the Mechanism? Or maybe they were stealing souls from the soulstalkers?

Like they'd stolen Ross.

Heather followed Ian's cart around the railing, moving toward another granite-like archway to the far left. Gemma tensed, her gaze wary. Heather kept her head down as she white-knuckled the cart handle and pushed the other cart behind Ian.

The place felt chaotic, souls and demons rushing back and forth, looking tense and stressed. Stressed out demons? That almost made her laugh out loud. What could possibly stress out demons?

As Heather pushed the squeaky cart around the Mechanism, she got a chance to peer over the railing.

She couldn't believe how different the caverns below looked now. Still dark and forbidding, but the demons had done massive excavations, carving out floors and tunnels, refining, and upgrading the cavern into an industrial complex.

How many souls had it taken to dig out all of this and haul away the dirt? How many carts full of dirt had Ian and Gemma carried out of these lower caverns?

Several scaffold-like platforms clung to the towering, engine-like machine that looked like a small skyscraper now. The platforms had three or four levels, each with a control panel filled with levers and buttons that winked blue and green. A heavy braided rope as thick as Heather's arm dangled from each platform. She watched as the demons moved platforms around by making the souls pull them into place with those heavy ropes.

Dozens of souls stood on the platforms and ran switchboards and control panels. Amber, blue, and green lights washed across the massive machine's oily surface, punctuated with a wink of red light.

Ian swerved away from the railing as hot air blew from a steam vent, smelling warm and musty.

Heather swung her cart out, away from the railing, moving around the gust of steam that misted the air. The air had a metallic, salty scent that mixed with the stink of burning oil as the machinery thumped and whirred like a dryer out of round.

Was she imagining that smell?

The cacophony of sounds combined into a single staccato beat that reverberated through the cavern, vibrating through her body. Into her teeth. The movement was oddly comforting, like the memory of her human heart beating steadily in her chest again.

And that frightened her.

Dozens of leathery, grey-skinned demons crowded the main floor, rushing around, shouting orders at the human souls as they ascended platforms like crazed monkeys. Other demons shifted human souls back and forth on the platforms like crates, positioning them around the Mechanism.

With demons shouting in their ears, the human souls grabbed the heavy ropes and dragged platforms into new positions. Demons were everywhere, so many more than she remembered, but they looked distracted and overwhelmed. Before, they seemed carefree and laid back, seeming almost amused by the souls in the cavern. They'd ambled through the space, observing everything with an almost fascinated smirk.

These demons seemed preoccupied and fearful, hurrying to get things done, reminding Heather of overworked factory workers. Every demon that passed her paid no attention to her presence. They didn't seem to care what she did as long as she was working. And right now, she wasn't ready to test that.

On this floor, the demons outnumbered the human souls three to one. She could only imagine what the other floors were like. And the demons had become drones just like the human souls. Their expressionless faces were thin and ashen, eyes empty and as hollow as the souls. No one seemed to disobey an order. No one even asked questions and the souls didn't hesitate to follow them.

Heather felt sick inside. What had happened here? Just what did this Mechanism do?

"Keep to your left," Gemma whispered against her ear. "We're not allowed in the corridors to the right."

"Why's that?" Heather asked as they reached a crossroad of three tunnels. She halted the cart as Ian turned into the left-hand tunnel.

"It's where the other demons reside," said Gemma. "And it's where the shiny black rocks are sent."

Heather frowned. "Other demons? What other demons?"

"The ones in charge," Gemma replied. "They tell these little demons and the souls what to do. They're taller. Softer. Red. They're cruel and put things into your head. I don't like being around them."

Heather's eyes widened. A hierarchy of demons here—in the Between?

"Heather, this way," Ian called, motioning her to the leftmost tunnel

Heather pushed the cart to the left, but movement in the right-hand tunnel caught her gaze. She turned to look.

At the end of the tunnel was a large, smoky room. Scalding yellow lights pierced the room in sharp but misty beams, shadows moving through the space. In the center of the room stood a large, round table.

She stepped away from the cart, moving toward the tunnel. She hesitated a moment and then took two steps into the tunnel.

Heavy, straight-backed chairs rose out of the darkness. A shadow. Movement. Wood scraping across rock.

She took another step toward the sound.

Ross stepped into the light, pausing at the tunnel entrance, hands on his hips.

Heather froze, clamping her hand over her mouth, fighting every impulse to run down that tunnel and throw her arms around him. And never let go.

But something felt...off.

His skin was pasty white, eyes shadowed and vacuous—as if someone had excavated all the passion from his soul and all the memories from his brain. The beautiful gold of his hazel eyes had grown dull and stony. Shadows framed his eyes and hollowed his cheeks. His angry expression was hard and distant, no trace of compassion or humility.

"No," she whispered. "No...Ross—what have they done to you?"

"Heather, now," Ian snapped. "Or we'll be digging in the coal fields."

Gemma grabbed her by the shoulders and pulled her back to the cart. Heather took hold of the cart handles as Ian moved down the left-hand tunnel. She hesitated, casting one last forlorn look at Ross, and then pushed the cart into the tunnel. But she couldn't help herself. She turned around for another glimpse of Ross.

Ross' enraged shout vibrated through the tunnels. He raged and screamed, spouting orders and shoving lesser demons around in the tunnel as a big group emerged from the room. Clutches of demons responded, marching down the tunnel and disappearing into other tunnels. Others spilled into the main room.

Heather had never seen him like that before. Horrified and sick to her stomach, tears welling in her eyes, she backed away from the cart. She wanted to run away from these caverns and this memory. Hide deep in the soul tree forever.

Ross wasn't a captive. He was in charge.

The demons did his bidding now. She had no idea what they were doing down here, but Ross was overseeing it now. He wasn't like Thraecius who'd been a foreman in the coal fields. He outranked demons and they obeyed him. Doing whatever horrible things he ordered. She didn't even want to know.

Fighting back tears, Heather followed Ian into the safety of a small room tucked at the end of the tunnel. Just big enough for four cots, two on each side, and a narrow walkway between them. A rickety wooden chair sat in between or at the end of each cot.

Gemma shook her hard. "Heather? Please! We've got to move."

At last, Gemma's words got through. Heather gave the cart a hard shove ahead and turned left down a wide tunnel with little chambers on both sides. A dozen or more by the time she reached the end. There were two doors. The left-hand door was open, carts lining each side of what looked like a storeroom. Ian put his cart into the line of carts and Heather did the same with her cart. She swiped the tears off her face and followed Ian and Gemma into the room to the right. With the four cots. Once inside, she sank into the far corner, shaking, arms folded against her chest.

She felt sick about Ross.

How would she save him now? It just seemed impossible. Impossible!

Gemma knelt beside her, a hand against her shoulder. Ian leaned over her, looking frightened.

"What's happened, Gemma?" he asked in a quiet voice.

"She saw Ross in the tunnel to the demon quarters."

"Oh no, I was afraid that would happen." He sat down on the floor beside her. "I wanted to tell you about him, to prepare you for what he's become."

Heather shook her head, not looking at either of them. "I can't save him now, can I?" She looked up at Gemma and Ian, tears flooding her cheeks. "It's all too late, isn't it?"

"Heather, listen," said Ian. "I know it looks bad, but maybe there's a way? Maybe we just need to put our heads together and brainstorm a bit?"

Gemma smiled, nodding at her. "Sì, there are ways into that tunnel, Heather. We must be a bit clever, but it's not totally off-limits to us."

"Gemma's right," said Ian, patting Heather's forearm. "There are ways into that chamber. I've been inside it before. And with things being so hectic right now, it might get easier. So, don't fret. And don't give up. I won't give up on Thomas if you don't give up on Ross. Okay?"

Maybe there was still a chance? She had to hold onto that sliver of hope as long as she could.

Heather nodded. "All right," she replied, brushing away more tears. "I'll hold onto that."

"That's the spirit!" Ian cried, clapping his hands together as he got to his feet. "All right then, you'll stay in our chamber, Heather. They put four of us together in each compartment. Ruomei disappeared some time ago and they took Thomas to the coal fields, so we've got space."

Heather scrambled to her feet. "Wait, someone disappeared?"

Ian nodded as he moved toward Gemma who sat down on one of the cots to the right. Ian sat down on a rickety wooden chair at the foot of one of the cots in the space. They had tied the two cots together to make one bed and turned it against the opposite wall.

"One day, Ruomei just wasn't here anymore. Gemma and I asked about her, but no one had seen her. We have no idea what happened. No one claims to have seen her and the demons just snicker when I ask."

Heather felt anger burn through her. "There has to be a reason. Souls just don't disappear! Unless they're dragged off by something."

"Maybe they've got her working in the coal fields?" Gemma said and stretched out on the bed.

Something about this disappearance frightened Heather. The demons had more than enough souls and with the chaos, she doubted anyone would notice a few souls disappearing. Had Ruomei escaped? Or had something happened to her?

Heather shuddered, a chill dancing down her spine. Had the demons done something to Ruomei?

Maybe she was hiding in the forest somewhere? Or had soulstalkers carried her off? Heather's stomach felt queasy when she remembered Knox trying to teach these lost souls—and the pale angels—how to defend themselves. Most of the souls had zoned out after a little while. With nearly 50 souls and about 30 pale angels, they would be no match for these demons and the army of souls under demonic control. She needed to talk to Zakhart, let him see this for himself. They needed another plan.

She sighed. And a much bigger army.

"So, what happens now?" Heather asked, sitting down on one of the cots.

"We wait for more tasks," said Ian. "There's no schedule or anything. It's quite random really. Demons aren't the most organized creatures I've ever met."

Gemma leaned back against the rock wall. "Just recently, things have gotten even more confused. Much less structure. Before, we all had regular shifts. We would dig in the new tunnels and cart away the dirt before they'd let us touch the Veils again. Now, we just carry away the dirt whenever a demon orders us to and that can be at any time. The rest of the time, we're free to spend as much time in the Veils as we'd like."

Ian sighed and rubbed his forehead. "When I was under the Veils' spell, I didn't mind the work so much. Perhaps because I didn't realize I was working. Now that I'm free of that influence, all I want to do is leave. But until I find Thomas, I shall endure the tedium."

"You're free to wander around or stay in your quarters—whatever suits you," said Gemma, motioning toward the hallway. "To be honest, Heather, I doubt they'll even notice you right now."

"Why are things so chaotic?" Heather asked.

Ian glanced at Gemma and shrugged. He rose from the chair and climbed onto the bed, gathering Gemma in his arms. She slid her arms around his neck and kissed him.

"Wish I knew," said Ian. "I think they have made some sort of breakthrough with that confounded machine, so the demons are pushing hard for even more improvements."

"What does it actually do?"

"Wish I knew," said Ian with another shrug. "They don't tell us anything. I find the monstrous thing disturbing and I worry that it'll be used against all of us very soon."

Gemma glanced at the door and then at Ian. She pulled in a quick breath and leaned toward Heather who sat on the bed opposite theirs, motioning her closer. Heather sat down on the bed beside her and Ian.

"I hear them talking sometimes," she whispered with wide eyes, her full lips pursed.

Ian's eyes grew wide, pupils dilating. He cast nervous glances at the door and back at Gemma.

"What have you heard?" Heather asked.

"They don't realize that the tunnels carry their voices long distances," said Gemma, her whispers sharp. "They are trying to get the Mechanism ready for some event."

"What event?" Ian asked.

Heather nodded for her to continue.

"Yesterday—or what felt like yesterday—I heard them reporting in, saying that testing was going well. The big one, Mulciber? He told the others to do testing. Faster. And to start in the coal fields. He said they had to be ready at a moment's notice. That things were moving faster than expected. They had to be ready."

"Ready for what?" Heather whispered.

"So, they *are* gearing up for something," said Ian through gritted teeth. He pulled Gemma tighter in his arms, his gaze moving from the hallway to Heather. "But your question remains, what are they waiting for? And why? Somehow, we must find out these answers before we leave here."

Two bells chimed, echoing down the hallway.

"We'll get the next one, all right?" Ian said to Gemma.

Heather sighed, bowing her head, the frustration growing. "I agree. They're demons, so we know they're not here to help lost souls."

"True," said Gemma, gripping Ian's arms as he held her. "I wish I'd heard more, but they stopped talking after that."

"So they're testing something in the coal fields. Any idea what that might be?" Heather asked.

Gemma shook her head. "None. I haven't ever been down there and neither has Ian. At least I don't think I've been down there."

"How do people get assigned to the coal fields?" Heather asked.

"I don't know," said Gemma. "I've only met a few people who worked in the coal fields. But there are frequent calls to cart rock out of the fields."

Ian nodded, sadness shadowing his eyes. "I don't know either," he replied, a heavy sigh on his lips. "But I've not seen them since their new assignment. And most never come back from there."

"What?"

Heather studied Ian then Gemma. Neither of them seemed even the slightest bit troubled by this news.

"So, every time someone you know gets assigned to the coal fields, you never see them again? Why?" Heather asked. "Do they get placed in different quarters? Do they get separated, and permanently housed on the lower floor? Someplace you two never go? Or... something else?"

Heather wanted to shy away from a horrible thought that was weaving its way through her fevered brain, but knowing she couldn't. It nagged at her now, like she'd left a gas burner turned on somewhere or left the garage door up.

A single bell rang through the hallway. Heather frowned. What was with these bells?

A faraway look touched Ian's eyes as he stared past Heather, deep in thought, tapping his forefinger against his chin. Gemma's face scrunched into a contemplative expression as she fiddled with the edge of a tan blanket with her long, thin fingers.

"I knew about five or six souls who'd been sent to the coal fields," said Ian, his words slow and contemplative. "Most of them had been spending less and less time in the Veils. I would hear them chatting as we hauled dirt out of the cavern. Asking questions. Arguing with a demon or two...whispering about leaving."

Gemma's mouth gaped and she stared at Ian, wide-eyed. "Yes! The ones that I knew had begun avoiding the Veils, telling me that the memories just hurt and they clouded their heads." She snapped her fingers. "Then boom! I did not see them anymore."

Heather rose to her feet, pacing now. "The demons were losing control," she replied, "so they moved those souls deeper into the cavern. To keep them from poisoning the others and...something else."

"Yes, they were causing trouble," Ian replied, nodding. "And they were increasing dissatisfaction throughout the ranks of souls."

Turning toward the door, Heather glanced out into the hall to make sure no one was eavesdropping. Another bell chimed. Ian and Gemma didn't react to the sound. Heather moved back to the cots and sat down beside Gemma and Ian again, her voice low now.

"Zakhart has always told me that demons can't control you unless you invite them in and give them permission," Heather explained and touched Gemma's shoulder. "There's absolutely nothing physically holding your souls inside this place. These demons could do nothing if every single soul just stood up and walked out."

No one spoke. Ian and Gemma were stunned silent by Heather's statement. She could see the disbelief staring back at her.

"Are you serious?" Gemma asked finally, her voice barely above a whisper.

"Very," Heather said, waving her hand toward the hallway. "Your souls can leave this place any time. But you've been so caught up in your own memories, so lost in the Veils, that you don't realize that you're working for the demons. That's how they trap souls and get them to do their bidding."

"You mean that Ian and I have trapped ourselves here?"

Heather nodded.

Another single bell rang through the hallway, startling Heather. She glanced toward the sound.

Gemma thrust her hands over her face, shoulders heaving. Ian put his arms around Gemma, stroking her hair, trying to calm her.

"It's not your fault, Gemma," said Heather, turning back to the cot. "The Veils are dangerous. I was trapped in them until Ross helped me escape. But he and I were able to walk out of here together. The demons tried to persuade us not to leave, but they were powerless to prevent it. Now, when they discover dissatisfied souls, they send them into the coal fields before the Veils' hold disappears."

"To test...something," said Ian. "But what could it be?

"Something forbidden throughout the realms," said a voice from the doorway.

Heather turned toward the sound.

Zakhart!

twelve

· · ·

ZAKHART STOOD IN THE DOORWAY, wrapped in the same, grey souls' clothing that Heather wore. His wings were concealed under the loose-fitting shirt, a small hump at his back. Knox stood behind him, leaning against the doorframe. Both of them looked angry and relieved. Heather swallowed hard, avoiding their probing stares.

Maybe she should have told them where she was going. If she had, they would have tried to stop her.

"Who are you?" Gemma asked, pressing herself deeper into Ian's arms, eyes wide, a hand against her mouth.

Ian slid Gemma behind him, blocking her with his body. "Identify yourselves," Ian snapped. "Now."

Zakhart rushed across the room and dropped down at Heather's feet. He hesitated a moment, his pumpkin-orange eyes watery as he gripped her forearms. Exhaling sharply, he clasped her to his chest.

"Heather," he said with a sigh, relief in his voice. "I've been out of my head worrying about you. Knox and I have been searching everywhere for you."

"I'm sorry, Zakhart," she said. "I didn't mean to worry you, but what are you and Knox doing here?"

The pale angel held her out at arm's length, looking her over and finally let go. He got to his feet, checking out the room.

Knox dropped down on the cot beside her, anger burning in his blue eyes.

"You scared the hell out of me!" Knox shouted. "I thought you'd been carried off by soulstalkers." Finally, he put his arms around her and hugged her. He let out a breath, laying his head against her shoulder.

Heather smiled, hugging him back. Her tough-as-bullets soldier looked rattled. Concerned. About her? Had Knox developed feelings for her?

He let go, wagging a finger at her, a stern expression on his face. "Don't you ever do that again, Heather! Goin' off on your own like that, tryin' to be a hero, can get you killed."

Heather glared at him. "I wasn't trying to be a hero, Knox. I was just trying to find Ross."

Ian cleared his throat. "Um, excuse me, Heather," he said, his voice shaking. "Perhaps you could introduce your friends? And allay my fiancée's fright. They are your friends, aren't they?"

Heather nodded, glancing at Ian. Gemma peaked over Ian's shoulder, her head pressed against his chest, arms tight around his waist. She was trembling.

"Gemma," said Heather, pointing at Zakhart who stood across from the cot, pumpkin-orange eyes fiery. His presence had probably terrified Gemma. "This is Zakhart." She lowered her voice to a sharp whisper. "He's a pale angel, sent here to help lost souls."

"There are no angels here! Only those horrid flying things!" Gemma's voice was trembling, her Italian accent thick now. "Where are his wings?"

Knox moved over and lifted Zakhart's silky, grey shirt. Underneath, his soft beige wings were bound tightly to his back. Gemma's mouth gaped and she loosened her chokehold on Ian.

"Forgive me for not displaying a halo," said Zakhart. "There's too much darkness here to expose it. But I'll try if it will calm your fears."

Gemma nodded.

Zakhart closed his eyes, lips moving as he whispered something. After a moment or two, brilliant white light encircled his head, casting sparks throughout the room. His face scrunched with concentration, hands balled into fists as the halo pulsated above his white hair. He let it spark for a few more moments and finally let it go, his body slumping. The light faded quickly until only an afterglow remained until it, too was swallowed up by the room's dim lighting.

"It's beautiful," Gemma said with a gasp and sat up. "Like your wings. They are so curved and sleek, not at all like the wind-ravaged wings of those nasty shadow creatures."

"Thank you," said Zakhart.

Heather nodded at Knox. "And Knox is another lost soul like me. From the soul tree."

"Pleased to meet you both," said Ian. He laid a hand against his chest. "My name is Ian and this is my fiancée, Gemma."

Everyone went quiet, staring at each other as the awkward silence grew. A single bell rang out followed by a door creaking open and footsteps pattering down the hallway.

"Zakhart," said Gemma, sitting on the edge of the cot, her legs crossed beneath her. "You said something about the demons. About something being forbidden."

"Yes, I did," said Zakhart, his voice calm and soothing as he sat down at the end of Heather's cot and turned to face Gemma, hands clasped in front of him. "I said that demons, like any ethereal creature, are forbidden from harming or interfering with any soul's progress—regardless of whether it's forward or backward. *Unless* that soul expressly requests their intervention."

Zakhart moved beside Heather, his gaze settling on her. He didn't speak, but his expression was intense.

"Zakhart," said Heather, leaning around Knox. "I think the

demons are harming souls down here. Some of the souls have essentially disappeared and no one's seen them since."

Worry shadowed the pale angel's pearlescent complexion. His eyebrows pressed into heavy lines. "Disappearing? How?"

Heather shrugged. "I'm not sure. But both Ian and Gemma say some of the souls lured into this place have vanished."

The pale angel crossed his arms, fidgeting. His expression became contemplative and he grew quiet. Heather could almost watch the thoughts tumbling through his brain as he got lost in thought.

"What if that's part of the demons' testing?" Heather asked. "Could this Mechanism be something that destroys souls?"

Ian frowned, shaking his head. "What would they gain by destroying souls?"

Zakhart's head snapped up, eyes wide. "Destroy souls? Even if they had the power—which they don't—that's forbidden! Only the Maker can create and destroy souls—or give that power to others. Like the ancient agent, Death and only the most trusted of angels." He shook his head, face contorting. "How would they have obtained such power? Was it even possible?"

The room went quiet again, a heaviness hanging over it. Ian and Gemma huddled together, confused and frightened as Zakhart sat down on a cot and slipped into a deep trance-like state, rocking in a rhythmic motion. Knox rose to his feet and paced the room, growing more restless. Heather got up from the cot and leaned against the wall, trying to make sense of everything.

Had the demons gained some sort of forbidden power? Were they actually destroying souls? How'd they get this power? A bargain with Death?

She sighed. Nothing made sense anymore.

For a long time, she waited for Zakhart to come out of his trance. When he didn't, she moved away from the wall to bring him out of it. Before he drew the demons' attention to his strange behavior.

"Zakhart," Heather called, shaking his shoulder until his gaze met hers.

She sat down beside him on the cot and spoke in quiet tones that only the pale angel could hear.

"The others say that these souls that have disappeared were first taken into the coal fields."

The pale angel's face pinched, looking exasperated. He shook his head.

"That's just not possible, Heather. There is no coal in the Between, I've already told you that."

"I know," said Heather, nodding. "I don't know what they're actually mining, but they carry hunks of shiny rock up from those fields every single day."

"Every day?" Zakhart said, frowning.

"Yes, they were mining that shiny rock the first time I was here," said Heather. "Pushing out cartloads of the stuff." She glanced at the others and dropped her voice to a tight whisper. "Did the demons somehow acquire the power of death when Death captured Ross?"

He shook his head violently, waving his hand in protest. "Heather! It's not possible!" he cried. "No one can acquire the power unless Death gives it to them or—" His voice broke, eyes wide as he froze, a look of fear washing over his alabaster face. "Oh, no."

He got to his feet, turning away as he whispered a staccato melody that carried through the room and dissipated into the hallway.

Heather ran to him, a hand on his shoulder, tugging at his shirt. "Zakhart, talk to me! Zakhart!"

The pale angel whirled around, grabbing her by the shoulders. "Heather, have you seen Ross and Mulciber?"

She frowned at him, shaking her head. "Just Ross, but only for a moment. I know he's here. I heard him screaming orders to the demons. That's what I wanted to tell you, that he'd been brainwashed or was being controlled somehow."

Zakhart squeezed his eyes closed. He rubbed a hand over his face, moaning. "No...this can't be happening," he said through gritted teeth. "It can't be happening!"

"Zakhart, what? What?" She shook him.

He steered Heather to the cot and sat her down, kneeling beside her, an arm around her shoulders.

"Heather," he said in such a dark, despondent voice that she held her breath, fearing what he was about to say. "When Razasha reached the Spiral, Death had pulled Ross free of it. She swung her scythe in a wide arc just as a clutch of demons surged out of the brush. One of them got in the way of the scythe, grabbing hold of Ross with both hands just as the scythe struck." He sighed. "I don't know if the blade struck the demon or Ross—or both."

"Why does that matter?"

"Because," Zakhart hissed. "If she missed Ross and hit the demon, the entire clutch banded together to absorb the blow. Capturing its power. If she hit Ross, then the demon and its clutch absorbed the blow from his body. Again capturing the power."

A chill tore through her chest, dread turning her fingers to ice. In the distance, a bell rang once.

"What does that mean?"

"Dear God, Heather—the demons have the power of death. All they need now is a way through the Spiral."

Heather felt her skin turning to gooseflesh. "Which they don't have. Right?"

Zakhart nodded. "Yes. But if they acquired that ability, then they would have the power to enter the physical world. Once there, they could command the power of death to kill humans and absorb their souls."

Heather grabbed his hands. "Zakhart, the Mechanism. What does it do?"

He squeezed her hands. "I'm not sure, but I'd guess it was an attempt to access the Spiral."

"We've got to find Ross. Find out what he knows."

"Yes," said Zakhart, his breath quickening. "Yes, that's right. Only he can tell us what happened when he escaped Death, but Heather, bear in mind that what you saw may not even be Ross. Demons can shift into many forms."

"But why would they shift into Ross' form?" Heather shouted, letting go of his hands. "None of these souls has ever seen him before." She gasped, the reality at last sinking into her brain. "Except me," she said.

Seeing Ross meant that the demons knew she would return. And they'd been expecting her. But why? What did they want from her?

Zakhart's face turned white, his pumpkin-orange eyes like eclipsed moons as he studied her face.

"They *were* expecting you, Heather," said the pale angel. "Counting on you to show up. Perhaps that's why they kept Ross alive—or took his human form. They were planning to lure you back here for some purpose."

He closed his eyes, intoning an aching melody that began as a major chord and sank quickly into a minor key that made Heather's skin crawl. What sort of message had he sent to the other pale angels?

"But why, Zakhart?" she asked, a hand on his arm. "What could they possibly want from me?"

Knox was on his feet now, arms crossed as he stepped beside Zakhart.

"Use you as collateral," said Knox, blue eyes hard and steely. "Maybe they want something from Ross and know you're a good prize to dangle in front of him?"

Zakhart nodded, pacing now, his face a mask of concentration.

"Possibly," said Heather. "Maybe because he's the only soul in the Between right now seeking the Spiral? They might force him to lead them to the Spiral or they'll harm me."

"That's possible," Zakhart mumbled, still pacing.

Knox thought for a moment, his mouth pressed into a line, brow furrowed. "Maybe Ross' soul is dead and they've taken his form so you'll try to rescue him? Then you'd bring home a demon to your safe spot."

"Yes, that's possible, too," said Zakhart, raising his forefinger into the air. He sang a handful of tenor notes, sharp as crystal, and sent them aloft. "I've asked someone to check and see if his soul has left the Between."

Heather's stomach knotted into a heavy ball of worry that made her belly ache. Was Ross gone? Lost to her forever? She folded her arms against her chest and bowed her head, her pacing frantic now.

Please, Ross, she whispered. *Please be all right. I need you.*

"But what about the disappearing souls?" Heather asked. "I think they're connected somehow."

"I concur with Heather," Ian called from the cot. "Gemma and I have seen this Ross many times from a distance. Saw him giving orders to the demons. Either he is under a quite powerful spell or he is in cahoots with them."

Knox grinned. "A sellout! Maybe he promised the demons to lead a bunch of souls here, including yours, Heather?"

Fire burned through her veins. Heather whirled around, glaring at Knox.

Knox was ready for her reaction. He grabbed her arms and forced her against the wall as she tried to swing at him.

"C'mon, Heather—you know I'm right."

Heather shook her head, rage burning through her. "No, you're not right!" she shouted, swinging her hands at Knox's face, but he dodged her slaps.

"Heather, face it—it's over!" His voice softened, eyes sad, sympathetic. "I'm really sorry, but that's probably not even your boyfriend anymore. It's probably a demon taking his form."

She glanced over at Zakhart who stared at her with grief-stricken eyes.

Tears welled in her eyes, her bottom lip quivering. "No, Zakhart," she said in a choked voice. "No...tell him. Please."

The pale angel looked at Knox and nodded his head.

Knox pulled her into his arms. Heather clung to him, feeling weak now as she sank against him.

Ross was gone forever. She had been too late to save him.

Knox cradled her, stroking her hair. "It's okay...it's gonna be okay, kiddo," he said, his breath hot against her ear. "I'm still here. And I'll be here for you."

She nuzzled her face against his chest as the first hard sob tore free. She felt so broken, so exhausted—so tired of fighting shadows and demons. When was this nightmare going to end? Why couldn't it have ended with her and Ross together? Why?

She couldn't hold back the tide of grief.

Knox let her cry until her voice grew raspy and quiet. He lifted her chin and wiped the tears from her face with the tail of his shirt. He smoothed back a lock of hair and cradled her face in his hands, staring into her eyes.

"It's gonna be okay, kiddo," he said, caressing her cheek.

She let herself sink into the blue depths of his eyes, the warmth of his comforting embrace, and the enticing, smoky scent of his skin.

Somewhere nearby, a bell chimed once.

Knox tilted his face, his lips finding hers in a slow, gentle kiss. She leaned into him, kissing him back, needing his touch to pull out of the swell of grief drowning her. The loss was just too much.

Then a thought pierced through her grief, blooming into a warm white hope within her. She pulled away from him.

"But what if he *is* still in there?" she whispered.

Knox chuckled, pressing his forehead to hers, his hands still cradling her face. "Then he's a very lucky man," he said.

Heather laid her hands on his forearms, squeezing.

"Thank you," she replied.

"But...when we're all back at the soul tree again, Ross is gonna have some competition." He let go of her face.

"Fair enough," said Heather.

When she glanced at Zakhart, he was smiling.

"Heather," he said, stepping over to her. "If I can get close enough to Ross, I'll be able to learn more about what's happening. I have some doubts. Usually, when a demon assumes a human form, it's an illusion portrayed for a handful of humans. Most of them aren't powerful enough to pull off a long-term illusion to fool everyone. But it could be a more powerful demon."

So there was a chance that it was really Ross under some sort of spell or control! She smiled, encouraged.

Zakhart laid his hand on her shoulder, squeezing. "But I don't understand why the demons singled him out. What about Ross makes him more valuable than every other soul in the Between? He's touched the Spiral, so that might be his value. He might be a trap set for you. Or he may be in league with them. We have to find the answer to that question, Heather."

"What do we do?" Heather asked.

The pale angel laid a hand against his chin. "First, I want to see these coal fields you've mentioned. Get a sample of this shiny black rock to take back." He glanced over at Ian and Gemma who sat wide-eyed and motionless on their cot. "We can do that and look for...what was his name? Thomas, right?"

"Yes, Thomas," Ian replied. He rose from the cot, Gemma clinging to his arm, and moved toward Zakhart. "He's my youngest brother. He disappeared after they sent him to the coal fields."

"Thomas, Ian's brother," said Zakhart, motioning at Ian. "If you and your fiancée would kindly lead us to the coal fields, we'll search for Thomas and gather some samples to take back. Then we'll try and get close enough to Ross to find out what's holding him here—and whether he's still human. If he's still human, we'll have to find a way to slip all of you, including Ross, out of here."

"That's workable," said Knox, standing behind Heather, hands on her shoulders. "First, we find Thomas then we check out Ross. What's the egress route?"

Zakhart raised an eyebrow. "Egress?"

"Exit strategy. How the hell do we get out of here?"

Everyone fell silent, faces lined with concentration.

"What about the carts?" Gemma asked.

Ian turned to stare at his fiancée. "What do you mean, love?"

Gemma's eyes brightened. "Everyone gets a cart. There are always mounds of dirt that must be taken outside and dumped. We place Thomas in one, Ross in the other, and fill all the carts with dirt. Then we push them outside and dump them."

"That's brilliant," Ian replied, hugging Gemma.

"Yeah, I like it," said Knox. "No one would pay any attention. When Zakhart and I entered the cavern, we passed a bunch of carts hauling off dirt."

"Agreed then," said Zakhart. "Ian, will you and Gemma lead us to the coal fields and identify your brother?"

"Certainly," said Ian. "There's a bell that rings, signaling when loads of dirt need to be carted away. One bell means dirt from the tunnels and two bells means carting loads from the coal fields below."

"We'll wait for two bells then," said Zakhart. "How frequent are the calls?"

"The single chimes happen all the time." A single bell rang again and Gemma smiled, pointing toward the hallways. "Alas, there is always dirt to carry away."

For a long time, they waited. The single bell rings were frequent, always followed by footsteps in the hallway outside the small chamber. Ian and Gemma sat together on their cot, whispering to each other. Zakhart and Knox paced the room, their voices low as they talked about how to increase training. Heather leaned against the wall near the door, her uneasiness mixing with guilt. She shouldn't have kissed Knox. She loved Ross.

She felt so confused.

"Seems like every day, Avana and her people lead a few more souls to the tree," said Zakhart.

Knox nodded. "Yeah, she's been great about that and about getting people outside to train. Even a few more new ones."

"Sadly, the soulstalkers are getting to them faster than we can," said Zakhart. "Avana and her people are now camping the entry point. The soulstalkers don't see them in their smoky form, so it's been easy to scare them off. For now. That won't last much longer."

"Where is the entry point?" Knox asked. "I've never really known."

"There are two trails that cross each other. One trail to the poppy fields and one trail into the soulstalker warrens. That's where all souls enter the Between."

Heather remembered that first night so vividly. The wind had been so strong, whipping through the tall, wispy grasses, and the forest had been so dark. The trees were all bare and looked gnarled and terrifying with their stark black shadows hanging over the grasses. She'd been so disoriented when those black wings soared past her, casting a rough, wavy shadow across her. She'd felt so lost and so scared. Until the amber lights winked through the forest like fireflies and moved toward her.

She smiled, tears springing to her eyes when she remembered Ross' tall, handsome frame and his light sandy hair. How he'd beaten down the soulstalker that had captured her. And with bright eyes and gentle hands, he'd led her to the great tree's safety. Asking nothing in return. Yet he'd given her everything he had to give—including his heart—while she was here.

Guilt burned through her, making her stomach ache. She'd given him her heart in return and then, when things got rough, she'd gone and kissed Knox. Why? She loved Ross with all her heart. How could she do that to him when there was still a chance to save him? They'd only had minutes to say what they carried in their hearts before entering the Spiral. There hadn't been time for promises and platitudes.

She felt awful now.

Behind her, the bell chimed twice. Twice!

She scrambled to her feet as Knox and Zakhart stopped pacing and turned toward the hallway.

"That was two bells," said Zakhart.

Ian and Gemma were on their feet now. "That's for the coal fields," said Ian. "We'd better hurry to make sure we get inside down there. Hurry!"

Ian motioned Knox to follow him down the hallway. In a few moments, they had two carts squeaking into the hallway. They handed them off to Gemma and Heather and disappeared into the storage room to get more until all five of them had carts.

"This way," said Gemma, pushing her cart down the hall as she turned right.

Heather and the others followed.

thirteen

. . .

HEATHER FOLLOWED GEMMA DOWN A LONG,
sloping tunnel, turning a sharp corner into a dark, serpentine cavern
that ended in a metal platform. Gemma swung the squeaky metal
gate open and directed the carts into the huge lift. It was wide
enough for three carts, so Heather helped Gemma squeeze three
carts into the space. Knox shuffled onto the platform beside Heather
and Gemma pressed the button.

The lift dropped, sending Heather's stomach into freefall as they
left Ian and Zakhart behind when the platform lurched downward,
dropping deeper into the rocky, dark cavern.

She gripped the cart with both hands, closing her eyes as the
platform creaked and swayed, a dull moan filling the dark shaft. The
air smelled dirty. Gritty. Like an old, dark basement.

It seemed like forever until the platform thumped against hard-
packed ground, jostling the three carts. One nearly turned over, but
Knox managed to keep it upright.

They pushed all three carts out into the dimly lit, high-ceiling
chamber, the air dusty and cool. Curved rock walls had been carved
out of stone. In the distance, the clink of pickaxes was a sharp, steady

rhythm as Gemma closed the rickety platform gate and pressed a button, sending the metal platform upward, out of the coal fields. It creaked and swayed until it finally lurched to a stop somewhere above them.

Heather listened to the thumps and creaks and finally, a buzz as the rickety platform lurched downward again, back toward the dark coal fields.

Knox stood beside her, watching with crossed arms as the platform swayed and groaned as it descended. He seemed focused on every sound, his gaze snapping to a flutter of movement, footsteps, and voices that echoed through the cavernous chamber. He was in a defensive stance, body like an over-wound wire, eyes scanning ahead and behind. Even through the blousy grey clothing that draped their bodies, his muscles were corded, jaw tight.

Heather understood. This place made her skin crawl, too. She felt like her every move was being watched, demons lurking in every corner.

The rickety platform groaned, gears and pulleys squeaking, Zakhart and Ian looking worried through the thin wire shell that surrounded the shaft.

It seemed like forever until at last, Zakhart's brilliant, pumpkin-orange eyes appeared in the coal field's dim light. The pale angel's eyes always had an inner glow that calmed Heather. She let out a breath as the platform stopped and Ian clamored out with his cart, Zakhart stumbling out behind him with another cart.

"All right," said Gemma. "We are all here." She pointed ahead to the right where a massive metal gate stood about thirty feet away. "Let's go inside and collect the rocks."

Knox laid a hand on Gemma's arm. "Wait, what exactly are we walking into, Gemma? How many demons? How many slaves?" He glanced back at the platform, pointing. "Is this the only egress point?"

"Sorry," said Ian, stepping over to Gemma. "We don't know a lot about the coal fields. But there is always a detail of demons down here, so be on the lookout for them."

"Sì," said Gemma. "That means about eight or so demons. The little ones. At times, there are a few of the larger ones. Two sometimes three."

Knox's face turned pensive, his brow furrowing as he nodded. "Okay, that covers the known patrols. How many workers? Is there some sort of foreman—someone in charge besides the larger demons down here?"

Gemma laid her hand against her face, her gaze becoming far away. Heather could almost see her counting.

"Usually, there is a soul they've turned against his or her people as the foreman," said Gemma as she leaned on her cart handles.

"The demons gloat whenever they are successful in turning one of us," Ian added.

"Like Ross?" Heather asked. "Do they force him to work down here? To oversee other souls?"

Ian sighed. "No, Heather, I'm afraid it's worse than that. He started down here. I saw him several times, shouting at souls to work harder and snapping a whip at us. Then later, he wasn't there. When I asked, I found out he'd been promoted, but I didn't know what that meant. There was no one to ask either."

Worse than Thraecius. Would that have been the former gladiator's fate, too, if she and Ross hadn't come here and rescued him? These demons seemed to enjoy pitting souls against each other.

"Ian," Knox said in a wary voice. "Do they know that you and Thomas are brothers?"

Ian's eyes widened and he shook his head. "Oh, definitely not."

"That's good news," said Knox. "All right, let's break up into two groups once we get past that gate and search for him."

"Agreed," said Ian. "Gemma and I must split up, to help identify him."

Knox nodded, pointing at Gemma. "Gemma, you stick with Heather and Zakhart. I'll go with Ian."

"Yes," said Ian. "You'll be safe with the angel. Knox and I can handle ourselves well enough."

"First group to find him," Heather replied, "send up a trill as a signal to head for the platform."

"A what?" said Zakhart.

Heather made a high-pitched sound, rolling her tongue. "Like that. Some sort of bird sound."

Ian imitated Heather's trill and Knox whistled a bird-like chirp.

"Perfect," she said, smiling. "Let's find Thomas."

The five of them pushed their carts toward the huge gate. It was an arched metal frame built into the rocky walls. The door was about eight feet tall and looked cobbled together from random sheets of metal and lots of thick, rusty metal bars. The gate was ajar.

Zakhart pushed the metal gate open. It creaked, rasping, a moan echoing as they pushed their carts into a small but cavernous chamber, rock on all sides. At least two dozen souls swung pickaxes at the rocky walls.

Heather counted the demons as she followed Gemma toward a pile of rock about ten feet away. Six. Seven demons. They were short, not even five feet tall. Thin bodies that reminded her of lizards as they scampered past, moving toward the souls swinging pickaxes. Completely ignoring Heather and Gemma. The demons picked and prodded at the souls, shouting orders as Gemma maneuvered her cart beside the pile of shiny black stone.

"Zakhart," Heather whispered, leaning close to him as she positioned her cart. "This is the stone I mentioned."

"This?" he asked, pointing.

She nodded, picking up a large piece of shiny stone, and placing it in her cart. She grabbed another one, about the size of a watermelon, and another one the size of her palm. After placing the big stone in her cart, she handed the small one to Zakhart who quickly tucked it into his robes.

The three of them loaded stones, glancing across the expanse to locate Ian and Knox who'd gone to the other side. Gemma motioned ahead, toward the next bin of stones.

"He's not here," Gemma whispered. "Let's move ahead."

Heather waited for two wiry grey demons to sprint past before she wheeled her cart around and pushed it behind Gemma, following her toward the next group of souls. Zakhart pushed his cart a few feet behind her.

The three of them trundled toward four bins and collected more stones as they hunted for Thomas, but he wasn't at any of these pickup points. As they approached a fifth bin, two large demons stormed toward them.

They weren't grey and leathery-skinned. Taller than the grey demons, they were broader-shouldered, black eyes flecked red. They lacked the almost animal-like snouts of the smaller grey demons and thick, clammy hides. No, their skin looked spongy, fleshy, less like cold-blooded amphibians. The softer, ruddy skin stretched over more human-shaped skulls. Their skin had a hint of the patterned appearance of the smaller ones and soot black hair that crowned their larger heads. Their eyes were devoid of any emotion.

"What are those things?" Zakhart hissed as he stopped his cart.

"Keep moving," Gemma whispered. "And don't stare."

Zakhart complied, pushing his cart behind Heather as the bigger demons swept past them. Heather and the others parked their carts beside the fifth bin and began loading the shiny black rocks onto the carts.

"Why would you ask that, Zakhart?" Heather asked, placing a large rock on Zakhart's cart. "You've probably seen every demon there is."

"I have," he said, his brow furrowed. "And none of them look like that. I've never seen those creatures before."

Heather stared at him. "What do you mean?" she asked, shaking her head.

"Whatever those things are," said Zakhart in a sharp whisper, "they aren't like the demons in the original blueprints. I've studied most of the Maker's schematics and I've seen all the creatures projected evolutions—including the demonic ones. Those things are not in the plan."

Heather's eyes widened. Maker? Schematics? What did all of that mean? And what did he mean by evolutions? Did angels and demons grow and change like humans and animals? She couldn't even wrap her brain around that.

"Angels and demons—evolve?" she asked in a quiet voice.

Zakhart nodded, touching Heather's arm. "Yes, Heather. The Maker never intended for guardians, stewards, and other balancing forces to remain static when everything else around them changed and grew. So that capacity was built into every ethereal creature—even demons. But changes to the schematics and their projected trajectories were only made by the Maker." The pale angel ran his fingers through his flowing white locks, his gaze on his cart. "I don't know what's going on here, but my angel senses are telling me that all of this was hidden beneath the Between for a reason. Along with the demons' plan."

"I thought they'd hidden below ground for a reason, Zakhart," said Heather, glancing behind her at the large demons as they disappeared through the distant gate.

"Mulciber hid these creatures he's been creating," said Zakhart. "Bet he never dreamed an ethereal being would discover his changes among a bunch of lost souls."

"Why is the Between so hidden and overlooked?" Heather asked, feeling forgotten.

Guess no one cared about humans who committed suicide. People that were sick and unable to find their way home again.

"The angels demanded it," said Zakhart. "It was important that there was an isolated place, cut off from the other realms' influences."

Heather sighed, picking up more rocks and loading them. "We tried to be like everyone else, Zakhart. We tried really hard. But every day was a fight against our own brains. Every day, it bombarded me with messages that I'm a waste of oxygen. That I'm worthless. Not worth the effort. Or it would ninja attack me at three in the morning when I'd wake up in tears, shaking because I felt so worthless and alone and couldn't ever imagine a reason why someone would want to be with me. And then my body would join the fight, leeching away my energy so I couldn't get out of bed. I'd sleep for hours, hoping like hell I wouldn't dream. Or have to face other people as that girl."

Zakhart moved beside her, sliding his arm around her shoulders. "No, no—you misunderstand me. The Between is isolated to protect already fragile souls."

"By allowing soulstalkers to hunt us as prey?" Heather replied.

He shook his head. "No, of course not! In the beginning, the Between was only forests and poppies. And Death. She walked the paths, after a time, to clear out the souls that had long given up. The souls whose lights had begun to fade. Those who no longer sought the Spiral of life."

"So there was a time when the Between was actually safe?" Heather asked, dropping shiny rocks into all three carts.

"Yes, it was quiet and safe," said Zakhart in a wistful tone. "And beautiful. Until the physical world changed and the Between became full of lost souls that didn't want to leave, didn't want to move on. They hid from Death and built structures, pretending to go through the motions of life. Death was overwhelmed, so she created some help."

"Soulstalkers," said Heather, shuddering at the thought of anyone willingly creating those things.

"Yes, Death created them as her agents, to help her prod the souls into action. At first, it was to spur souls to action, but most just hid deeper in the forests. And the numbers of souls grew even higher."

"Why so many lost souls?" Gemma asked.

Zakhart bowed his head. "We were still trying to understand why when Death violated the Maker's decree and created more and more shadow creatures. more sand runners gathered more poppy dust for more soulstalkers until soulstalkers gained the power to grant the final sleep. This concentration of shadow creatures drew demons. A few were to be expected, but not the numbers I've seen in this cavern. Especially now. Bit by bit, the demons eroded Death's control of the shadow creatures. And shadows themselves. Upsetting everything."

"These demons have created something organized and progressive down here," said Gemma, loading more shiny stones.

"That's what I find chilling, Gemma," said Zakhart. "It's more than the settlement or crude compound that was here previously. That I reported to my superiors. It's become almost a military operation."

"And they're experimenting on humans," Heather said, walking away from the bin to take hold of her cart. "From the looks of these other creatures, I'd say they were experimenting on demons, too."

Gemma's eyes widened. "Sì, like Hitler experimented on humans."

Zakhart winced. "A terrible image, but it fits. These demons appear to be creating more advanced demons. By stealing human design, they are trying to blend these demons in with the humans beyond the Between. Maybe that's the purpose of this Mechanism. I just don't yet know what it does. For everyone's sake, we need to lay this place bare and discover what they're doing here. Before something terrible happens."

"Zakhart," Heather replied. "Do you think that Ross is part of their experiments?"

For several, long moments, Zakhart stared at the ground. Finally, he lifted his gaze to her face, nodding.

"Yes, Heather. I think he's part of their testing. From the looks of those larger demons, I'd guess that they're trying to merge human form with demon form. It's like they've taken key characteristics of humans and somehow—applied them to demons. I don't know how or why they've done this, but I find it very disturbing."

Heather did, too, especially with Ross in their hands.

"Are these things just projecting illusions or are their features real?" Heather asked.

"For the world's sake, I hope they are illusions."

A whip snapped against Heather's thigh. She yelped, whirling around.

Two of the smaller, grey demons with clammy, lizard-like skin glared at her. The one with the whip raised the weapon over its head, pointy snout and steely eyes sparkling in the dim light.

"Stop the slacking and get to work!" the demon shouted.

The other demon hissed and glared at all three of them, pointing toward the carts.

Heather grabbed her cart and wheeled it around, hustling toward the next bin. Gemma yelped as the whip bit into her shoulders. She shoved her cart forward, Zakhart behind her.

The two demons watched until all three of their carts were gathered around the next bin of shiny rocks. One demon turned away, heading across the coalfield toward more carts. The demon with the whip hovered, watching as Heather snatched a big, heavy rock in both hands and heaved it into her cart. Gemma and Zakhart picked up rocks, too, shuffling them into their carts.

Satisfied, it turned away, swinging the whip back and forth as it walked.

Heather glanced ahead, at the rocky wall curving around the expanse. In the center of the chamber, stalactites hung above rubble piled into six-foot mounds. Knox and Ian were in sight now, only three rock bins separating them.

Heather stepped in front of Gemma, blocking the line of sight with the demons so Gemma could look for Thomas. The dusty air clung like a mask against her face, coating her lips and hands with a fine sheen of grit. And it smelled like Grandma Billot's dark basement where Heather used to play as a kid. It made her uneasy—like Grandma's basement. She rubbed her hand across her mouth, wiping away the dust.

"He's not here, either," Gemma whispered, sounding exasperated. "We've almost caught up to Ian. What if they'd done something to him?"

"We'll keep looking," said Zakhart. "We can't give up yet."

He picked up a small, shiny rock and tucked it into a small pouch beneath the silky folds of his shirt.

Heather and Gemma returned to the bin, emptying rocks into the three carts. After they'd emptied the bin, Heather nudged her cart forward, Zakhart and Gemma following, and approached the next bin.

Knox and Ian were much closer now. Knox stared at her from his cart, winking when Heather's gaze met his. She smiled, nodding at him. He looked boyish with that mop of dusty brown curls, intense eyes so blue in the thin wash of light.

The next bin was only half full of shiny stones.

Heather and Zakhart worked slowly loading the rocks while Gemma walked around each soul digging rock at the walls.

"Heather!" Gemma whispered. "Come quick!"

Heather rushed to Gemma's side as she pointed toward a man slumped against the wall, struggling to swing his pickaxe. He fumbled it up onto his shoulder and used his whole body to swing it against the thick, rock walls. The metal pickaxe clinked against a pocket of shiny black rock, barely nicking it.

"Is that him?" Heather asked, motioning Zakhart over.

"Sì," she cried, clapping her hands together as her eyes filled with tears. "That's Thomas."

Heather turned and let out a trill. Several of the workers paused to stare at her a moment then returned to the drudgery of digging. She watched them struggle and her chest ached.

"Zakhart," she whispered.

The pale angel stepped toward her, leaning down as Heather whispered in his ear. She nodded toward the workers.

"Isn't there any way to free these people? It's not right. These people were already despondent when they arrived in the Between. And to be preyed on by demons, forced to work like this...it just isn't right. That's not any kind of second chance to me."

Zakhart lifted his hand into the air and a glowing white cloud of light appeared in his palm. He blew softly on it and it rose into the dank air, dissipating into a mist that fell across the workers in the cavern. The glowing particles landed against their bodies and clothes, flickering a bit, and then went dark. Only two or three of the workers had a slight gleam of light to them as they hacked at the walls with their pickaxes.

Heather frowned. "What was that?"

The pale angel turned to her, his expression softening. "Heather, not everyone who takes their life is a lost, desperate soul that gave up. Many souls in the Between did great evil in their lives. When the time came to deal with the consequences, they ended their lives to avoid punishment. Incarceration. Instead, they took the easy path out of their situation. They came here without learning from their actions, without feeling remorse, and with no intention of changing anything about themselves. Without remorse and a change of heart, they will never leave the Between."

"Why?" Heather asked.

"Because the Spiral will never appear to them. This refusal to change or show remorse made them easy prey for demons. There's little I can do for them."

"You didn't even try?" said Heather, shaking her head.

Zakhart's face pinched with anger, his face flushed as he crossed his arms.

"Of course, I tried," he snapped. "We all tried. We showed them over and over what they did and why it was wrong. They ignored us. They ignored what they did. And I'm not perfect." He bowed his head, sighing. "All of us strive for white wings and robes, but you wouldn't believe how many shades of ivory and cream exist before reaching true white."

Gemma pulled her cart over against the rocky wall and dropped to her knees beside Thomas.

"What does that mean?" Heather asked.

Zakhart motioned her toward the carts and she followed him as he spoke.

"When I first came here, I met a man. He was in his thirties, pudgy, balding and he looked lost and alone, wringing his hands as he hid in the tall grasses. I towered over him as I flew into the grass and crouched in front of him. He threw his arms over his face, shouting, and begging for mercy. I took his hands and spoke to him in a soothing voice, telling him that everything would be all right. That I would help him find a safe place. Then I asked why he'd taken his life."

Heather stared at the pale angel. "What did he say?"

"He stuttered through an explanation in his native tongue and I listened, expecting a sad tale and someone who needed my help. And he didn't disappoint. He told me that he'd been a kind and gentle man who'd loved his family, that he'd done his best to take care of them, but it just got too difficult and he couldn't handle it anymore. So he hung himself."

Heather frowned. "That's so sad."

Zakhart bared his teeth and pounded his fist into his hand. He was so angry that he was shaking. Heather had never seen him angry like this before.

"Sad? It was sad all right. Because it was all a lie. I looked into his soul and the blackness that met my eyes made my stomach lurch. His family? They were four teenage girls he'd kidnapped off the streets and chained up in a spare bedroom for twelve years."

"What?" Heather cried. "Are you serious?"

Zakhart nodded. "He fathered four children by these girls that he'd stolen from other families. Tore them apart for his selfish, sick fantasies. Every time he told his lies, he bought into them a little deeper each time. But I looked into his thoughts, his memories. He joked with his roommate about it. He was proud of what he'd done. No remorse at all. And he claimed that he'd never be caught. But one day, one of the women got free and he was arrested. In custody, he told his sob story, but no one listened. He was convicted and sent to prison. Not even a month later, he killed himself. Even in the presence of an angel, he refused to tell the truth." The pale angel sighed, his arms falling against his sides. "I left him in the tall grass and watched as a soulstalker carried him off. That cost me a shade of white on my wings and a reprimand for giving up too soon."

Heather saw the remorse in Zakhart's eyes. "Lots of regret over that?" she asked.

"Not at all," he replied, his gaze darting to Heather's face. "I'd do it again if faced with a soul as black as his. But I feel terrible for those young women." His eyes burned with anger still, his mouth taut, jawline sharpening. "This man was proud of what he'd done and no matter how sorry he claimed to be, his soul and his mind showed me otherwise. I was told later that another angel rescued him from the shadows and spent a great deal of time with the man."

"What happened to him?" Heather asked.

"The other angel wasted months on the man, but the man never stopped lying. He never took responsibility for what he did to those girls, so the other angel ended up washing his hands of the man."

Heather motioned at the other workers. "So, you're saying there are people like that man right here? Working the coal fields?"

Zakhart nodded. "They're everywhere, Heather. Blackest souls I've ever seen. By choice. Most of them are in the Red City."

Heather backed away toward Gemma who had taken the pickaxe out of Thomas' hand. She noticed that a faint gleam of light clung to Thomas' clothes.

"This one shouldn't be here," said Zakhart.

The sound of footsteps made Heather turn. Ian and Knox approached, their carts parked beside the bin. Knox was behind him, watching both sides of the coalfield for demons.

"Thomas!" Ian cried, rushing past to kneel beside the exhausted man. He clasped his brother to his chest. "I've found you at last."

"Ian?" the younger man said in a gravelly voice.

"Sssh," Ian hissed, getting the man to his feet. "That's a good lad. We need to get you to safety."

Zakhart reached out and laid his hand on Thomas' chest, closing his eyes. A surge of light swirled from his palm into Thomas. The ray of light made a deep, scritching sound as it scrubbed across Thomas' chest and limbs. Static electricity popped and crackled as the light moved across the young man.

For several seconds, the light pulsed over Thomas who seemed to grow weaker. Ian had to hold him up. At last, Thomas heaved a sigh that deepened into a sputtering cough. He spit up some sticky black stuff, his stomach lurching. It spilled onto the rocky floor and turned into an inky black puddle, a sour, sulphury scent in the air.

Gemma and Knox turned away. Heather flinched, covering her nose.

"What is that?" Ian cried, turning his head away from Thomas.

"I'm not sure," said Zakhart. "But I had to get him to expel it before we take him out of here. Otherwise, the demons would have easily pulled him back into this cavern if I hadn't."

Thomas moaned, his knees weak. He began to shake, teeth chattering as his face turned from shadowy to pasty white.

Zakhart nodded toward the distant metal gate ahead, helping Ian hold up his brother. "Let's get these carts out of here. Ian, get Thomas behind one of those carts. Gemma, you and Heather take another one."

Heather and Gemma hurried toward the full carts and struggled to turn them around. Thomas walked between Zakhart and Ian toward the remaining carts. Ian directed his younger brother to a cart and stood beside him. Thomas steadied himself, legs and arms still shaking, and took hold of the handle.

"You gonna make it, kid?" Knox asked from the cart in front.

"Quite," Thomas said, nodding. "Let's get on, shall we?"

Knox waved his hand, motioning for everyone to move out. The carts creaked and thumped over the hard-packed ground as they moved at a brisk pace toward the gate.

Three clutches of grey demons skulked along the edge of the coal fields, whips in hand as they passed. The demons threatened the souls digging with pickaxes, swinging whips in sharp snaps over the souls' heads, voices throaty and grating.

"Get to work! Faster!" one demon shouted in a raspy voice.

"There are worse things than the coal fields!" another called, snapping its whip. "Faster!"

Heather winced. What was worse than this place? Were there parts of the Between she hadn't seen before?

None of the demons even turned toward them as they pushed five carts full of stones toward the gate. And the lift beyond it.

"When we get up to the main level," said Gemma. "I'll show you where we dump the rocks."

Knox shoved open the gate and pushed his cart through, Heather and Gemma close behind. They drew closer together and headed toward the lift. It took some arranging, but they fit three carts into the lift. It rocked and creaked as it made its way up out of the coal fields.

Heather felt awful as the platform rose, leaving Zakhart, Ian, and Thomas behind. Thomas slumped between Ian and Zakhart, his face pale and faded, eyes so deep and shadowed in their sockets. He looked almost skeletal, like something had drawn away his soul's life force, a breath at a time.

Did Ross look like this now? Or worse?

She felt the heat of Knox's hand on her shoulder, squeezing. Reaching up, she folded her hand over his as the platform moved upward.

"Don't give up, kid," he whispered.

Somehow, he knew what she'd been thinking as she stared at Thomas.

"Thanks," she said, letting go of his hand.

When the lift door opened, Knox pushed his cart out and helped the others get their carts off the lift platform.

This level was crawling with demons!

Gemma closed the lift door and pressed a button. With a sharp buzz, the platform clunked downward again, toward the others.

Demons scrutinized them as they passed, slowing down, and staring.

Knox and Heather stalled, pretending to move rocks around in the carts to keep them balanced as the platform thunked and clamored back up from the coal fields.

She could barely breathe as the demons crowded through the

tunnel and passed by the carts. More and more of the larger, angrier ones with spongy skin that was an odd washed-out color. Some looked like cooling lava, others like sunbaked clay. One or two looked pinkish almost putty-colored like a shaved rabbit. Their skin looked clammy, almost shiny like a wet lizard.

Only when everyone had returned from the coal fields and gotten their carts off the platform did Heather's tension begin to dissipate. Her hands stopped shaking when all five carts moved down the tunnel. Away from the coal fields. And the demons.

Gemma led the way this time, waving everyone forward as she and Heather shoved their carts in motion.

Heather kept her gaze focused on the cart, not making eye contact with any of the demons, but she couldn't help looking at every soul that she passed, hoping to see Ross. Gemma kept her head down, too as they moved through the crowded tunnel.

"Up ahead, to the right, is a short tunnel with a chute at the end," said Gemma. "That's where we dump the rocks."

Heather nodded, her grip like steel on the handle as a short, dim-lit tunnel appeared ahead. No more than ten feet away. Gemma picked up the pace, Knox and the others matching it, wheels clunking and squeaking.

Gemma was almost running as she veered right with her cart.

Heather pulled hard, maneuvering her heavy cart into the tunnel. A wooden ramp led into the downward-sloping tunnel, wide enough for three carts at a time. The cart's wheels thumped over it onto hard-packed soil as they passed two carts coming from the opposite direction.

Heather counted each cart as it rolled over the ramp and looked at each soul that passed. An old man with wild, white hair.

Thump. Knox was through.

A middle-aged man with dark hair and dark eyes, a blond woman beside him. Shadowed faces smeared with soot.

Thunk. Ian was in the tunnel.

Two young men, one with red hair and one with light brown hair and a beard, shuffled ahead of two lanky teenage boys. One had shaved hair and sad blue eyes. The other was dark-skinned with thick black hair. Their faces were shadowed, eyes hollowed, cheeks sunken. Like Thomas. They were barely visible as the tunnel darkened.

Thump. Crunch. A sharp cry. Thomas.

C'mon, Zakhart! Hurry!

Heather gritted her teeth and tightened her grip on the cart handle, listening for the last cart.

Four more carts passed, an old woman and two younger men with black hair and dark faces. The old woman plodded ahead of the cart, the two younger ones pushing it. Their eyes were downcast, faces lined, and shadowed. A man and woman pushed the third one. Followed by a teenage girl at the last one. They were pale and shadowed, their forms faded like over-washed jeans.

Bump, thud. The final cart entered the tunnel. She smiled. Zakhart.

Heather couldn't help but wonder about these souls as they passed by. Could they be saved? Or were they truly lost, like the ones Zakhart showed her in the coal fields?

At the end of the tunnel was a thick, rusty metal door. It looked oily and smeared with black sooty splotches, like burn marks. Gemma stopped the cart about a foot from the door and grabbed the long bar handle mounted vertically on the metal door.

As the metal door opened, a blast of heat roiled out of the opening, flames leaping and crackling.

Heather froze, heat tingling against her cheeks, baking into the folds of her grey clothes, and soaking into her feet. The massive fire that burned behind it was so bright that her eyes watered.

"Heather!" a sharp voice shouted in her ear.

The flames were so tall, churning, and crackling with shades of vivid oranges and fierce yellows edged white. Somewhere in the tangles of flames, the bright blue fire flickered. So alive. So vibrant. It made her feel alive again.

But underneath that warmth was a putrid smell. Worse than six-day-old tuna salad. Worse than a bloated opossum carcass on the side of the road.

Her face screwed up against the foul, rotten stench, but she couldn't turn away from the warmth against her skin.

Like a towel hot from the dryer. So comforting. So peaceful.

"HEATHER!"

Something shook her hard, turning her body away from the door. She closed her eyes a moment, the sudden chill cutting through her. She opened her eyes, staring into Zakhart's fearful gaze.

"What?" she snapped, confused, and hating the cold that wrapped around her body again.

Zakhart bit his lip, his face a mask of worry. "Do you know what that is?"

Heather frowned. "No. What?"

Only then did she realize that Zakhart was shaking.

"Zakhart? What's the matter with you?"

He turned away, hands over his face, shoulders shaking. The wings beneath his clothes twitched, wanting release. He leaned against the wall and she followed him as the others emptied their carts into the roaring flames behind the door. She laid her hand on his arm.

"What's wrong?" she asked the pale angel, shaking her head.

"That's not a furnace, Heather," he said, his eyes full of fear.

"What is it?" she asked.

He could barely speak. "It's where...where...they come from. The demons."

Heather's eyes widened. "What do you mean?"

"It's a door into their realm, Heather," he said, an ache in his voice. He pulled one of the shiny stones off a cart. "And this?" he said, holding it up to her. "This isn't coal. It's fuel though—like coal. And they are mining it out of those cavern walls."

"What is it, Zakhart?" she asked.

In the fire's glow, the shiny substance twinkled like it was compacted from a swath of stars out of the heavens. It looked strange and otherworldly. Dread trembled through her stomach.

"Those souls mining below? The demons slowly suck away the life force from their souls as they work. Until every bit is gone. Leaving primordial bits of shadow that harden into a shiny, rock-hard substance."

Heather felt sick now, a deep ache rumbling through her.

Zakhart gritted his teeth, tears running down his face. "They burn spent souls for fuel, Heather," he cried. "As fuel!"

Someone shouted. Footsteps clattering through the tunnel.

Heather turned as a grey-skinned demon leaped out of the flames and skittered into the tunnel. Its skin smoked and burned, charred and smoldering as it loped down the tunnel and rushed into the main hallway.

She turned back to Zakhart. He still had the stone between his fingers, holding it up in the dim light as it flickered with hellfire.

"They're also making demons from the remains of souls," he said in a defeated voice and hung his head.

Zakhart's voice carried through the deathly quiet tunnel, shuddering through Heather.

Something terrible had happened to the Between. Horrible things had been simmering here since the first time she'd passed through this strange place. Until now, the creatures of light had been unaware of the dark factory churning below the lost souls that were struggling to survive their first deaths. A dark factory that was quietly harvesting these lost souls, luring them from the Spiral and the final sleep, and pumping out a shadow force to rival the heavens.

The look of devastation on Zakhart's face told her that the light had a terrible fight on its hands. A battle of ethereal proportions was coming. And all the world's lost souls were caught in the middle.

It was so much worse than Heather had ever imagined.

fourteen

. . .

"LET'S GET OUT OF HERE," Zakhart whispered. "Now!"

"We can't," Gemma cried. "All these carts are still full."

Zakhart whirled around, those orange eyes turning otherworldly, glowing with terrible fury.

Heather knew not to argue with an angry angel—even a pale one.

Zakhart lifted his hands into the air, summoning white bolts of light in each. He flung them at all the carts, turning the shiny rocks to dust. He blew out a breath of white fire that churned into a whirlwind that swept up the dust, turning it into rays of light that floated away.

"I've released all of those souls," he said. "I'll let Puriel sort them out for now. But the archangels of death: Azrael, Sidriel, Turiel, and Sariel need to know." Zakhart's eyes narrowed. "Believe me, they will be furious when they hear about it. Especially Azrael."

Heather saw the pain on Zakhart's face every time he stared at that metal door. Finally, he turned away like he couldn't look at it anymore and grabbed an empty cart. Heather and the others each grabbed a cart and pushed it out of the dim-lit tunnel.

AFTER THEY'D PUT THE CARTS BACK IN PLACE, THEY ALL huddled in the cramped space of Ian and Gemma's slave quarters. Thomas lay on a rickety wooden cot, only a thin grey mattress on it. He still looked weak, but already, that faded look of his body began to sharpen and grow more solid.

Zakhart was distant and detached, staring off into a haze of what looked like troubled thoughts as Ian took care of his younger brother. Knox fidgeted beside Gemma, talking quietly about the layout of the compound. He looked focused on developing an escape plan.

Heather tried to focus on the escape plan, on Zakhart's troubled demeanor, and Thomas, but all she could think about was Ross. The man she loved was nothing like the person she'd seen in that tunnel. Enraged and spouting orders.

She'd seen so many horrible things since she'd been back in the Between. Felt so many conflicted emotions. The entire time, she'd feared that this whole battle could end with her losing Ross. At the time, she'd listened to that tiny voice inside her head, the one telling her that the angels believed she could save Ross. That they wouldn't drag her back to this desolation and hopelessness if they hadn't thought Ross could be saved.

Now, she'd never felt so lost.

Heather walked over to Zakhart and slid her arm around his waist in a gentle hug.

"I don't know what to say right now," she said in a quiet voice. "Other than I'm here if you want to talk."

"Neither do I, Heather," he said in a tired voice and rubbed the bridge of his nose with thumb and forefinger. "I've failed the very people I swore to protect. I've spent so much time in the Between, hoping to save the souls here, but I never even noticed the hive of demons forming here." He sighed. "As a guardian angel, I really suck."

"Zakhart, no!" Her grip around his waist tightened. "Without you, Ross and I would have never found the Spiral. You saved me, Zakhart! And Ross. And so many others by coming to the Between to help. And by coming here, you found this horrible place."

He didn't look convinced. She nudged him with her elbow.

"Just think about what would happen if no one knew. Or tried to help. You're the only one who bothered to come here. Don't forget that. None of the angels wanted to be here, remember?"

Zakhart's face darkened, the shadows thick across his pearlescent face, furrowing across his smooth brow.

"You're right, Heather. But none of the others in the realm of light even know about this. Razasha and I first came here as part of our training. It seemed like the best place to start. The archangels of death don't know what's happening here. They need to be told. And they need to eliminate this primordial spirit of Death. Replace her with the army of compassionate angels of death that cross humans over with love and patience." He sighed. "Most of them anyway."

"You were in training when you came here?" Heather asked.

The pale angel nodded. "Razasha and I were brand new stewards in the ranks of Guardian angels. Former Watchers. I started coming here to help the humans that had given up. To understand what happened here. How souls end up here and...how we could prevent souls from remaining in the Between."

He turned around, facing the small room, his gaze softening as he watched the other souls huddling around Thomas.

"I brought other lesser angels here, too—the few who seemed interested. Sadly, there weren't many." The hint of a smile rose and fell on his lips. "I even dragged some of my superiors here."

Heather frowned. "How'd that go?"

Zakhart shook his head, rubbing his hand against his forehead. "Not well. They said it was...functioning as expected. Another angel afraid to tangle with Death herself. An ancient primordial spirit from when angels and humans were new creations. Our angels of death would have a lot to say about this setup. They wouldn't be afraid to help. And the Archangel of Death, Azrael will be furious when I tell him about this place."

That unearthly creature coming at her with wild eyes and a razor-sharp scythe had been terrifying. Having angels handling human deaths made much more sense.

"Death became part of the Between and over time, angels forgot about the entire realm, including any souls that ended up here. It's appalling, but the work of seraphim is not to be questioned. Right or wrong, they answer only to the Maker."

Seraphim? She had no idea about angel hierarchies. "What are seraphim?" she asked.

Zakhart's pumpkin-orange eyes widened. "Forgive me," he said. "You know nothing about my realm, do you? Seraphim are the highest order of angels—except for Throne angels that guard the Maker. They govern all other angels, including the lowest rungs: Watchers and Stewards. You know us as Guardian Angels."

So, Zakhart saw himself as the lowest-ranking of angels. Did that mean he had no say in what happened here? Or about the other Guardian angels with him? Like Razasha and Halea? And the others like him?

"Is that what you and Razasha were training for?" Heather asked. "To be Guardian angels?"

Zakhart nodded. "This time, Razasha and I came prepared. When we brought you back, we brought our teams. Halea is part of Razasha's team, hoping to become a steward soon. We've been training the team to help souls *before* they get here and how to help the ones already here." He bowed his head, his voice tired again. "It seemed like the best way to do the greatest amount of good."

"It's a good thing you did, Zakhart," said Heather, patting his arm.

He nodded. His face lightened, a slight smile curving upward.

"Maybe there's still time to squash the demon assault?"

"There is," she said. "There has to be."

It was nothing more than a gut feeling, but she'd always trusted her gut. She wouldn't change that now.

Zakhart hugged her back.

"What do you think the demons have done to Ross?" she asked, hoping he might have some idea what they'd done to him.

"Oh, Heather," he said. "I'm so afraid for Ross."

"Why?" she asked with a gasp.

A pained expression rose on Zakhart's moon-pale face. "What if they've devoured his essence and are using an illusion of him to manage the other lost souls."

A cold chill rushed over her.

"Maybe they have him toiling away in some dark corner of this cavern where he'll never be found—like Thomas. Or they have control of him, using him like they used Thraecius. There's no telling what's happened to Ross. All of the possibilities are bad, I'm afraid. Very bad."

Heather could only nod, turning away, her emotions too raw to speak. She folded her arms against her chest and walked away.

"Heather," he called, "I'm sorry. I wish I could give you better news."

She nodded, holding her rage and grief inside as she slumped into the corner and folded herself into a protective ball.

In a few moments, Knox was bending down beside her, a hand on her shoulder.

"Rough news?" he asked, dropping down on the floor. He slid his arms around her. She buried her face against his chest, shaking, and he put his arms around her, holding her.

"I'm here, kid," he said. "You're not alone."

She swallowed the raw sobs clawing through her lungs and scraping their way up her throat. She was shaking, so cold that she ached all over.

Knox held her until exhaustion had softened her grief.

"I gave up a perfectly good life to find him, Knox," she said with a moan. "I gave up everything he sacrificed himself for and from the beginning, it just wasn't enough. And I can't stand it."

Knox leaned against the wall, his arms tightening around her.

"Sometimes we give our all and nothing changes. Like some of my buddies in Afghanistan. They gave their all. Some of them are buried far, far away and they'll never come home again. But they didn't stop to ask if it would be enough. They gave all of themselves freely, trying to protect their homeland from a threat, never imagining how much of it was a lie. Not realizing how much that story would change when they arrived. So they did their best to do the right thing. Even if it meant giving all of themselves to do it."

He lifted her chin and with the tail of his shirt, he wiped away her tears.

"I thought I could save him, Knox," she said, staring up at him, his blue eyes filled with pain and sympathy. "I really thought I could save him."

He smiled. "I know you did. But sometimes our all just isn't enough. Do you know how heroic I think you are?"

"Me?" she cried. "Why would you think I'm heroic?" She sat up, staring at his handsome face and those big blue eyes, her body against his.

"Like you said," he replied, running his fingers through her hair. "You turned everything around and escaped this place. Yet, knowing what this place was, you gave up your new life to come back and save someone you love. That's a hero in my book."

Heather shook her head. She'd never thought of herself as heroic. If anything, she felt selfish. At times, she felt so guilty for leaving the physical world like she did to come back here. Thinking about the sudden pain she'd caused Hannah's family made her wince. Even though Zakhart told her that Hannah would have died at fourteen, she still felt bad for the sudden way they lost her. So she could come back here and save Ross. Not knowing that it was all too late.

She was terrified that the demons had already destroyed him.

"You brought me back from the edge, Heather," said Knox in a soft voice, laying his face against her hair. "Cooled the rage that's been an overpowering force in my life. Helped me care about other people again. And myself. Thank you."

He pressed a gentle kiss against the side of her face.

"You helped me, too, Knox," she said and laid her hand against his cheek. "More than you know. You've kept me from giving up when things got bad. You and Zakhart. Thank you."

She kissed him on the cheek. He blushed, a smile brightening his face.

"And look how much you've helped the other lost souls," said Knox.

Heather put her arms around Knox and held him close.

"Without you, most of them would be sleeping with the poppies now," Knox whispered in her ear. "Cora. Javier. Especially Zoe. And don't forget Gemma and Ian. And Thomas. So, your trip here wasn't wasted, kid. Believe me."

She never believed it was wasted time, but the fact that it might be too late to save Ross ate at her. Hurt her heart.

A shadow fell over Heather. She glanced up. Thomas was standing over her, looking shaky and thin.

"Thomas?" said Heather as she let go of Knox and sat up to face the young man.

He had a long face like his brother's, but shadows hollowed his cheeks and recessed his soft hazel eyes. Flecks of gold and green brightened them against his washed-out form. His brown hair was cut short at the nape and at his ears, his bangs long, hanging in his face, not slicked back like Ian's. His silky grey clothes were ragged and torn, soot-stained, and filled with holes. He looked so young, light beginning to warm the shadowed edges of his face, softening his almost skeletal look. Like his soul was returning from the demons' hold. He crouched beside her, hands clasped in front of him.

"Heather...Knox," he began. His voice was smooth like hot chocolate, his British accent soothing to her ears. "I wanted to thank you for freeing me from the coal fields. I don't know what would have happened if you hadn't rescued me."

Heather smiled. "You're welcome."

Knox clapped the young man on the shoulder. "Glad we could help, kid," he said.

Thomas nodded then turned his attention to Heather. "Forgive me for intruding, but I couldn't help overhearing your conversation with Zakhart. And just now with Knox."

"It's fine, Thomas. I'm not upset," said Heather. "This room is so tiny...it's impossible to have a private conversation."

"You mentioned someone named Ross?"

Heather nodded.

"Like my brother, I've seen Ross many times in this cavern, but only briefly."

"You have?" Heather cried, gripping his arm. "Tell me, what have you seen?"

She looked up to see Zakhart hurry over. He sat down on the floor beside Heather.

"Thomas, please—tell us everything," said Zakhart. "Even the slightest detail might be important."

"Yes," Heather added, rising on her knees. "He's the reason I'm here. Please, tell me everything you know."

Thomas nodded, clearing his throat. He sat down on the floor facing Heather and crossed his legs. Ian and Gemma came over now, sitting beside Thomas. Ian put his hand on his brother's back.

"I first saw Ross the day they took me out of this room."

"That was some time ago, brother," said Ian, glancing at Heather.

Thomas shrugged. "I'm not sure of the time. It's too difficult to judge here."

"Quite," said Ian. "I tried to mark the event in time as best I could. For every shift Gemma and I worked, I put a black slash on the wall near the bed."

"I thought that's what you were doing," said Gemma.

"By my count, that was nearly *twenty* days ago," said Ian. "As much as there is the passage of a day here."

Heather felt her body tense as her frustration intensified. "Then what?" she added.

"The grey demons took me to the Mechanism," said Thomas, running a hand through his bangs, pushing them out of his eyes. "Where two of the larger demons waited. The grey ones forced me to stand on a black square plate on the floor. It looked shiny and metallic."

Zakhart winced, closing his eyes.

"When I stood on the plate, a metal cage came down over me. I felt something pressing against my entire body as the machine hummed. The sound vibrated through me, making my teeth chatter. That's when I saw him. Standing in front of the cage. Staring right through me. As if the cage was empty. Like he did not even see me."

Heather twisted the hem of her shirt into a knot around her fingers, her breath hanging on Thomas' every word.

"He walked up to the cage, standing so close that I could have touched him if my hands had been free. His eyes were strange. Black. Not a trace of color to them."

"No," Heather moaned. "He has the most beautiful, golden hazel eyes you've ever seen. When he laughs, they're so bright, like the autumn sun sparkling through turning leaves."

She sighed. And when he looked at her, his eyes filled with love. For her. And when he held her, those eyes sparked like embers, his touch tingling hot against her skin.

"He didn't say a word, Heather," Thomas continued, leaning toward her. "He walked around the cage, arms behind his back. At last, the humming sound stopped, the vibrations dying away. He stepped back, standing beside two of those larger demons. One of them asked if everything was satisfactory. Ross said it was adequate. Then he snapped his fingers. The two demons jumped as if startled—or terrified. Ross said to implement it and turned away, walking back toward the forbidden hallway. Every other time I saw him, he was touring the coal fields with at least three demons at his side. Large and small alike."

Heather dropped her head in her hands. "How can this be happening?"

Thomas shrugged. "I confess, this makes no sense to me. Why would demons let a human—run the show as it were? And if it were true, why would any human sell out his kind like this? For fleeting moments of power. It makes no sense at all."

"What happened to Mulciber?" Heather asked. "He was in charge when Ross and I came here the first time. He was the one who attacked me and then Ross as we were leaving the cave. What changed?"

Zakhart went quiet, his face taut with concentration. Knox had been silent, too, letting Heather absorb Thomas' observations, but now, he spoke up.

"A coup, maybe?" Knox offered. "Maybe Ross got together with some others to overthrow this Mulciber and take over? If it is him, why would he continue the demon's operations after they'd inflicted this pain on him."

"Who is Mulciber?" Ian asked. "I've never heard that name before."

Heather sighed. "He didn't identify himself as in charge, but it was obvious by how the other demons acted that he was the leader. But his attack on Ross had been brutal. And Ross would never tell me exactly what they did to him."

"At first, Ross was friendly to us in the coal fields," said Thomas. "Kind. Charming. Sympathetic. Souls trusted him. Responded to him, especially when the demons left him alone with us. But later, he became distant and angry. Keeping his distance. Then he stopped coming to the fields. We would see him only in the room with the Mechanism. Or shouting orders from the forbidden hallway."

"That's so strange," said Heather as she leaned against the wall and wrapped her arms around her knees. "That last part doesn't sound like Ross at all."

Zakhart nodded, that far-off look still in his eyes. He didn't even seem like he was listening, but he always responded to Thomas' words.

Thomas folded his hands into his lap. "Heather, if I were you, I would storm the forbidden hallway and see exactly what's in that room. Or rather who is in that room."

"Thomas!" Ian cried. "That's a terrible suggestion."

"It's the only way to know what's afoot, dear brother," said Thomas.

"Thomas is right," Zakhart said finally.

Everyone turned to look at him.

"Okay, pale angel," said Knox, sitting up straighter. "Why do you agree with Thomas here? That's a radical and dangerous plan, don't you think?"

"When we walked through the room with the Mechanism with our carts," Zakhart said as he glanced around the room at the faces staring back at him. "I felt a strange energy. It made me very uneasy. It grew stronger when we reached the crossroad. The strange energy was magnified there. I took a step or two toward the forbidden hallway and the energy pulsated against my body, almost repelling my light. My wings shuddered, spasming against the darkness I sensed there."

Heather frowned at him. "What does that mean?"

Zakhart shook his head and shrugged. "That something dark and deadly is here in the Between—that shouldn't be here. And I feel it... inside this place. But I won't know until I've examined that room."

Knox got to his feet, brushing off traces of soot and dust from his clothes. Heather sprang up beside him. Ian and Gemma helped Thomas stand.

"All right, we've got an objective now," said Knox. "Enter the forbidden hallway."

"Agreed," said Heather, brushing dust off her clothes. "If Ross is still in the Between, that's where they've got him." She glared past Zakhart into the hallway. "And I'm going in there after him if I have to bring down every demon in this place."

Zakhart nodded as a smile rose on his angelic face.

"I've been analyzing the egress routes ever since I stepped into this place," said Knox, motioning toward the door. "So, I know how to get us out of here. I propose that we hide Thomas, Ian, and Gemma in the carts, under a healthy layer of dirt. Heather, Zakhart, and I will push the carts outside to the dump site. You guys climb out and Zak's winged buddies safely carry the three of you off to the tree."

"It's Zakhart," said the pale angel in a polite voice.

Knox grinned. "Then me, Zak, and Heather come back inside. We storm this forbidden hallway and find out what's there. Then...we either grab Ross and run like hell or we find out that he's in league with these assholes and we leave him to rot. With the dark thing you're sensing, angel. Or something else that we won't figure out until we've seen that hallway."

Heather glared at Knox. "What kind of plan is that?"

"The best one I got, kid," he said. "We have no way to recon the target or gather intel on the objective. Plus, there's only one way in or out of this place, so most likely, we've only got one shot at this."

A chill rushed down her spine. One shot. Was Knox right about that?

"To minimize casualties," Knox continued. "We evac all the innocents and focus on the objective. Concentrate on the target."

Heather turned to Zakhart. "Zakhart, what do you say?"

"Let me think." The pale angel put his arms behind his back and paced the room in silence.

"I want to stay and help you," said Ian. "It's the least I can do after you saved Gemma and Thomas."

"Me, too," said Gemma, gesturing toward the hallway. "I can help you fight them."

"Gemma, no!" Ian shouted, his gaze snapping toward her, anger on his face. "It's much too dangerous."

"Ian, please," she cried, grabbing hold of his hands. "I can provide directions. Or even a distraction or two. I want to help. And what about the other innocent souls trapped here like us? What happens to them?"

"Gemma, we don't have enough people to rescue everyone in this place," said Knox, holding out his hands. "I don't even know if we have enough for *this* job."

"Knox is right, love," said Ian. "There are too many demons to try and empty this cavern of innocent souls."

"But we can't just—leave them like this?"

Gemma launched into a string of Italian phrases that Heather didn't understand. Ian interrupted her, also speaking Italian, Thomas joining the argument.

The conversation made Knox's eyes cross. He shook his head and leaned against the rough rock wall. "I'll just let them talk amongst themselves while I plan our escape." He cupped Heather's chin a moment. "Hopefully with Ross."

Heather reached up and gripped his hand. "Thanks," she whispered.

Knox nodded and watched Zakhart pace through the room as the argument in Italian escalated.

Finally, Zakhart stopped his pacing and moved back to Heather and Knox. "I've consulted with the other angels," he said. "They're quite disturbed by this news."

"Not surprised," said Knox. "What do you think of the plan I've proposed?"

Gemma's shrill voice carried through the room, making Zakhart cringe. Knox seemed to block it out.

"It's so risky, Knox, but you already know that," said Zakhart. "Nevertheless, I don't see any other option. And I'm bothered by leaving innocent people in demon hands. But we're no match for all these demons. We need to gather a stronger force to fight them."

"Agreed," said Knox, leaning against the wall. "As soon as the screaming's stopped, we'll get this moving."

"If it ever stops," Zakhart replied with a nod and cast a look at the argument still in progress—in Italian.

"Count me in," Heather added.

"Enough!" Ian shouted as he crossed his arms and turned away from Gemma. "It is unwise and I forbid it, Gemma! End of story."

Gemma stamped her feet. "Not end of story! I will do what I must, Ian Arrington James!" She whirled around, storming off toward the hallway as Ian turned around, looking shocked, his mouth hanging open.

"Excuse me," Knox said quickly and stepped in front of Gemma, intercepting her before she entered the hallway. "Gemma, I just wanted to say thanks," he said, flashing a charming smile, those blue eyes piercing.

Gemma paused, her brow furrowed. "What? Oh. Grazie."

"I mean, your help so far was instrumental in saving Thomas," Knox continued. "I'm glad we got to him in time, but to be honest, I'm a little worried about his condition."

Her eyes widened. "His condition?"

Knox nodded. "Yeah, he's pretty vulnerable right now. I'll feel much better when we get him out of here and back to the tree so the angels can treat him. I'm afraid he'll relapse if he stays here any longer."

"What can I do to help him?" Gemma asked, glancing over at the frail young man who walked toward the cots against the wall.

"You've looked after him so well here," said Knox. "I was hoping you'd shepherd him back to the tree and get him help."

Heather watched Knox charm Gemma into doing the opposite of what she'd been planning. Guy was good.

Gemma crossed her arms. "But the others here, they need me."

Knox motioned at Thomas who slumped onto one of the cots, looking weak and exhausted.

"I think he needs you more right now. Don't you think? And what if the demons get to him again? He might not survive a second attack."

Gemma's eyes grew fearful as she glanced from Thomas to Knox.

Thomas groaned, stretching out on the coat. He closed his eyes, looking restless.

Gemma's eyes turned sad. Finally, she nodded at Knox. "You're right. I'll make certain that he gets to the tree safely."

"Thank you," Knox said, sighing as he brushed a dark curl off his forehead. "That takes a lot of weight off my shoulders. Will you walk us through the layout of the forbidden hallway before we smuggle you, Ian, and Thomas out?"

"Of course."

"Thanks, Gemma," he said and moved back to Heather and Zakhart.

As he passed Ian, Knox winked at him. Ian mouthed a thank you to him and went over to sit by his brother. In a few moments, Gemma joined him and the two made up quietly.

"Okay, situation neutralized," said Knox in a half-whisper. "I vote we go now. Get these people outside and on their way back to the tree. Then we'll head for our objective."

Zakhart nodded. "I'll get everyone moving while you two get the carts."

"Roger that," said Knox as he moved toward the doorway.

Zakhart walked over to Gemma and Ian who sat beside Thomas on the cot.

Heather followed Knox into the hallway and headed toward the storage room where they had parked the carts.

fifteen

· · ·

THE TRIP down to the lowest level to gather dirt was a long trip through a confusing array of dark tunnels until they reached the cavernous digging site. Heather was surprised by the number of huge mounds of brown earth piled along the tunnel. And the dozens of souls digging out another new tunnel.

Gemma had already shown Knox the route out of the caves and the layout of the Mechanism chamber. She had also led him past the entrance to the forbidden hallway, a place that Heather had only seen from a distance. When Knox was satisfied that he could find his way out of the caves again, he gave the okay to head into the tunnels.

By now, Heather trusted Knox without question. Until now, she hadn't realized how much she relied on him. And as much as she loved Ross, she couldn't deny that she had feelings for this good-hearted, take-charge soldier with the wounded blue eyes.

"Let's do this," said Knox, pointing at the carts.

Gemma hesitated as Knox helped Ian onto a cart. With a nod from Ian, she moved toward Heather's cart and Heather helped her onto it. She lay on her side, curled in a fetal position. Zakhart lifted Thomas in his arms and laid him down on his side in another cart.

The pale angel pressed his hand to Thomas' face, creating a bubble of light around him.

"It will help with the claustrophobia," Zakhart whispered, patting Thomas' shoulder.

Thomas nodded and covered his eyes with his hands.

Zakhart moved to the other carts, laying his hand against Ian's head, engulfing him in a bubble of light. Finally, he moved to Gemma. He cast one last look at each cart and then picked up a shovel.

With a crunch, his shovel bit into the nearest pile of dirt. He carried it over to the first cart and began sifting dirt over Thomas. Following Zakhart's lead, Heather and Knox grabbed shovels and quickly filled the other two carts, covering Gemma and Thomas. When they'd filled all three carts with loose soil, concealing the three souls, Knox motioned for them to turn around the carts and hurry out of the tunnels.

Heather struggled to swivel around her heavy cart, trying not to jostle Gemma around as she pushed the bulky cart forward behind Knox. Zakhart was behind her now, the three of them plodding through the maze of tunnels.

"Sure you know the way?" Heather asked Knox.

"I do," he replied. "But feel free to shout out if I make a wrong turn."

"It's not like I can Google the directions," Heather said with a chuckle.

Knox snickered. "Zakhart's the next best thing to the internet."

"He's better than that," said Heather. "He brings the results to you."

They laughed, expecting a response from the pale angel, but Zakhart just shook his head.

"Very funny," Zakhart said finally. "You know the internet was my idea, don't you?"

Heather rolled her eyes. "Of course, it was, Al."

"No, truly, it was," Zakhart replied. "I suggested it to Gabriel back in the 1950s. I told him how great it could be to connect humanity with a network of more than just voice. That it would let the angels communicate with them easier." He grimaced. "Gabriel thanked me for my suggestion, but told me to let humanity find its own way."

"Mind. Blown." Knox made an explosion sound through his teeth and glanced back at Heather, shaking his head.

Heather couldn't hold back her laugh. Zakhart blushed.

"No one believes me," Zakhart lamented. "I'm an angel—incapable of lying."

"But very capable of stretching the truth," Knox muttered.

Heather tried to hold back another laugh, but it spilled out, echoing through the tunnel as they approached the archway into the Mechanism chamber.

Everyone fell silent now.

Zakhart's frame stiffened, shoulders thrust back, eyes squinting. Heather held her breath when they passed through the arch into the chamber where the Mechanism chugged and bellowed greasy black smoke. The room had a burnt, sulfury scent that was acrid and cloying, burning her throat as Heather hurried through the chamber behind Knox who jogged toward the main tunnel that led outside. The carts creaked and groaned, but the sound was hushed by the hiss of steam and thump of machinery.

No demons came after them, tried to chase them, or even stop them as they passed through. When they reached the tunnel leading outside, they encountered a steady line of souls pushing empty carts back inside. The tunnel was wide enough for three carts, but seeing the endless line of souls passing by on the other side unnerved Heather.

She counted the steps to the exit. Never had she felt as claustrophobic as she did inside this tunnel. And frightened.

Finally, Knox was at the door, shoving it open. Heather quickened her pace, smiling as she rolled through the doorway, seeing trees and swampy marshes ahead. They followed a few carts ahead of them around a stand of trees to a huge pile of dirt behind the rocky hillside.

When they stopped moving, Knox reached into the dirt in his cart and dug Ian out. Heather scooped the dirt off Gemma while Zakhart got Thomas free. The three of them furiously brushed at their clothing and faces even though Zakhart's light bubbles had kept the dirt out of their noses and mouths.

Zakhart turned his face into the wind and sang a series of clear, tenor notes. The wind rose, carrying the melody aloft, and swept it away.

It seemed like only minutes until Heather saw figures on the horizon, winging their way toward the outcropping.

Razasha appeared first, Halea behind her. And a male angel that Heather hadn't seen before. He hadn't been at the tree. His hair was white, wings a pale ivory, his robes a matching silk that billowed in the wind. His large eyes were brilliant copper.

The three pale angels set down beside Zakhart and exchanged a quick harmony.

"Please, get these three souls back to the soul tree," said Zakhart. "Thomas was attacked, as I explained. Razasha, please evaluate him. He may need more healing light to counteract whatever those demons did to him."

Razasha trilled a few notes then nodded her head as she took Thomas into her arms.

"Angels!" Gemma cried, her voice soft, eyes filled with wonder.

She dropped to her knees and clasped her hands together. Halea knelt beside Gemma, wings at full span, and Gemma stared, wide-eyed.

Gently, Halea held out her hand to Gemma. The petite woman hesitated a moment then took hold of Halea's hand. The pale angel lifted her into the air.

"I never dreamed I would see angels here," Gemma replied.

Ian smiled as the other pale angel lifted him into his arms.

"Heather," Gemma called. "I hope you come back with your man."

"Thanks, Gemma," Heather replied, standing closer to Knox.

The angels took to the air and winged off, disappearing over the trees. Zakhart turned back to Heather and Knox, pushing up his sleeves. His back went stick straight, his chest puffed out, determination hardening his features.

"Let's storm this place and see if we can still save Ross." His voice was tight, angry.

Heather had never seen him so determined. He meant business.

"Let's move," Knox replied, motioning Heather ahead of him while he watched their backs all the down the path leading back toward the demon cave.

Heather held her breath as they approached the door. Zakhart yanked it open, stepping inside. She entered behind him, Knox at her back.

She felt out of breath, her entire body trembling as they rushed down the main tunnel toward the Mechanism. The room was crawling with demons this time, souls scurrying back and forth around the Mechanism that thrummed mercilessly, its gyrations vibrating through the walls and into the floor.

The demons ignored them.

Hadn't the demons noticed that they didn't bring back the carts? That they'd left them outside? If demons only controlled human souls that had let them take over, how did they maintain control of so many? Especially when they didn't seem to be paying full attention to everything happening around them.

Heather couldn't believe the number of souls that had let the demons inside. Let them have control. Was Mulciber watching everything? Or was something else about to trap them here in the Veils forever? Like they'd trapped Ross?

Zakhart moved around the Mechanism's railing toward the crossroad, where the two tunnels met. Heather felt her stomach twist into a knot, her mouth dry, fingers cold as she glanced into the short, dark tunnel that led off to the right.

The forbidden tunnel.

She gritted her teeth, inhaling sharply, and set herself.

Zakhart summoned a shimmery swath of white light between his hands. It sparkled like translucent organza as he threw it across Heather and Knox. Zakhart waited until the white light settled over them like a salve against their skin. With a nod, the pale angel motioned them forward.

Heather took a deep breath and entered the forbidden passageway.

sixteen

THE SHORT PASSAGEWAY was pitch black, an eerie gold light ahead. Walking through this darkness was like trudging through mud, each step harder and harder to take.

"I've never felt darkness this powerful in the Between before," Zakhart whispered.

Zakhart halted, his hands pooling with liquid light. He tilted his hands, pouring the molten white liquid onto the ground, illuminating an inky black stickiness. Like the gunk that Thomas had thrown up. Heather couldn't help but wonder if this passageway was paved with the remnants of souls.

"Light protect us," Zakhart said in a pained voice.

The glowing liquid sloshed over the black ground, catching fire. Pure white flames burned a path through the sludge.

"Is this what I think it is?" Knox asked, sounding disgusted.

Zakhart nodded. "It is. Soul remnants. There is so much evil here. I placed the highest protection on us that I possess. Be very careful. After this, I don't know what might lie ahead."

Crouching, Heather crept through the passageway, Knox at her shoulder. He was calm and focused, his face a tight mask of concentration as he listened for demons and watched for any hint of movement. He kept reaching to his side. For a weapon? Every time, his hand came up empty and he stiffened.

Discomfort pinched his face. He seemed out of his element without a weapon right now.

The ashen trail through the sludge softened their footsteps, the eerie light slipping closer. No more than a hundred feet away.

A shadow passed in front of the light, the form looking human. Male. Ross?

She bit her tongue, wanting to call out to him, but she kept quiet, maintaining her slow, steady pace toward the archway ahead.

They had gotten halfway down the passageway when the human form passed in front of the light again, still a hazy figure. Footsteps tapped against stone. The faint sound of moans echoed from the chamber ahead.

As the distance slipped away, dim light approaching, a stone archway rose out of the mist. The square blocks were carved with strange symbols. Jagged swipes and violent scratches covered the stone as if made by claws. As Heather moved closer, shadows shifted. They were fluid almost writhing with life as they oozed in front of the archway.

Revealing faces carved into the blocks.

Grotesque, contorted faces. Human faces, male and female, frozen into twisted expressions of agony. Terror. Fury. Others looked insane. Leering. Maniacal. The shadows distorted and flowed across the stones, giving the faces a terrifying animated, strobed movement as if they were alive.

Heather looked away, concentrating on the ashen soil that stopped abruptly at the doorway.

Knox's hand went to her shoulder, tugging, and she stopped, watching the hazy, shuffling figure pace through the eerie light again.

Zakhart laid his hands on hers and Knox's shoulders and she felt a warm pulse of energy flow from his hands into her neck. It streamed upward into her throat, warming her mouth and nose as it traveled into her eyes and flowed out of her forehead and back to Zakhart.

She heard his voice in her head.

As long as my touch is on you and Knox, the three of us can communicate without words. Zakhart.

This is much cooler than texting, Knox's voice filled her head.

Heather couldn't help but smile.

I've given both of you the brief gift of extraordinary vision, Zakhart's voice echoed in her head. *To see through the shadows, in the dark—and past demon illusions. Their illusions are dangerous, so be careful. This gift only sees through tricks to the eyes. Not to the mind. And Heather, you are the most vulnerable because of your connection to Ross.*

I'll be careful, Heather answered.

Whatever is beyond this archway is very powerful. And very dangerous. Remember, demons can twist everything but your heart. Remember that. Both of you.

Understood, said Knox. *How long will this gift last?*

Angels can always speak to you without words, Zakhart replied, *but you won't be able to do the same when I let go. So, let's take a good look into the chamber and figure out a plan. Understand?*

She and Knox agreed at the same time. With the warm vibration of light in her eyes, Heather stared through the misty abyss ahead.

A large disc hung from the ceiling, casting eerie streams of sickly yellow light through the room. The disc rotated, turning slowly through the room, casting the eerie light that caused thick shadows to shift in a constant sweep. The high-ceiling chamber was larger than Heather had expected. An opening stood at the far end of the chamber. As she swept her gaze through the room, Zakhart's gift picked out the edges of the space, revealing walls that had been hidden in darkness.

It's huge, Knox said in her head. *Must be fifty, sixty feet across.*

The walls look like the stones in the archway, Heather replied.

And these constantly shifting shadows make them look like they're moving.

I'm analyzing the stones right now, Zakhart replied. *There's something very odd about them.*

You mean beyond all the demons and the creepy, Jeffrey-Dahmer-crime-scene décor? Knox.

Knox was right. The cylindrical chamber was beyond creepy with its walls built from those huge blocks of dark stone carved with faces and symbols. Shadows undulated through the room, giving strobed life to more of those horrible, contorted faces. Humans, demons, and many other creatures she didn't recognize.

Muffled sounds emanated from the chamber. Were they moans? Heather couldn't tell.

I could so do without more of those faces.

Me, too, Knox. Zakhart.

All along the wall, spaced about three feet apart, huge, grey slabs of stone stood, stretching from floor to ceiling. Set between columns of the smaller blocks and blackness, the slabs were concave carvings of full-bodied figures. Soulstalkers. Small demons. Large demons.

Really? Like the faces aren't enough? Knox. *Now, we gotta stare at life-size monsters. Awesome.*

This is a whole new level of creepy, said Heather.

What are these things? Zakhart sounded disgusted and a little unnerved. *I haven't spent a lot of time around demons, but the higher-level angels have shown us images of the lower realms—even the Nether Core—but none of the architecture looked like this.*

Nether Core? What was that? Heather hadn't heard Zakhart mention these things before.

Even the angel doesn't know. We're screwed. Knox.

Heather's gaze flitted from one slab to the next, making note of each carving. A sand runner. A creature she didn't recognize. Demon. Empty slab. Demon. Empty slab.

At the flutter of shadows, something billowed through the darkness, catching her attention.

She squinted, letting Zakhart's gift sort through the shadows and outline the walls against the darkness. One of the slabs was covered with a white tarp that undulated in the shadows.

One of them is covered, she said.

Again, she stared around the room, studying the walls, staring deeper at the columns of blackness interspersed with the face blocks and life-sized, inverse carvings.

What's beyond those black spaces? Heather asked. *Are they just shadows? Or alcoves?*

No one responded.

Zakhart? Knox? Heather asked again.

Sorry, kid. Even with Zakhart's angel eyes, it's just too dark.

Something lies beyond them. Zakhart. They might be archways into more rooms.

Again, a figure passed underneath the light, disappearing into the writhing shadows. Heather froze.

That's a human figure. Knox. Ross, maybe?

I can't tell, said Heather. *I need to get closer. Zakhart, where are the demons?*

I feel their presence. They're close. So utmost caution, Heather.

Knox, we need to get closer, said Heather. *You have a plan?*

Sorry, kid, I'll have to leave this one to Zakhart, Knox answered.

Why? Heather asked.

Too much at risk, he replied.

On the count of three, we all go in, said Zakhart. *I'll watch out for both of you—and for demons. Knox, you watch Heather. Heather, you look for Ross.*

That's as good as it gets, Knox replied.

Zakhart set himself. *Ready.*

Taking a deep breath, Heather stepped beneath the archway of faces. Under the light. Knox was at her shoulder.

"I'm right here, Heather," he said. "No fear."

Standing under the light, Heather watched as the black spaces took shape. Archways into three alcoves. As the shadow stepped in front of the light again. From the alcove ahead.

And it was Ross.

"Ross!" Heather cried, rushing toward him.

"Heather, no!" Knox shouted.

He was in motion as she reached out toward the tall, sandy-haired, boyish guy she'd fallen in love with.

Ross turned, squinting at her, a dullness in his eyes. His vivid gold-hazel eyes looked tarnished. Empty. His form was skeletal and faded. Worse than Thomas. His clothes were in tattered shreds. She touched his skin. It was as cold as ice as he stared through her. Like he didn't recognize her.

"Ross, it's me!"

Don't say your name, Heather! Zakhart's voice shouted in her head.

"Is it really—you?" said Ross and his voice ached through Heather.

"Don't you recognize me?" she asked.

Lie to him. Tell him the wrong name.

Heather glanced over her shoulder at Zakhart, giving him a confused look.

"Ross, it's me! Remember? It's Jessie."

A smile rose on Ross' face. "Jessie? You were here with me the first time. We came from the tree together, didn't we? My memory's so fuzzy." He rubbed his eyes. "I've been here so long."

Her skin began to crawl. She took a step back. This wasn't Ross.

Ross moved toward her.

"Stay back," she said, her eyes hard. "Don't you touch me."

He held out his arms. "But Jessie! It's me! Ross."

With lightning reflexes, he grabbed Heather's wrist, his grip like iron. His skin was cold, clammy. Like a wet lizard. She shuddered.

Or a demon.

Heather lunged at Ross, slamming into him as hard as she could propel her body. She and the demon toppled to the floor.

And the illusion slipped.

It flickered like a lost cable signal, revealing a large demon beneath Ross' face. Its skin was the color of terra cotta, black horn buds above its black, steely eyes.

She kicked and punched the demon as Knox leaped into the fight.

Zakhart was through the archway now, acrid stench of ozone floating in the air as he flung a ball of white light at the demon. The light crackled and exploded.

Something inhuman screeched, the human illusion falling completely away.

Knox pulled Heather back as the demon twisted and contorted until it gave up Ross' image and sank back into its true form.

Heather glared at it as it stood up. Mulciber.

"You played me, my dear," Mulciber said in his buttery smooth voice, pointy teeth showing as the demon flashed her an appreciative smile. "I didn't expect that. Well done."

Mulciber tucked his arms behind him as he walked through the chamber. Zakhart held more liquid light in his hands, ready to strike as the demon moved with cautious steps.

"What is this place?" Knox demanded.

"My private chambers," said Mulciber, pacing around the chamber. "Where I do my studies and work in my lab. I've been perfecting my human illusions." He laughed, a deep, gravelly sound that scratched across her ears. "Amongst other experiments."

Heather couldn't stand it anymore. She stormed over to Mulciber. "Where's Ross?"

A leering grin rolled across his face. "He's around here somewhere."

Zakhart was beside her now. He faced the demon, shaping the liquid into a ball of light. The pale angel dropped it on the floor at Mulciber's feet. It exploded into a cage of light around the demon.

Mulciber looked shocked.

Go! Zakhart's voice reverberated through her thoughts. *Search the alcoves before Mulciber calls the whole population of demons down on us. He doesn't realize I'm blocking him right now, but I can't hold this for long.*

Heather and Knox separated. Knox veered left, Heather rushing to the right. Inside the alcove, she found six or seven souls chained to the wall. She picked them out in the darkness thanks to Zakhart's extraordinary gift of sight surging through her and Knox. She checked each soul. They had all faded away, beyond her help.

She rushed back out of the alcove and ran past Mulciber toward another alcove opposite the archway.

It was just like the one on the right, several souls chained and faded away. But the flash of sandy-blond hair to the left caught her attention. She turned.

Ross! Faded and skeletal like Thomas, hanging by his chains. Flickers of light still burned in his gold-hazel eyes.

She ran to him and pressed her hands against his face.

"Ross! Oh, God, Ross! It's me."

His gaze turned toward her, staring.

"Stop...tormenting me—Mulciber," he muttered, his voice raspy and weak.

"It's me, Ross," she said, leaning toward his face. She pressed her lips to his, her hands cradling his face.

His eyes welled with tears. "Heather?" he squeaked out. "It can't be you. You disappeared—into the Spiral. I made sure."

She stroked his face, kissing him again. "But I came back," she whispered.

His face contorted with misery and he shook his head. "No... Heather? Why?"

She wrapped her arms around him.

"Because someone once said to me that he loved me more than his own life. When I reached the other side, I realized that I felt the same way."

"No," he moaned. "The fact that you were safe was the only

thing—keeping me going. Why'd you...throw away your new life like this?"

"Because I love you," said Heather.

His whole face brightened. She kissed him again.

"But I said it first," he said in a raspy whisper.

Heather laughed, reaching out to unfasten the shadowy cuffs holding him against the wall. One by one, she broke them all and Ross collapsed against her. He was too weak to move.

Knox appeared in the doorway. "Kid, you found him?"

She nodded. "Help me, please."

She saw the pain appear in Knox's wounded blue eyes. He hesitated a moment and then rushed over to take hold of Ross. Together, they supported Ross between them, hurrying out to the main chamber. Where Zakhart held Mulciber in a cage of light.

Take Ross out of here. Now. Zakhart's voice rang through her head. *I'll follow you out.*

"Zakhart, no!" Heather cried.

It'll be okay, he said.

"You promise?" she asked, backing away from Mulciber, Ross and Knox beside her as the three of them crept toward the archway.

Zakhart smiled, his gaze settling on her as she moved past him. His face was tense, pumpkin-orange eyes squinting.

I promise, he said.

That better not be a lie, she said back to him.

She paused at the archway, not wanting to leave the pale angel behind like this.

Could angels die? No, she couldn't think about that right now.

Knox gave her a gentle nudge forward.

Tightening her arm around Ross' waist, she backed out of the chamber, Ross still between her and Knox. When they reached the short passageway, they turned and ran.

seventeen

. . .

PULLING ROSS ALONG BETWEEN THEM, Heather and Knox bolted through the intersecting passages, into the chamber where the Mechanism towered like a skyscraper. They dashed around the Mechanism's railing that overlooked the lower levels, clouds of steam and coiling streams of greasy black smoke roiling to the upper levels. Settling around them as they dodged souls and demons.

The opening to the main tunnel loomed ahead.

The way out!

Heather gritted her teeth and pushed harder, legs pumping, breath heaving. Ross stumbled beside her. His hand was locked tight in her right hand. Knox held Ross up between them, his left arm wrapped around Ross' waist, keeping Ross on his feet.

She expected them to be swarmed by demons at any moment, but the other demons barely even looked up at her and Knox. Zakhart's light cage must still be active, blocking Mulciber from communicating with the other demons. She hated that Zakhart wasn't right behind her, but she understood why he'd stayed behind now. If he'd released Mulciber from that cage to escape with them, this room might look very different right now.

Heather, Ross, and Knox pounded down the main passageway, passing a line of souls and carts on both sides as they rushed toward the cavern's exit.

Ross seemed to slip in and out of awareness, his speed waning, but Knox and Heather pulled him along, Heather's hand locked in Ross' grip. She refused to let go of him this time. She'd get him back to the soul tree and take care of him. When he was ready to travel, they'd leave for the Spiral.

Hopefully with Knox and the others.

The door leading outside was in sight now.

Knox ran harder, Heather keeping pace.

"What'd they do to him?" Knox asked.

"Not sure," Heather answered. "Zakhart will know."

Knox slammed his hand against the door and shoved it open.

Heather grinned. They were out!

Swampy marshlands rose around them, dusk hanging thick through the murky woods outside the rocky outcropping. The wind was gritty, smelling like dirty rain, but it was cool against her face as she, Ross, and Knox careened down a footpath leading through stands of spindly saplings and thickening grasslands as they ran away from the cave. They kept running until the swampy ground felt solid and the trees and brush had gotten dense and leafy.

Knox motioned toward a huge stand of tall bushes. She and Ross veered toward it as Knox dropped to his hands and knees and crawled inside, pulling Heather and Ross in after him.

They crouched in the brush and waited. For Zakhart. Nobody had stated it, but it was understood. They weren't leaving without Zakhart either.

Ross lay on his side beside Heather, shaking, eyes closed. He was so weak and disoriented, the color of his skin pale and ashen. She laid a hand on his forearm. It was cold and clammy.

What had the demons done to him? How long had he been in that place, scared and alone, being tortured?

She put her arms around him and huddled against him.

The Between was deadly silent. No soulstalkers screeched overhead. No hush of wind rushed through the sea of grasses. The air smelled dirty, almost pungent with swamp water and decaying plants.

It seemed like forever until wings whispered down the path. Knox stuck his head out.

"It's Zak," he announced and crawled out of the brush.

Heather left Ross on his side and stepped out of the bushes. Zakhart's robes were torn and sooty. His alabaster face had a thick black mark across his left cheek, but he was smiling.

"You're safe!" Heather cried, rushing toward him.

She threw her arms around the pale angel and hugged him.

"I told you I'd be fine," he said, letting her go.

Zakhart reached up to the soot-stained rags he wore and tore them away, revealing his creamy white robes beneath. His wings sprang free, unfurling to their full span and height.

"Ahhh," he said, stretching arms and wings. He flexed his wings, flapping them hard, and then folded them against his back again. "Much better. How's Ross?"

Heather motioned him over to the bushes as she and Knox lifted Ross out of the brush. They laid Ross in the grass as Zakhart knelt.

"He's not good, Zakhart. Something's still wrong."

Concern furrowed the pale angel's brow as he bent down and turned Ross onto his back. Ross' eyes were closed. And he was still shivering.

Zakhart pulled open the tatters of Ross' grey shirt. Ross' ashen skin was leathery and cold, stretching tight over his body. His breath rasped against his chest.

Heather gasped and stumbled backward. "What's happening to him?" she demanded.

"Ross," Zakhart called, patting his face. "Ross, wake up. It's Zakhart. Hear my voice and wake up."

At last, Ross' eyes rolled open. His irises were pitch black and he seemed to look right through Zakhart.

"Zakhart, his eyes!" Heather cried.

She knelt beside Ross, taking his icy hand in hers.

Zakhart shook his head. "I'm not sure, Heather. But I think that something's attached itself to his soul."

"That's because he's still mine," said a raspy voice through the trees.

Heather got to her feet as Zakhart and Knox turned.

Mulciber!

The pale angel wrapped his wings around Knox and Heather, arms stretched out to protect them.

"Did you think we'd simply let all of you just walk out like that?" the demon asked, lifting its arms into the air as clutches of the smaller grey demons appeared behind him.

Heather stopped counting at ten, moving closer to Zakhart. Knox's back stiffened, jaw set as his body shifted into a defensive stance. Zakhart turned his face to the sky and sang a piercing string of tenor notes that became a discord. He was calling the other pale angels to him! She hoped they'd get here in time.

The demons began to advance on them. Zakhart held his ground. Heather bent into the defensive stance that Knox had taught her, watching every movement, listening to every sound. Zakhart kept his gaze solely on Mulciber.

Mulciber, the ruddy-skinned demon stepped out of the force of grey demons and held out his hand.

"Ross, to me!" Mulciber spoke with a throaty growl like he was summoning a dog to his side. "We have more work to do." The demon pointed a gnarled finger at the ground in front of him. "Ross! Now!"

Ross moaned, struggling to rise from the ground.

"No," he said through gritted teeth. "I won't!"

But his body refused to obey him, instead responding to Mulciber's commands.

Ross fought, struggling to his feet, but with unsteady steps, he moved away from the brush. His face contorted, teeth bared as he fought against the command with all his strength, but his legs kept moving toward Mulciber. Ross seemed powerless against the summons.

"I refuse," Ross said with a moan, his entire body convulsing. "I. Refuse."

Mulciber grinned. "Of course, you do, Ross. Now, come along. I have many more experiments that require your—participation." A husky laugh swelled out of the demon's belly, a smug look on its angular, pointy face as it motioned Ross forward.

Heather wanted to smash in Mulciber's face. She grabbed Ross' hand, yanking him backward, but he broke her grip and lurched forward again. Ross cursed at the demon, shouting his frustration, but he couldn't stop his body from moving toward Mulciber.

The large, ruddy-skinned demon crossed its arms and tapped its shriveled foot in impatience, but it seemed amused by Ross' futile struggle to disobey the command. Mulciber grinned every time Ross shouted at him.

Ross stepped around Zakhart and the pale angel grabbed Ross' shoulder, pulling him back. But Ross moved toward the demon again. Zakhart wrapped both arms around Ross' waist, holding him in place. Ross fought against the hold.

"I'm sorry, Zakhart," Ross snarled, swinging at the pale angel. "I can't control it. I'm sorry."

Zakhart held him tight, dodging Ross' flailing arms and fists, but even the pale angel's hold was slipping.

Knox stepped in front of Ross.

"Me, too, Ross," he said, cocking his fist.

Knox clocked Ross hard and Ross crumpled under the blow. Knox yelped, shaking his fist. Finally, he cradled his fist against his chest.

"Nice work, Knox," Zakhart replied. "Well done."

Mulciber rolled its black eyes. "You're just wasting time. He'll return to me as soon as he regains awareness. You can't stop him."

Mulciber waved the clutches of demons forward again.

"Gather them all up and bring them back to the caves."

The demons hesitated.

"Do it!" Mulciber shouted.

"The angel..." one of them squeaked out.

"We weren't invited in," another rasped.

Mulciber splayed its gnarled, clawed hands. "I declare the Golden Order at an end. Over! Behold, the new order where no consent is required! With no king on Hell's throne, I create a new order in this realm. The Umbran Order of Shadow. Ruled by me. My demons and I will mold these lost souls into our image and make them useful again."

The arrogant demon held out its arms, a grin curving across its darkening face.

"Take them," Mulciber ordered. "Take them all."

The grey demons swarmed forward.

Heather set herself, Zakhart's wings still protecting her. The pale angel lifted his arms, eyes glowing pure white as he summoned a ring of pure light that became a white shield of light around them. Zakhart pulled his arms closer together to control its range. Sweat dripped down his face, arms shaking as he held the shield around them.

Waves of demons bounced off the crackling dome of light.

At the edge of Heather's concentration, rhythmic beats echoed through the quiet. Growing louder. Closer.

Distracted, Heather glanced up at the sky.

Angel wings thumped through the dark sky. Heather grinned as three angels soared above the treetops, dropping out of the sky to land in front of Zakhart.

Razasha, Halea, and the male angel that had carried Ian back to the soul tree stood in front of Zakhart, ready to fight.

"Right on time," Zakhart replied and nodded toward Mulciber and the swarm of demons. "Mulciber, allow me to introduce Razasha, Halea, and Lairz. We'd love to stay and chat about your delusions, but we have better things to do. And so does Ross. He won't be staying for your demented little party. Ever again."

Zakhart chirped a quick command to Razasha who lifted Heather into her arms. Halea picked up Knox, hovering above the ground while Lairz summoned a shield of crackling white fire that burned between him and the demons. Zakhart let his shield drop. He moved to Ross, scooped him up from the ground, and rose into the sky.

Again, Zakhart sang two or three tenor notes.

Lairz hesitated a moment and then leaped into the air, wings stretched wide, as his shield dissolved. He followed behind Zakhart and the other pale angels as they soared out of the swamplands, leaving the confused demons staring up at them.

Fury burned dark and wild in Mulciber's steely eyes. The demon stared up at the sky, watching until Zakhart and the other angels put a lot more distance between the swamp and the forest.

The pale angels followed the small, clear stream that cut across the Between and ambled through the woods toward a pitch-black forest. When the first heartlily blooms gleamed orange on the horizon, the pale angels swerved deeper into the woods, toward the ring of soul trees that skirted the edge of the black forest.

At the top of the soul tree, in Heather's little nook, Zakhart laid Ross on the bed. On top of her lavender comforter. Razasha and Knox crowded around the bed on the left side. Looking anxious, Avana slid past Zakhart on the right and stood beside the headboard. Heather sat on the right edge of the bed and leaned against the pillow where Ross' head rested. Halea and Lairz stood at the foot of the bed. Lairz looked stoic, like a bodyguard, hands behind his back as if standing vigil while Halea paced, wings twitching, her alabaster face shadowed.

"I can't believe you found him, Heather," said Avana. She reached out and brushed a lock of sandy hair off Ross' leathery forehead. "But what's happened to his body?"

Heather shook her head as she stroked her fingers through his sandy-blond hair. "Wish I knew."

"I've never seen something like this before," said Zakhart, glancing at Razasha. "Have you?"

Razasha laid her delicate, pearlescent hands against Ross' ashen, leathery stomach. The skin puckered, a strange pattern of black dots and slashes crisscrossing like a rash across Ross' skin. Looking like demon skin.

"It's like they're slowly changing him into a demon," Razasha remarked, frowning as the pattern appeared on Ross' thighs. "Or some other shadow creature."

Heather stroked Ross' bare shoulders. They looked wider and more muscular than she remembered. His arms had begun to elongate, too, beginning to look misshapen and out of proportion.

"Even his body is changing," she replied, pointing at his arms. "I don't understand. What did Mulciber do to him, Zakhart?"

"What's happening to him?" Zakhart said with a moan. "I'm sensing a bunch of that black sludge within him. Like Thomas. Only much, much worse."

Razasha pressed both hands against Ross' chest and closed her eyes.

"I'll concentrate on that first."

Zakhart nodded as Razasha cast a sheaf of white light like a blanket across Ross.

Heather stared at the mutations afflicting Ross, Mulciber's words rushing back to haunt her. *We will mold these lost souls into our image and make them useful again.*

Mold them into our image? What did that mean? Images of those full-sized slabs of stones drifted back to her, inverse images of demons, humans, and sand runners.

Inverse images? A chill cut through her like a glacial wind. Molds. Those carvings were molds!

"Zakhart!" she cried. "Remember what Mulciber said? Something about molding souls to their image. Do you remember that?"

"Unfortunately, yes," he replied, casting thin trails of light across Ross.

"And the walls of that chamber—they had full-size images of shadow creatures."

"What about them, Heather?" Zakhart asked, running his fingers across the deepening pattern on Ross' right forearm.

"They were inverse carvings," she continued, "More than just creepy decorations. Zakhart, they were molds!"

It took a moment or two for Zakhart to absorb her comment as he struggled to help Ross. Finally, he jerked his head up, staring at Heather, the wheels in his head turning.

"Molds," he said in a quiet voice. He stared at her in silence for several moments as he strung long strands of light along Ross' motionless frame. "Hmmm. Sludge. Shiny rocks. Are they molding souls into facsimiles of Between creatures? Soulstalkers that do Mulciber's bidding instead of Death's. Sand runners that harvest pollen and plant new poppies according to demon orders and not Death's? Oh, no...this is bad."

Razasha chewed her lip as she spun up thin threads of white light and laid them side-by-side across Ross' chest.

"Creatures that will blend into the Between," said Razasha. "So creatures of light think everything is normal. That things are as they should be."

"All the while, they're building an army in the Demon caves," Zakhart said. "Where they already control the Veils."

"It's also a great way to harvest—I mean, steal many more souls," said Heather as she glanced at Ross. "They can send out packs of those creepy soulstalkers to gather souls. Soulstalkers that answer to them. Looks like they've only created soulstalkers so far. Ross was probably their first transformation."

"We've got to make sure he's their last, too, Heather," said Zakhart.

Heather gripped Ross' hand as the strands that Razasha and Zakhart had spun became a matrix of glowing threads that stretched across Ross' body. When they were finally done, the lattice of white light looked like a weaver's loom.

"What is that?" Heather asked.

"It's a filter," said Zakhart, pushing the threads up and down, repositioning them so that the weave was tight.

"Zakhart and I are going to flood Ross' soul with a surge of pure white light," Razasha explained. "To flush all that demonic sludge from his body and hopefully wash away whatever it is that's changing his body."

"And controlling him," Zakhart added.

Razasha caught Zakhart's gaze and held it. "Ready?"

"As soon as Heather lets go of Ross' hand."

Heather hesitated, squeezing Ross' hand. Taking a deep breath, she held it and pressed Ross' hand against his side. Letting go.

Lifting his hands, palms up, Zakhart held them over Ross. Razasha laid her hands on top of Zakhart's, closing her eyes. Pure white light radiated from their hands, the glare blinding. Heather squinted, her eyes tearing up as a shrill hum thrummed through the nook. She couldn't look away as Razasha and Zakhart sang a complicated string of harmonies, the light building in writhing layers around Ross.

Zakhart sang another harmony that melted into a multi-layered chord. Its ethereal resonance sounded like dozens of voices sang at the same time. As one complex chord.

Then he counted back from five.

At one, Zakhart and Razasha jerked their hands down hard, slamming their palms against the matrix of light. A spark exploded into a torrent of glowing liquid light that churned, drenching Ross. He tossed and seized against the currents of pure white light that ran through his body until sticky, thick black sludge extruded through the matrix of light threads, bubbling up in heaping gobs. Like squeezing clay through a dough press.

Zakhart and Razasha took turns zapping the black goo into a grey powder. Lairz and Halea pitched in, using gold flashes of light to burn away the dust when it had piled up too high. After a while, the sludge trickled away to flecks that Lairz burned away quickly.

"Something's still there," said Zakhart with a moan. "It's resisting our light energies."

"Halea and I will add our energy to the mix."

Halea frowned, shaking her head. "I don't know those chords, Lairz. I've only heard that melody once."

Zakhart exchanged a look with Razasha, but he didn't reply.

"But this young man needs us," said Lairz.

Halea took a step back, waving her hand at him.

"Halea it's our duty," Lairz snapped, anger rising in his deep copper eyes. "They come first and we're sworn to help them at all costs. They're the Maker's favored."

"But I don't know the melody," Halea said, backing away. "I won't be able to help. I'm sorry." She turned and rushed out of the room.

Lairz sighed, swiping angrily at his long white hair. He spoke three bass notes that vibrated through the room in rich, velvet tones. In a moment or two, another pale angel flitted into the room, someone Heather didn't recognize. She had dove-grey hair that coiled into ringlets, her eyes a muted copper. Her taupe wings were small and velvety, feathers gently tapered.

"I'm here, Lairz," the pale angel cried, rushing over to the bed. "What can I do?"

"Diri, thank you," said Lairz, his anger dissipating. He motioned at Ross. "His soul is in danger. I need your help."

"Of course," said Diri.

Lairz held his hands, palms up, above Zakhart's and Razasha's.

Diri quickly thrust her hands on top of Lairz's hands as he toned the same melody that Zakhart had just sung, his voice in a much deeper octave.

"Do you know it?" Lairz asked.

Diri shook her head. "No, but I'll pick it up."

Lairz smiled. He pulled in a breath and sang the bass notes that thrummed through the room in velvety tones. Diri added her alto voice to his, sliding along the chords and quickly finding the harmonies when needed until the white light flowed between their hands.

Lairz counted backward from three as he and Diri lifted their hands into the air. At zero, they both slammed their palms against the matrix of light, releasing a second torrent of liquid white light that slammed against Ross' body. It mixed with the remaining force of light, churning and spinning until the shadowy edges of something dark floated up and bumped against the matrix of light.

"There!" Avana shouted, pointing. "I see its shadow."

Slowly, the strange thing bobbed upward, smashing against the matrix with every churn of light. It was sort of round and slightly elongated, larger than a fist. It throbbed in a steady, hideous rhythm that horrified Heather.

"Keep up those currents," said Zakhart. "When that thing appears again, I'll tear it free."

Lairz and Diri nodded, increasing the force while Razasha kept more light pouring into Ross' body.

"It looks like Mulciber attached some sort of dark essence to Ross' soul," said Razasha.

Zakhart shook his head. "Not an essence. That's a demon heart."

A demon heart? Heather gasped, horrified by that thought.

The demon heart bobbed up and sank twice. Zakhart poised his hand above the light matrix, waiting.

Lairz grunted and once more, he and Diri slammed a wave of light against the matrix of threads.

The demon heart popped up like a submerged beach ball.

Zakhart plunged his hand through the light matrix, his fingers closing around the beating black mass.

Using all his strength, Zakhart tore the demon heart out of Ross' chest.

Ross' eyes snapped open. He screamed in pain and collapsed against the pillow as Zakhart carried the beating thing away from the bed. It dripped inky black liquid with every squeeze of its shadowy tissue. Zakhart encased it in a ball of white light, strangling it until it stopped beating.

Almost immediately, it began to shrivel, turning to ash.

Zakhart squeezed the ball of light between his palms, crushing it into powder. He zapped the powder with a spark of white light, destroying every trace.

"It's over," said Zakhart.

The light matrix dissolved, the watery white light dissipating into rays of gold that faded to a soft glow and then disappeared.

"Mulciber's hold on Ross is gone, Heather," said Zakhart.

Heather threw her arms around the pale angel, hugging him hard.

"Thank you," she whispered in his ear.

"Thank *you*," said Zakhart.

She let go of him, staring into his eyes. "Why thank me?"

He took her hand in his and squeezed it. "Without your sacrifice, we wouldn't have uncovered any of this. And without you, I might have sunk to the bottom rungs of the angel hierarchy and stayed there. Before you called out to me, I was feeling useless."

"I couldn't have done any of this without you, Zakhart. Never forget that."

He smiled.

"She's right," said Knox. "You're the most kickass angel I've ever met." He smiled. "Okay, you were the only angel I'd ever met. It's been a pleasure fighting at your side, bro." Knox extended his hand to Zakhart who shook it.

"Unfortunately, our fight is just beginning, Knox. So, we'll have the privilege of fighting together for some time." Zakhart leaned down and whispered in Heather's ear. "Without you. You've done enough here, Heather. When Ross can travel, you follow those bracelets to the Spiral. You and Ross have earned it."

"Really?" Heather cried.

Zakhart nodded at her. "All right, everyone, let's leave Heather and Ross alone. Let him recover."

Everyone filed out of the room and Zakhart closed the door behind him. Heather pulled the comforter across Ross and crawled underneath it, snuggling against him, and cradling him against her body.

eighteen

. . .

NIGHT HAD FALLEN in the Between when Ross opened his eyes. Heather held him close, protecting him with her body, holding onto him so no one could take him from her again. She wouldn't let Mulciber or anything else take Ross away from her again. Now that he was finally back in her arms.

"Heather?" Ross said in a weak voice, turning toward her, those gold hazel eyes so wide and filled with surprise as he slid his arms around her, pulling her against his chest. "It's been so long. God, I missed you. That separation nearly broke me."

"I'm here now and we're together again," she said, unable to hold back a grin as she stroked his hair. "I've waited so long to feel you next to me again."

"You went through so much for me," he said in a tight voice.

She pressed her fingers against his face, tracing the familiar bridge of his nose, the soft arch of his brows over those smoldering ember-like hazel eyes as she pressed feather kisses across his cheeks and down the curve of his jaw to his chin. She nuzzled her face against his neck, sipping his neck, and then his warm mouth again.

"I was so terrified I'd never see you again," she said in a half-whisper and laid her face against his chest.

His hot hands sizzled across her skin as he pulled her closer. She ran her hands across his chest, her lips finding his again in burning mouthfuls. His hands burned against her cheek as he cupped her face in his hand.

The leathery patterning was gone from his skin and the once ashen hue had turned incandescent and silky again, like she remembered it. Warm and pulsing with threads of light, like the memory of the human heart that had once filled his chest. Broken into so many pieces just like hers and given up in despair.

She hadn't realized that the beating heart sensation had been a memory until she returned here without Ross. Now, finally, in his arms, the visceral memory of her beating heart filled her chest again. No one else—including Knox—could fill that void but Ross.

He rolled her onto her back, his mouth against hers in a searing kiss. His hands slid across her bare skin and she pressed her body against his, needing to feel the weight of his body, the heat of his hands.

Heather wrapped her arms around his neck. His touch was gentle but urgent, breath hot against her lips. She couldn't get close enough to him. Couldn't hold him tight enough.

He shuddered, laying his head on her chest. "God, Heather—I thought I'd lost you forever," he said, his voice breaking.

His shoulders heaved, a sob bubbling up. He buried his face in her hair and she felt the tears against his face.

"When you let go of my hand in the Spiral," Heather whispered, "my heart broke into a million pieces."

Ross pressed his mouth against her ear. "If it takes me a lifetime, I'll put them back together one piece at a time until it's whole again. If you'll let me."

Taking his face in her hands, Heather kissed him hard on the lips. "I gave up everything for that chance, Ross."

"I've wanted to hold you like this for so long," said Ross.

His mouth smashed against hers in desperate, white-hot gulps as if he couldn't breathe without her. She kissed him back with almost bruising force, urgent hands stroking his face, frantic fingers twisting in his sandy hair as his body pressed her hard against the bed.

The muffled groan startled her as Ross sank against her.

"Ross?" she replied.

No response.

"Ross? Are you all right?"

Several moments went by before he spoke. "Yeah," he said finally in a shaky voice. "I'm okay. Just a little dizzy, that's all."

Heather rolled him onto his side. "You've been through a terrible ordeal, Ross," she said. "You need to rest."

"It's okay," he said with a charming smile. "I'm fine."

"Rest," she insisted, curling up against him again, and brushed her fingers through his sandy-blond hair. "We've got a long trip tomorrow."

Ross squinted at her. "Trip?"

She pulled up her sleeve, revealing the glowing bracelet around her wrist. "This bracelet will lead us right to the Spiral," she replied. "We're getting out. Together. Like we were meant to last time."

He was grinning now, his fingers tracing over the glowing cords.

"Now, rest," said Heather, kissing him on the cheek.

Ross slumped against the bed, spooning against Heather this time, his arms wrapped around her waist. She rubbed his forearms until he closed his eyes.

In the darkness, she watched the steady rise and fall of his chest. He probably hadn't felt that much calm in such a long time. Knowing that they were leaving this place for good now.

Together.

When the sky had lightened, Heather and Ross rose from the bed and walked down the stairs of the new soul tree together. She held his hand, showing him the smaller tree and its layout. They stood in the main room, hand in hand, while Heather pointed out the souls to him.

Knox sat in front of the fireplace, laughing and telling jokes with Ian, Gemma, and Thomas. Zakhart leaned against the wall, Razasha beside him. Zoe sat across the room, pink unicorn in her arms, looking worried. On the couch, Cora sat with Barb and Javier, the pale angels, Diri and Lairz beside them.

"I almost expected to see Ester and Matthew on that couch," said Ross, smiling.

"So did I," said Heather with a chuckle.

"The angels did a great job on the new tree," he replied.

Zakhart walked over to them as Knox got to his feet and joined them.

"Zakhart," said Ross, extending his hand. "Can't thank you enough for what you did for me."

Zakhart pulled him into a hug. "Just glad it worked. I take my job very seriously."

Ross glanced at Knox and the two men exchanged a strange look that Heather couldn't read, but she saw Knox glance from Ross to her.

"Knox, thank you," said Ross, extending his hand. "I wouldn't have escaped without your help."

For a moment, Knox stared past Ross, his gaze unblinking as it settled on Heather. He smiled at her as if they'd spent a lifetime together. Heather winced, feeling the attraction between them. Finally, he nodded and shook Ross' hand.

"You're a lucky man," Knox said, clapping Ross on the shoulder. He pointed a finger at Heather and forced a smile and Heather saw the pain behind it. "Now, you be careful out there. And don't let your guard down."

Knox stepped up to Heather and pulled her into a powerful hug that made Heather weak in the knees.

"Thank you for everything, Knox," she said, holding him tight and then letting him go. "I couldn't have done this without you."

"Damn right you couldn't," he said with a smirk. "Be safe, you two. Hopefully, we'll see each other again someday."

Heather and Ross walked through the tree, saying their goodbyes. Razasha gave her a big hug and wished her well as Zakhart walked them outside. He hugged Ross and then Heather. Heather took his hand and squeezed it hard.

"I'm gonna miss you so much, Zakhart," she said, her eyes filling with tears as he pulled her into another long hug.

"I'll miss you, too, Heather," he said and rubbed her shoulder. "We've been through an awful lot together, haven't we?"

She nodded, tears threading down her cheeks. "I can't imagine my life without you."

Ross put his arm around her as Zakhart reached up to wipe away the tears.

"I'm your Guardian angel, so you won't have to, but you won't see me for a long, long time, Heather." He patted them both on the shoulders. "All right, go now. Those bracelets will take you right to the Spiral. Don't delay, okay?"

Heather nodded. "Do I just look for a color change?"

Zakhart reached down and slid one off her wrist. He tossed it against the ground. The strands untwisted, joining together into a gold thread that snaked across the ground and into the forest. It would lead them right to the Spiral.

"It'll take you right to it. Be safe in the light."

"Bye, Zakhart," said Heather, leaning up and kissing him on the cheek.

Ross took her hand and they turned away from the soul tree, Zakhart standing in the ring of trees as they walked away, toward the stream. She felt a horrible sadness inside as she turned away from Zakhart.

Footsteps crunched across the grass behind them. Wind whispered through the trees.

Heather smiled. Zakhart wanted to say one last thing. She turned around, wanting to hug him one more time.

Zakhart stood in the grass, waving goodbye, those pumpkin-orange eyes burning bright against the dusky sky.

"Let's go, Heather," said Ross, tugging on her hand.

Heather waved one last time and they moved on toward the trees.

But the shadow to her left made her turn.

Mulciber leaped out of the brush, a clutch of demons behind it. The demon grabbed Heather, but Ross pushed Mulciber backward. And shoved her behind him.

"Thank you, Heather," Mulciber rasped, stepping back. "You accomplished something for me that I've been trying to do for centuries."

Zakhart ran toward them, calling Heather's name as Ross fended off the demons. Heather held onto Ross, shaking off their holds.

She felt Zakhart at her shoulder as Mulciber reached out, a dark force pressing through her chest and into her soul. It felt like something had grabbed hold of her heart and squeezed it. And pulled its hand back again.

Between Mulciber's shriveled fingers was a bright gold spark.

"Thank you for bringing this back to me, dear Heather," said Mulciber grinning.

Heather glared at the demon. "What are you talking about?"

"You didn't know it, but you carried poppy petals into the physical world for me. I hid the petals in your sleeve."

"What?" Zakhart cried. "It's forbidden for realms to touch like that. What have you done?"

Mulciber cradled the spark in its scaly hands as the light shriveled into a charcoal grey pearl.

"The demon essence is complete now. It can grow here and in the physical world."

Zakhart's eyes grew wide, his mouth falling open. "No, Mulciber!" His face flushed with fury. "I'll never let you plant poppies in the human world."

The demon laughed, holding its belly. "Next season's harvest of human souls will be the best ever. And I have you to thank for that,

Heather." Mulciber glanced at Ross. "It's such a shame our testing couldn't continue with you, Ross." His gaze shifted to Heather.

Something moved in the corner of her eye.

"I think we'll take Heather instead."

Ross bared his teeth, fury burning in his eyes. "Like hell, you will."

A flash of black.

Heather turned as something dark slammed into her and Ross, knocking them to the ground. She got to her feet, struggling to regain her balance when Ross grabbed her around the waist and lifted her to her feet.

"Heather!" Ross' shout crackled through the forest.

But it wasn't Ross that had her around the waist.

And suddenly, she was rising.

She twisted around, staring into the fluid black eyes of a soulstalker.

"No! Ross, help me! Zakhart!"

She screamed, clawing and biting, but she couldn't break the soulstalker's grip as it carried her off, the poppy fields thick below as the sky darkened.

Ross' anguished scream was the last sound she heard before the soulstalker dipped low on the horizon and disappeared into the darkness ahead.

The End of Reprise, Book 2: The Spiral Series

The story continues in...

Avenge, Book 3: The Spiral Series (Coming Soon!)

Dark forces control the Between. Forcing Heather to choose between Ross and Knox.

NOVELS BY LISA SILVERTHORNE

Standalones:

ISABEL'S TEARS

LANDFALL

PACIFIC BLUE TATTOO

A Game of Lost Souls series:

THE CINDERELLA HOUR

THE PRINCE CHARMING HOUR

THE EVER AFTER HOUR

THE FALLEN HEARTS SEASON

THE RISING SPIRITS SEASON

THE ETERNAL SOULS SEASON

THE ROYAL WEDDING HOUR

THE HEAVENLY HONEYMOON HOUR

THE DIVINE NEWLYWEDS SHOW

THE CELESTIAL COUPLES SHOW

The Spiral series:

BETWEEN

REPRISE

SHORT STORY COLLECTIONS

THE SOUND OF ANGELS

THE MAGIC OF ORDINARY THINGS

SCIENCE FICTION WRITING AS L.S. SILVERTHORNE

Standalones:

REDISCOVERY

Experiencing True Purple series:

RECOMBINANT, Book 1

HELIX, Book 2

FORTHCOMING

A Game of Lost Souls series:

The Enochian Apocalypse Show, Book Eleven (9/3/23)

The Angelic Anniversary Hour, Book Twelve

The Perdition Picture Show, Book Thirteen

The Spiral series:

Avenge, Book 3 (Coming Soon!)

Ruin, Book 4

Descent, Book 5

The Resurrectionist Papers:

A ROMANTIC FANTASY MYSTERY SERIES

Grave Reckoning, Book 1

Corpses Delicti, Book 2

Stiffed Again, Book 3

SCIENCE FICTION WRITING AS L.S. SILVERTHORNE

Experiencing True Purple series:

Splice, Book 3 (8/13/23)

Cipher, Book 4

Renascence, Book 5

SHORT STORY COLLECTIONS

Timeless: 8 Time Travel Romances (Dec 2023)

Get Isabel's Tears FREE for joining the mailing list!

Don't miss another book by Lisa Silverthorne!

Subscribe for news on my new book releases.

No spam or wasting your valuable time.

Only occasional book releases and special fiction promotions.

Or Follow Me on BookBub for new book alerts!

about the author

LISA SILVERTHORNE has published over 20 novels and 150 short stories and novelettes in many genres. She is the author of **A Game of Lost Souls** series, **Experiencing True Purple** series, the new **Spiral** series, and the upcoming **The Resurrectionist Papers**. She lives in Las Vegas, Nevada.

Before you go, you are invited to please leave a **review of this book**!

Reviews are a wonderful way to help an author. They are also an exciting opportunity to share your honest thoughts with other readers, so **please post yours,** in as many places as possible!